The Holiday House

ROMANTIC WOMEN'S FRIENDSHIP FICTION

FIVE ISLAND COVE
BOOK ELEVEN

JESSIE NEWTON

feel good fiction

ELANA JOHNSON

Chapter One

Eloise Sherman's fingers flew over the keyboard as she tried to restore the reservation system at the Cliffside Inn. The constant ding of the bell at the front desk competed with the cheerful holiday music playing softly in the background, creating a cacophony that grated on her nerves. She glanced up from the computer, forcing a smile as yet another guest approached her desk with a question.

"The woman at the front desk said you could help us reset our pool key." The man there looked hopeful, especially as he already wore his swim trunks and a rashguard. The woman at his side carried two towels, her sunglasses pushed up onto her head.

"Sure." Eloise's voice came out calm despite the growing tension in her shoulders. The keying software only worked at this desk, and she'd been waiting for the replacement for the front desk for a week now.

She quickly made the new key for the man and his wife, and as she handed the key back, she said, "Thank you for your patience."

"Sure," the man said easily. "This place is really great."

Pride filled Eloise as she smiled and said, "Thank you. We appreciate that."

They both smiled their way away from the desk and down the hall that led to the pool at the back of the inn. Eloise had kept it open last winter when she realized there were no other swimming pools available in Five Island Cove during the months of September through April.

Well, there was one at the Cliffside Inn, and her bookings had stayed consistent throughout the winter when they'd dropped in previous years. The pool got used plenty, and Eloise could justify the additional maintenance costs by the number of guests she had staying at the inn during the traditionally slower, non-touristy months.

Once they'd gone, Eloise returned her attention to the computer screen. The software for bookings had completed the update, and she clicked the button to launch it. "Please let this work," she muttered. If her reservation software didn't work, guests couldn't make online bookings, and that was obviously a huge problem.

The site refreshed as it updated, and Eloise quickly navigated to an incognito window to try to make a reservation for her family coming to Five Island Cove in January.

When she made it all the way to the payment screen without an issue, she grinned and leaned back in her chair. Her rest and respite didn't last long, as she quickly sat up again, clicking away from the problems at the Cliffside Inn and over to the spreadsheet she'd been working on for the personal trip to The Starlight Manor on Rocky Ridge.

Aaron had gotten time off, and around the holidays, that had taken a real miracle. The house could sleep fifty-four, and Eloise had been tasked with making room assignments for the Christmas getaway she and all of her friends and their families were taking this year.

She'd rented The Starlight Manor for twenty-three days, and she had a solid confirmation from everyone that they'd be there this weekend, and then again starting on December twenty-third and running through the twenty-sixth.

Others would be in and out, with a few people, including Eloise, going for all twenty-three days.

Why did I think I could manage this? she wondered as she took in the color-coded boxes with names and dates in them. *Who takes a month-long vacation anyway?*

But Eloise desperately needed time away from Cliffside. She wasn't sure she wanted to spend all twenty-three of those days with Kristen, Robin, AJ, and Alice, but she'd told herself time and again that The Starlight

Manor provided plenty of space for Eloise to be alone when she needed to be.

Plus, maybe she did need the strong bonds with her friends to feel like herself again.

She sighed, pushing a strand of long, dark hair behind her ear, and clicked over to the tab she kept open with the floor plan of The Starlight Manor.

Her worries eased instantly. One, Eloise loved floor plans, and two, she adored sprawling Victorian mansions. The one on Rocky Ridge had become a rental property about a decade ago, but no one in El's friend group had ever stayed there.

Even Alice, who'd once owned a home on Rocky Ridge, and Maddy, who lived there now, had never been. The house sat high on the bluff, on eleven acres, without another house in sight. She needed a code to get past the gate, and a quiet excitement burned inside Eloise at the thought of being there tomorrow night.

There, and not here.

She and Kristen had first come up with this idea a few months ago, and Eloise had dedicated time to it every day since. She could just see cozy winter nights by the outdoor fire pit, laughter-filled dinners, and the chance to reconnect with her friends, with Aaron, Billie, and Grace, away from the demands of everyday life.

In the past week, however, Eloise felt like the details would drown her. Just pull her right under and choke the life out of her. From the various arrival times, to where couples would stay, when their children would be arriving and where they'd stay, could overwhelm anyone.

And then, meals had to be considered, as Rocky Ridge didn't have a grocery store on it. A tiny little food mart was all, and Eloise had called them three times to find out when they stocked their shelves, what kinds of fresh produce and meat they carried, and if they got extra shipments during the holidays.

Barring another tsunami like they had a few years ago, there should be plenty of food for the party at The Starlight Manor and the regular residents of Rocky Ridge.

Eloise still planned to take a load of groceries with her tomorrow, and she'd shipped some muffin, cookie, and bread mixes from the inn here to the manor to arrive two days from now, on Saturday morning.

"El."

She looked up at the sound of Maggie's voice. She ran the front desk on weekday mornings, and Eloise had rejoiced the day she'd started, just this last spring. She'd cleaned up their digital filing system, and everyone who came to the inn seemed to like her. Making a good first impression with front desk staff went a long way with guests, and Eloise smiled at her.

"What's up, Mags?"

"Room four needs extra towels, and housekeeping says they don't have any."

Eloise got to her feet. "That can't be true." Her laundry room hummed away twenty-four hours a day, it seemed, and a random Thursday morning—even if it was the week after Thanksgiving—wouldn't exhaust their towel supply. "I'll go check the laundry room and take them up."

"I can do it if you get the towels."

She opened the top drawer of her desk and reached into the back on the right side to get her keys. As she made her way from the front, public-facing part of the inn to the back facilities, she remembered that Goldie had not come in this morning.

"No wonder we don't have towels." Eloise groaned as she fitted the key in the lock and pushed her way into the laundry room. The towels collected from the room turnovers that day sat there, but since Goldie hadn't come in, no one had started them.

Eloise got the job done, and she managed to find three clean towels hiding in a high cupboard next to one of the industrial dryers. She grabbed those, set an alarm on her phone to come back and switch the laundry, and took the towels out to Maggie.

She'd just finished that task when her phone rang. Robin's name sat there, and Eloise wanted to swipe the call to voicemail. But that would only prompt Robin to try again, so she tapped on the call and lifted it to her ear. "Hey, Robin."

"Heya, El," Robin chirped, almost like the bird she was named after. "I wanted to run the meal plan by you for the first week at The Starlight Manor. I've got some great ideas, but I need to know about any dietary restrictions. Oh, and are we still planning that big welcome dinner for Saturday night?"

El's head spun at the speed at which Robin spoke. She should be used to it by now—and she was. So she took a big breath and said, "Yes, to the big welcome dinner on Saturday night. Everyone is confirmed." She could practically hear Robin's pen make a scratching noise as she made a check-mark on her clipboard.

She planned weddings for a living, and Eloise could appreciate a woman who could manage so many details and a bridezilla. So the meal planning for the duration of the stay at The Starlight Manor had naturally fallen to Robin.

Kristen had suggested her, actually, and Eloise didn't care who managed the meals as long as she didn't have to.

She returned to her desk, where she sat each afternoon to be available for guests as they checked in and prepped for dinner. She worked here from three to five-thirty every afternoon, and most days, Billie and Grace did homework nearby or went to help Shirley in the kitchen.

Today, Aaron had picked up the girls from school and taken them home. They'd all join Eloise at The Starlight Manor tomorrow, and her joy started to rise again.

No one came over with another problem or question, and Eloise pulled out the physical binder she'd be taking home with her tonight. Color-coded tabs separated sections for accommodations, activities, meals, the Christmas gift exchange, and more. She flipped to the page detailing room assignments, one last thing to take care of before everything kicked off tomorrow.

She picked up her phone and dialed Alice, hoping she wasn't with a client or on a call. Alice worked out of her home as a family rights lawyer, and she'd be spending a lot of the next twenty-three days working from the manor or not at all.

"What's up, El?" she asked in lieu of hello, and she sounded cheerful enough.

"Hey." Eloise tried not to sound too apologetic. "I had you and Arthur down for the Orion Suite, but, well, AJ requested a basement or first-floor room, and the only one that's comparable to what she and Matt have now."

"Okay," Alice said slowly.

"They're in the Andromeda Room," Eloise said next. "And it's almost the same exact room, but on the top floor." She trapped her breath for a moment, and then pushed it all out. "Will that be a problem?" Eloise didn't want to make Alice and Arthur start their vacation with disappointment.

"Does it have that charming little window seat?" Alice asked.

"Yep," Eloise said with a grin. "It sure does. And it's just as lovely, with bigger windows that overlook the ocean."

"I'm sure it'll be fine, El. We can climb the steps."

"It won't be as noisy up there, that's for sure."

"Then it sounds like I'm winning." Alice laughed lightly, and Eloise wasn't sure why she'd been so nervous. "Are you and Aaron and the girls still going tomorrow?"

"Yes," Eloise said. "You and Arthur are taking the ferry after school tomorrow?"

"Yes," Alice said. "And I can't wait. I've rescheduled all my clients for next week to the week after, and I just want to walk on the cliffs, and go to the black sand beach, and do all my Christmas shopping online."

Eloise laughed with her. "This sounds like the dream vacation."

"Right?"

"See you tomorrow," El said, and the call ended. She set down her phone, her gaze drifting to the framed photo on her desk. Her and Aaron from last Christmas, flanked by their girls as the four of them sat on a bench and put on ice skates. Everyone smiled—even Billie—cheeks rosy from the cold, eyes bright with laughter. She wanted the same thing this holiday. Not just a vacation that almost felt like a staycation, but a chance to make memories before Billie graduated and left Five Island Cove.

She still had a couple of years of high school left, but Eloise knew how fast time could pass, how much the things Billie owned would not matter. But memories lasted. Experiences mattered.

The phone on her desk rang, and that meant only one thing: someone from the kitchen needed her.

Anyone else would simply come talk to her, and her friends and family would use her personal cell.

You chose this life, she told herself as she reached for the receiver. "This is Eloise," she said in a crisp, professional voice.

"El, I'm so sorry," Shirley said in a rush of words. Something beeped on her end of the line, like an oven timer going off that she couldn't quite get to. Eloise shot a look toward the doorway halfway down the hall as she stood, but she couldn't go help while holding the phone.

"But Alex called in sick, and I need some help in the kitchen."

"Of course," Eloise said smoothly. "I'm on my way." She hung up and promptly strode over to the check-in desk. "Maggie, I have to go help in the kitchen, okay? If you need me, come get me."

"Yes, ma'am," Maggie chirped, her fingers moving back to the keyboard, where she was setting up the auto-reminders for next weekend's reservations.

Then, she turned to face the emergency in the kitchen, her heart beating like hummingbird wings in her throat. Of course. Because managing a fully-booked inn and planning a month-long vacation wasn't enough, now she had to figure out how to cover an important staff absence.

She then allowed herself just one moment of frustration. She closed her eyes, took a deep breath, and then slowly released it, imagining her stress flowing out with the exhale.

You've got this, Eloise.

She heard it in Aaron's voice, as he'd ever been her champion since she'd returned to the cove and they'd reconnected. And when she went home tonight, she wouldn't be back here at the inn for a while.

With renewed determination, Eloise opened her eyes, smoothed down her skirt, and ran a hand through her hair. She tucked The Starlight Manor binder into her take-home bag, promising herself she'd leaf through it leisurely tonight. Right now, her inn needed her full attention.

In the kitchen, Eloise donned an apron and moved to Shirley's side. "Tell me what to do." The beeping had been silenced, praise the heavens, and Eloise took in the myriad of prep bowls on the stainless steel counter. Her culinary skills were rusty, but she could take trays out of the oven, set timers, and follow directions.

Shirley placed a recipe in front of her. "Everything for this salad is prepped. I just need it put together and put in the fridge." She indicated the enormous bowl down on the end of the counter. It sat empty, waiting for all the ingredients of the red pepper pasta salad, and Eloise nodded resolutely.

"Got it." She read through the recipe quickly, then stepped down the counter to get the bowl. She added everything line by line, checking and double-checking before she emptied the three bottles of Italian dressing over the vegetables and pasta.

That done, she covered it with plastic wrap and

opened the industrial-sized fridge to set it to chill. "Okay," she said. "What next?" She turned and met Shirley's eyes.

Shirley nodded to the door Eloise had come through, and she turned that way. "Aaron." Relief and happiness filled her as quick as water rushing over steep cliffs, and Eloise moved straight into his arms. "Hey, what are you doing here?"

Behind him, Billie and Grace bickered as they tried to enter the kitchen too. "Dad, you're in the way," Billie griped. She managed to squeeze past him, and she and Grace went to help Shirley.

Eloise stepped back and gazed at her husband. "I never texted you back," she said, realizing it as the words came out.

"Thus, why we're here." Aaron grinned at her and held up a brown paper bag that could be holding anything. But somehow, Eloise knew he'd brought her favorite treat. "Do you have ten minutes to sneak away and take a break?"

She turned back to Shirley, who'd already set both Billie and Grace to work. Their eyes met, and Shirley nodded, clearly back in control now that she'd had some help with a salad and a couple of pairs of hands to keep assisting.

So she took the bag and said, "This better be that white chocolate raspberry cake," before she led Aaron out of the kitchen and away from the front of the inn.

She had a private office in the back for when she didn't want to share her cake—or her husband.

"How are things here?" Aaron asked.

"Hectic."

"So we're ready for The Starlight Manor."

Eloise pushed into her office and rounded the desk to take her seat. She sank into it with a sigh and smiled up at her husband as he followed her, crowding right into her space. He leaned down and took her face in his hands, a fascinating look of adoration on his face. "Yes," she whispered. "We're so ready for a vacation."

Aaron's mouth slipped into a slow, sexy smile. "And we have the Cassiopeia Suite, correct?"

"Correct, Officer." Eloise grinned at her husband.

He touched his smile to hers, and Eloise simply loved kissing Aaron. He slowed the world to exactly the speed she needed it to be moving, and her love for him soared as he pulled back and said, "All right, then. Eat your cake, and let's get back to the kitchen before someone burns it down."

Chapter Two

~

AJ Hymas reached up and grabbed the bar above the window as the RideShare driver navigated the winding road leading to The Starlight Manor. The afternoon sun kept getting covered by thick clouds, and she peered out the window just as the world brightened again.

In the toddler carseat AJ had brought from Diamond Island, her three-year-old son clutched a stuffed dinosaur in his chubby fingers. Asher squealed as he threw his arms out and babbled, "Rawr, mom-mom, *raaaawr*."

She smiled at her tow-headed little boy. "We're almost there, buddy." She reached over and smoothed his hair back off his forehead, and he looked at her with big, bright eyes.

As the SUV rounded the final bend, The Starlight Manor came into view, and AJ's breath caught at the top of her lungs. The house rose out of the dark cliffs, a perfectly manicured lawn with trees, shrubs, bushes, and flowers surrounding it.

An oasis on the rock.

They continued to go up and up to the mansion, and AJ couldn't wait to see the backdrop of the ocean against the beautiful greens, golds, and whites of the grounds and the house. A large turret rose on the left side, with the wrap-around porch extending from there, past the front door and all the way around the corner on the right end.

Mystery and wealth emanated from the house, and Christmas lights adorned the eaves, already twinkling softly in the cloudy day.

"Wow," AJ said to herself, the sound of her voice barely reaching her ears. Something made her skin prickle, and the driver turned into the circle driveway.

"Here you are," he said, and AJ bent to retrieve the diaper bag she took everywhere with her since Asher had been born.

"Thank you," AJ said, holding her phone to the payment console. It beeped, meaning she'd paid for her ride, and then she started the process of getting herself and Asher out. She told herself that she was staying here for the next few weeks, and she wouldn't have to do this every day.

She unbuckled her son and gathered him into her arms. "Momma's going to put you on the grass, and you need to stay there."

"Okay," Asher said, though AJ wasn't convinced that he even knew what she'd said.

She set him down and bent to be at eye-level with him. "Stay right here while I get out the bags, okay, baby?" She smiled at him and returned to the SUV to get the carseat. With that on the driveway, and the driver helping with her two suitcases, AJ had her things sooner than she'd anticipated.

She took an extra moment to take stock of everything, then stepped over to close the back door. "Thank you," she told the driver again, and he smiled at her as he rounded the trunk of the SUV, closed it, and then got behind the wheel.

AJ smoothed back her hair and tightened her ponytail. The familiar gesture grounded her, reminding her of the countless times she'd done the same before stepping in front of a camera during her sports journalism days.

"All right, Asher." She smiled at him, shouldered his bag, and reached for his hand. "Let's go find our room." She towed one of the suitcases behind her, willing to leave the other and come back and get it once she had Asher more contained.

Before she reached the bottom step which led up to the porch, the front door of the manor swung open, and Kristen Shields stepped outside. "AvaJane," she said, her tone maternal and warm and welcome.

AJ grinned at her and bent to Asher. "Go get Grammy Kristen, baby."

Asher squealed again and started up the steps, being

careful to take one at a time with both feet. Kristen met him at the top, her silver hair glinting in the weak sunlight. "Well, hello there, my baby boy." She giggled as she pulled Asher into a hug, and AJ turned to get her other suitcase.

Matt would be here for the weekend later tonight, but he had to work at the golf course he owned and operated at least a few days each week. Because of that, AJ had asked for a suite with room enough for all three of them, so Asher wouldn't have to be on his own in the house somewhere.

Eloise had assigned her to a ground-floor room with the biggest master closet AJ had ever seen on a floor plan, and her plan was to put Asher's bed in there while she and Matt used the bed in the suite.

"You are so big," Kristen said, turning to go into the house. AJ pulled one suitcase up the few steps, then returned for the other, and she pulled them both into the house. She'd planned to arrive right at the time they could get into the house, but she was still figuring out how to get everything ready to go on time, even now, three years after Asher had been born.

Inside, the grand foyer boasted a massive crystal chandelier overhead, and AJ tilted her head back to admire it. As she did, the lights flickered ever so slightly. A buzz. A shake. Flicker, flicker, and then the bulbs burned properly.

"I wouldn't want to be the one to change those light bulbs," she said to herself, a quick smile following the statement. She pulled her suitcases across the pale pink tiles on the floor, taking in the beauty of the art—all oceanic-themed among the astrological decor above. Seagulls flying above the azure ocean, a gorgeous painting that seemed to move the way waves did. A small table sat underneath the painting, and a long tray waited there, with labeled compartments.

Get your keys here, a sign read, and AJ paused there to read the signs for each set of keys.

The top row were for common areas of the house— *main house keys, library, home theater, indoor pool and hot tub, game room, kitchen pantry, basement kitchen pantry, sunroom, gym, backyard shed.*

The bottom row of compartments on the tray held the keys to each of the bedrooms in The Starlight Manor —*Andromeda Suite, Orion Suite, Aurora Borealis Suite, Cassiopeia Suite, North Star Suite, Gemini Suite.*

Other room names sat there too, and while AJ had looked with interest at the floor plan Eloise had sent out, she hadn't memorized it. She'd requested a suite for her, Matt, and Asher, and she'd been assigned the Orion Suite.

She plucked the keys from the section of the tray, and the lights above her went out completely. She startled and looked up, something cold running down her arms.

This place is old, she told herself.

"Jean's upstairs getting Heidi settled for a nap," Kristen said as she came into the foyer with Asher in her arms. The little boy now had teddy-bear-shaped cookies in his hands, and no wonder Kristen was his favorite. "Did you get your keys?" She glanced over to the tray.

AJ held them up. "Yep, got 'em."

Kristen smiled and said, "I've been here about twenty minutes, so I can show you where it is."

"Where are you staying?"

"The Nebula Room," she said. "It's on this level too."

AJ didn't say she was glad Kristen didn't have to navigate steps, though she was. "How many bedrooms are on this level?"

"Three," Kristen said. "The main suite, and two smaller bedrooms."

"Who's in the other one?"

"Julia," Kristen said. "Since Liam can only come over Christmas."

AJ nodded at Kristen's back but didn't say anything. She took in the rich carpet on the floor in the living room, noted the plush couches that looked like she could sink all the way to the floor, and the TV that shone like black oil above a piece of wood furniture that probably held board games, books, and DVDs behind the closed doors.

She couldn't even imagine the amount of money it had taken to put together just the family room, and AJ only had a moment to glance into the kitchen as she went by. She told herself she had plenty of time to examine every single thing in the house, from the rugs to the dishware to the brand of toilet paper they'd stocked in the bathrooms.

Kristen led her down a hallway with a full bath on the right, and they passed another door labeled *Comet Room*. Beside the bathroom sat the Nebula Room, and at the end of the hall, Kristen paused and nodded to the Orion Suite.

AJ smiled at her, trying to calm some of her nerves. She wasn't even sure why she felt anxious at all. She'd have plenty of help with Asher over the coming weeks, as she wasn't the only one coming for the duration of the rental agreement.

Eloise would be here, as would Robin, Kristen, and Jean. Their loved ones would come and go, though they'd all be here by tomorrow night's opening dinner, and El had said everyone had confirmed for Christmas Eve and Christmas Day too.

Sometimes AJ really enjoyed being in a big group setting, and other times, she simply wanted the peace and quiet she got at her bungalow on Diamond Island. But as she entered the Orion Suite, she realized she'd be able to get away from anyone and everything that bothered her while here at The Starlight Manor, simply by walking down the hall and entering this room.

And the door locked.

"I'll let you get settled," Kristen said. "When Robin gets here, she's going to want to dive right into the decorations."

"Sure," AJ said, manhandling the bags into the room

behind her. The space opened up into bright whites and soft grays, sky blues, seafoam greens, and the hint of golden sand. The tightness in AJ's chest expanded out, as she loved the beach. It calmed her, knowing that something bigger and stronger than her was in charge, so when she felt weak and small, it became okay.

"This is so nice," she said, drinking in the king-sized bed, the window seat that overlooked a flower garden, and the soft light coming from the lamps flanking the bed. She had a nightstand on either side of the bed too, and the bathroom opened up on her left, past the sitting area, which housed a full-sized couch and a recliner.

"Mom," Asher said behind her, and AJ turned to find him toddling toward her. "Rawr, rawr." He no longer carried his dinosaur, and AJ scooped him into her arms.

"We'll find your Roar," she told him, turning toward the closet. "Let's see where you're going to sleep." She smiled at her son, knowing full-well that the three-year-old would end up on Matt's side of the bed when her husband wasn't there. Sometimes when he was.

As she entered the closet, she paused as the sound of whispers met her ears. Her pulse rioted, making it hard to listen, to try to catch the words. The sound stopped a moment later anyway, and AJ looked from corner to corner of the closet.

She opened the nearest door, expecting to find something there. What, she had no idea. A leftover tape recorder playing spooky Halloween sounds? Something.

She found nothing.

By the time she finished checking every drawer and opening every door, Asher fussed to get down. She set him on his feet and told him, "Stay in the bedroom, bud." She turned in a slow circle one more time, trying to decide what, if anything, to do.

If she told Kristen or Jean or Robin she'd seen lights flicker and closets whisper, they'd think she'd gone crazy.

"Momma," Asher said. "Spy-er. Spy-er." He held something up in his hand, and AJ's stomach plummeted to her shoes.

"Is that a spider, buddy?" AJ dashed out of the closet and into the bathroom. She grabbed some of that luxury toilet paper and returned to her son. "Let me have it, sweetheart." She didn't want to touch a spider, dead or alive, but she couldn't let her three-year-old proudly present it to everyone who arrived at the manor.

She managed to squeeze the spider out of his chubby fingers, and she folded the tissue over again before she grinned at him. "We don't touch the spiders," she said. "You tell Mommy, okay?"

"Okay," Asher said, and he went with her to flush the spider. "Potty, Mommy."

"Yep," she said. "Let's go." She helped him up onto the toilet, and he was such a good boy, he'd been pretty easy to potty-train. Once he finished, and she washed his hands—and hers—she set him on his feet and said, "Let's go find Auntie Jean."

She could unpack later, as AJ was still pretty used to living out of a suitcase.

As she followed Asher out of the room, she caught sight of the constellations painted up the wall and onto the ceiling. She noted the star-covered pillows on the bed and couch that she hadn't before, and she appreciated the light fixture on the ceiling—a big, six-sided star that was only one among a whole belt of them painted into the ceiling.

The Starlight Manor really didn't leave a single detail untouched.

Out in the family room, she found Jean sitting on the couch with Kristen on the other end, Asher on her lap. "Hey," AJ said brightly. "How are you?" She leaned over and hugged Jean, who patted her on the back.

"Good," Jean said. "Real good."

"This place is *incredible*," AJ said as she sank onto another matching couch.

"Isn't it?" Kristen asked. "Eloise really outdid herself finding this place."

"Is she here yet?"

"She and Aaron and the girls were going to lunch and a movie before catching the ferry," Kristen said. "Then, they were going to stop at that little store and get a few groceries."

"Oh." AJ sat up and pulled her phone out of her pocket. "I found out you can order online and they'll deliver anywhere on Rocky Ridge."

"Out here?" Jean asked.

"They said anywhere." AJ tapped to get to the tab she'd saved. Something comforted her about being surrounded by friends, even if Matt's steady presence was noticeably absent. She missed him then, and she navigated away from the store's website and to her text string.

Miss you, baby. Can't wait until you get here tomorrow.

"All right," Robin called from the foyer of the house. "I'm here!" Her voice seemed to echo through the whole house—all four stories—and all three of them in the family room turned to greet her as she made her way to them.

She carried a pale pink overnight bag over her shoulder, and she dropped it as she entered the room.

"We made it." Joy poured from her, and AJ couldn't help smiling as she got up to hug Robin hello. Jean and Kristen did the same, and then Robin said, "Okay, let's get this place spruced up."

"I help," Asher said. He walked over to Robin and looked up at her with his big eyes wide open. "I help." He reached up and tugged on her shirt, and Robin finally crouched down in front of him.

"Of course you can help, my tiny friend. Come on." She took his hand and led him over to the card table in the corner. "You can help me by bringing over things to hang on the tree."

First, they had to move the table and position the tree in the corner where it had been. Then Robin put a

25

box of white Christmas balls in front of Asher and showed him how to check for the hooks. Thankfully, all the balls AJ could see had them already, and honestly, she expected nothing less from this place.

The tree came prelit, so all they had to do was listen to Robin tell them where to put each ornament, and since AJ didn't want to be in charge, she didn't mind having someone tell her what to do.

She hung the garland along the mantel the way Robin said, and she took the red bows from Asher after placing a kiss on his nose that made him giggle. She loved her boy, and they'd just finished with the garland that went up the railing on the steps leading to the second floor when Robin and Jean cried out nearly in unison.

She went down the few steps quickly. "What is it?"

They both stood by the Christmas tree, which now had no lights winking from the boughs. "The lights just went zap," Jean said.

"Oh, no," Robin said. "We can't have a tree with no lights." She planted her hands on her hips, like her will alone could relight the tree. "I'll call Duke and tell him to bring some strings from our house."

"Should we take all the ornaments off?" Jean asked.

AJ simply took in the tree, which stood twelve feet tall. They'd stood on a chair to decorate the top, and there was something off about a Christmas tree that was supposed to be lit up but wasn't. A shiver ran down AJ's arms, jumped to her back, and then squirreled up her spine.

"El is almost here," Robin said, her attention on her phone. "She has pizza." She sighed as she lowered her device and stuck it in her back pocket. "We're basically done here."

"Too bad about the lights," AJ said as she joined the others around the tree. "I saw the chandelier lights in the lobby flicker when I got here."

"Maybe this place hasn't been used in a while," Jean said.

"Maybe the Christmas tree is just old," Kristen said.

"Maybe," was all Robin said.

"Momma, cracker," Asher said, and AJ picked him up, grateful for the distraction. Thankfully, no one had disbelieved her about the chandelier lights.

She took her son into the kitchen and easily found the bag of teddy bear cookies Kristen had given Asher earlier. She'd clearly brought her favorites, as a bag of coffee grounds, a small bunch of bananas, and a box of protein bars sat against the wall with the cookies.

Gratitude filled her, because surely Kristen hadn't brought those for herself. No, she'd thought of Asher and brought his favorite snack.

"I should get some things from that little store," she said to Jean as she joined her in the kitchen. "Did you get anything? We could put in an order together."

"I brought a few of Heidi's things," Jean said. "But not enough for very long." She smiled and took a few of the teddy bear cookies too. "So yes, let's go get some things in the morning."

"Or put in an order," AJ said.

"Or that."

"Pizza," someone called, and it had to be Aaron, as he was the only man in the last group set to arrive today. Sure enough, he came around the corner with a stack of pizza boxes in his hands, and his girls followed with drinks and smaller boxes.

Billie, in all her nearly silver-white-haired glory, put a case of lime-essenced soda water on the counter and said, "Mom said she'd make citrus coolers. Virgin, of course."

"Of course." AJ stepped into her and hugged her. "How are you, Billie? Did you have a good day of playing hooky?"

"The best." Billie grinned as she pulled back. Then she moved out of the way as Grace put the smaller boxes on the counter.

"These are dessert pizzas," she said. "Dad got cookies and cream, peach pie, and cinnamon sugar."

"Sounds amazing," Jean said.

Eloise finally entered the kitchen, and she carried a big, lidded, plastic tote. "There's more in the car, you guys. Go on and get it."

"I can help," AJ said, and she went with Billie and Grace to get the groceries El and Aaron had stopped for. That done, the RideShare driver left, and when AJ returned to the kitchen, she found someone had strapped Asher into a booster seat at the kitchen table and given him a piece of pizza cut up into smaller chunks.

"Thanks for feeding Asher," she said to the whole room, and surprise jumped through her when Aaron answered with, "You bet."

She should know better than to put anything past the Chief of Police, and she gladly took the citrus cooler from El. "Which flavor is this?"

"Grapefruit-lime," El said.

AJ took a sip of the ice cold beverage, the fizziness combining with the sour grapefruit and making her whole mouth tingle and rejoice. "Mm, this is so good."

El grinned and proceeded to make another drink, this one orange-peach. She gave it to Grace when she came to get seconds of the sausage and potato pizza and her first round of dessert.

"What are you having?" El asked.

AJ took in the array of pizzas. "I think that supreme is calling my name." She smiled at El, who peeled a paper plate off the stack.

"It's the green peppers and olives," El said. "I know what you like." She put two slices on the plate and handed it to AJ.

"It's so good to see you, El." AJ rounded the end of the island and leaned in to hug her friend. "Thank you for all the work you put into this."

"I hope it goes okay," El said, and AJ heard the undercurrent of worry in her tone.

She stepped back and tried to look as casual as possible. She certainly didn't want El to know she'd just switched into reporter mode. "Why wouldn't it go okay?"

"Oh, you know," El muttered as she popped the tab on another can of soda. "With all of us in one place?" She threw AJ a side-eyed look. "It's not like we all agree about everything right now."

"True," AJ said, because it was true. "But it's the holidays. Everyone will be on their best behavior."

"Sure," El said, but she sounded like she believed AJ not at all. "Now, tell me what happened with the chandelier? Kristen said you saw it flicker, and I'm sending an email to the host about any initial problems we've noticed."

Chapter Three

"This place is beautiful," Robin Grover gushed into the phone as she paced in her suite. Her husband had found a dock for his fishing boat on the western side of Rocky Ridge, and he'd be here tomorrow about noon. "You're going to love it."

"I can't wait to be there," Mandie said, her voice sounding even further away than it was. She reached up and ran her fingers through her ponytail, then worked the band out. Relief cascaded through her scalp, and she scratched the spot where she'd secured her hair so tightly for so long.

"How are finals going?"

"Most of mine are next week," Mandie said. "Charlie's have already started, and they are going to be the death of us." She whispered the last several words.

Robin took a deep breath, inhaling the scent of pine and cinnamon that permeated the air. "I'm sure he'll do great," she said, infusing as much positivity in her tone as possible. "He's incredibly smart."

"That's what I keep telling him."

"Jamie can't wait until you get here."

"Is she okay in the bunk room with Billie and Grace?"

"Of course." Robin had worried about her youngest daughter for a couple of days, as Billie and Grace wore blouses and skirts, designer jeans and name-brand sneakers, while Jamie had been wearing more navy blue and black than any other color. She only had a few friends, and she certainly hadn't gotten multiple invites to Homecoming the way Billie had. "We got most of the Christmas decorations up tonight, and we'll fill the house with food tomorrow."

She put a smile on her face and moved over to the sleigh-style bed here in the Aurora Suite. She sank onto it and sighed. "I brought too much stuff, of course."

"Of course you did," Mandie teased. She laughed, and Robin sure did like hearing such happiness from her twenty-year-old.

"Well, I'll let you go," Robin said. "I'm on muffin duty in the morning."

"Okay, Mom. Love you."

"Love you too." Robin ended the call and lowered the phone. She'd already spoken to Duke after escaping to her third-floor suite, and Robin didn't usually have any problem being alone.

Tonight, though, inside the manor, the world

seemed so big. So wide open and... She looked over to the window, got up, and went to stand at the glass. "Dark," she murmured.

The night on the horizon practically radiated with blackness, as no other buildings stood nearby The Starlight Manor. Thankfully, the outdoor pool lights glittered and danced, moving to and fro as if fairies themselves swam about.

She'd gone to bed when everyone else had retired to their rooms too, and since Arthur had come on the ferry after he'd gotten out of school, Robin didn't feel like she could go over to Alice's suite and chat.

No one else had arrived who'd been assigned rooms on the third floor, which left Robin with only Alice and Arthur. Jamie's bunk room was situated in the basement, three full levels below Robin. But she'd only thrown her a single nervous glance, and then she'd headed downstairs with her bag, right on the heels of Billie and Grace.

Robin forced herself to go through the motions of getting ready for bed. Brushed her teeth. Pulled on her pajamas. Checked her calendar for the next couple of days. Only then could she climb into the king-size bed and lay down. She sighed as she gazed up to the ceiling, a soft smile coming to her face as the constellations that had been carefully and masterfully painted on the ceiling came to life.

With the blankets and mattress as fluffy as they were,

she felt like she'd be sleeping in the clouds, and the next thing she knew, her alarm roused her.

Robin opened her eyes and reached for her phone to silence the song she woke to each morning. Disbelief tore through her that she'd slept so soundly all night, but the clock read six-thirty, and the darkness beyond the glass seemed to be one step above black—and getting lighter.

She showered quickly, dressed, and headed down the flights of stairs to the kitchen. The scent of coffee greeted her on the second floor, and her smile had appeared before she found Kristen in the gourmet kitchen. "Good morning," she said.

Kristen gave her a soft, kind smile. "Morning."

Robin poured herself a cup of coffee without asking if she could, and she relaxed into the sip of straight-up, black brew. Then she stirred in a couple of big spoonfuls of sugar, left her coffee to "cure" as Duke said, and went to get out the boxes of muffin mix she'd brought.

"Since you're the only one up," she said as she put the assortment on the island next to her mug. "What do you think we should have today? I have cornbread, blueberry, pumpkin, and chocolate chip."

Kristen looked over to her from the kitchen table. "With the crowd we have here this morning, I'd go with blueberry and chocolate chip."

"Asher loves the chocolate chip ones," Robin said with a smile.

"So does Heidi."

Robin did a quick count of how many people would

be at breakfast that morning—fourteen—and decided two boxes of muffins would be plenty.

Kelli, Shad, and their kids would be arriving this afternoon, as would Tessa and Julia. Duke, Matt, Maddy and Ben, Laurel and Paul, and Clara and Scott should all be here by lunchtime, and Robin's nerves vibrated through her stomach.

She and El had spoken about having everyone in the same room and how that might go, because both of them wanted this holiday at this house to be nothing short of magical.

Laurel had been tasked with finding a local Five Island Cove charity or charitable event they could work with or contribute to, and Robin hoped that project could unify them.

She hoped Alice wouldn't say anything to rile up AJ, and she prayed AJ could keep her cool if the conversation went in a direction she didn't agree with. For the most part, Kelli and El didn't speak up unless absolutely necessary, and she supposed she could learn to curb her tongue about certain topics too.

And you will, she told herself. Because she wanted this Christmas to be the most amazing one for all of them.

The muffins came out perfect, and Robin started with the sausage patties and a pound of bacon. The scent of that usually got everyone out of bed, and this time was no exception.

By the time she pulled the last crispy slice from the

pan and turned to set the paper-towel lined plate on the island, all of the adults had arrived in the kitchen.

"Wow, Robin," Arthur said with a big smile. "Thank you so much for making breakfast." He stepped over to the fridge and pulled out the cream, as well as a square of butter. "What else do we need?"

"Muffin!" Asher yelled, and that caused Heidi to add her voice to the morning.

"I'll get you one," Billie said kindly, and she took Asher from AJ and started to buckle him into a booster seat at the table.

"No one has to wait." Robin gestured Jamie and Grace forward. "Come get something to eat. Everyone, come get breakfast." She stood out of the way while a line formed and conversations broke out. She wasn't sure what about providing a meal for people caused so much satisfaction; she only knew it did.

So she slow-sipped her coffee until everyone had a plate of food, and then she took a few slices of bacon and the last blueberry muffin over to the table. El had saved her a seat, and she slid into it with a quick look at her best friend.

"Thank you, Robin." El leaned her head against Robin's shoulder for a brief moment, and then she put another chunk of chocolate chip muffin on the table in front of Heidi.

"I really want this to be the best Christmas ever." She only spoke loud enough for Eloise to hear.

"Me too," El murmured in return. She took a bite of

her sausage and gave Robin a somewhat anxious look. "Do you think Charlie will propose?" She shot her gaze down to Alice and then focused on Robin again. "I asked Alice, and she acted like she had no idea."

Robin's throat turned into a narrow straw. "I don't know either," she said, doing everything in her power not to look at Alice and Arthur only a few seats down. "But my best guess? Yes, a proposal is coming soon. Mandie said they've talked about getting married next summer."

"That's only a handful of months away."

"Good thing she knows a really great wedding planner." Robin gave El a quick smile, and she squeezed El's hand as she returned it.

The familiar weight of responsibility settled on her shoulders, as Robin carried things she probably shouldn't. After all, she couldn't guarantee that everyone would get along here at The Starlight Manor. She couldn't even make them. And for someone like Robin, who loved to be in control of things and situations, and yes, even people, she'd been learning to let go of some things.

Or rather, she needed to do so—and she had plans for the New Year to help with this very thing.

One, she couldn't tell Mandie how to live her life. Either she'd marry Charlie or she wouldn't. She'd keep living with him while they went to college. No matter what, the world hadn't ended when they'd moved in together, and they seemed really happy together.

Two, she couldn't control her friends. Having them all back in Five Island Cove for these past few years had only solidified that for her, and Robin had been trying to love each one of them for exactly who they were—not who she wished they were.

As breakfast finished up, Arthur, Aaron, and Reuben went into the kitchen to clean up and do the dishes, and Robin went into the foyer to get the meal binder she'd brought with her. She returned to her spot at the kitchen table and flipped open the cover.

Beside her, El set down her coffee cup and started to laugh. And laugh, and laugh, and laugh.

Robin glared at her and flipped a plastic sleeve with today's date on it. "What?" she clipped out. "AJ said we're going to get groceries this morning, and in case you have forgotten, we're feeding almost forty people tonight."

"Who could forget that?" El rolled her eyes and got up. "I want to show you my binder."

Robin grinned at her retreating back, then switched it to Kristen. Everyone else had vacated the table, with some of them headed downstairs to the game room and indoor pool, and the moms of little ones going to get them dressed for the day.

"She has a binder?"

"It's an incredible sight," Kristen said. "Just you wait."

Sure enough, El came out of the mudroom, which

led into the garage, carrying a two-inch binder with red and green tassels hanging from it. Christmas *tassels*.

Robin started to laugh again, and El proudly held up her binder like it was a shield and would protect her in battle. "Wow," Robin said between her giggles. "What is in that thing?"

"Everything," El said as she rejoined her at the table. "The room arrangements, WiFi codes, how to restart the individual routers, how to heat the hot tub, who to call in a pool emergency."

"The important things."

"The floor plans." El chose a tab and flipped a bunch of pages to the basement layout of the manor. "I love floor plans."

Robin leaned over to study the page too. "There's something about them," she agreed. "Oh, there's a spa in the pool and hot tub area downstairs?"

El searched the page and then pointed to what Robin had already seen. "Yeah, it looks like it."

"I'm glad you told us to bring our swimming suits." It wasn't an item Robin normally packed with her in December.

"Do either of you want to go for a walk around the grounds?" Alice asked, and Robin looked away from Eloise's amazing binder to find another of her best friend's tugging on a pair of gloves that probably came from a high-end department store.

Alice exuded charm and sophistication, even when

simply putting on a sweater and gloves to go for a winter walk.

"I do," Robin said, eyeing Alice's black sweater. "Let me grab my jacket." She closed her meal planning binder and took it into the foyer, where a coat closet also housed her jacket. Back in the main part of the house, she glanced over to the hallway that led down to the bedrooms.

"AJ hasn't come out yet?"

"She put Asher in the tub," Alice said. "She said she doesn't want to go on a walk this morning." They exchanged a glance, but Robin wasn't quite sure what Alice meant to say. She could ask once they left these walls behind. "She said maybe later."

"Okay," Robin said cheerfully. "El, you coming?"

"Yep." She turned from the sink, where she'd been washing her hands. Her binder had likewise been put away. "We can do the groceries when we get back."

"Lunch is on-your-own today," Robin said. "So yes, we can go get what we need once we get back." Worry instantly stole into her thoughts, because she'd planned a three-meat taco bar, and she wanted to get enough cod— or maybe mahi mahi—for it. She should've gone first thing this morning to get the freshest fish.

Calm down, she told herself as Eloise pulled on her sweatshirt and the three of them left through the back sliding door. They exited onto a sprawling deck, covered by plenty of roofing. The outdoor pool waited at the bottom of a set of three steps, glinting and dazzling in the morning sunlight.

Beyond that, a stretch of cement housed a gas fire pit with two dozen Adirondack chairs stacked nearby. Cobblestones led through the grass toward the back of the property, with the bare branches of the trees jiggling slightly in the post-breakfast breeze.

Robin exhaled, all of her worries about what kind of fish they ate in their tacos that night simply floating up, up, and away. "I really need this holiday house." She linked arms with Eloise and brought her closer. "Thank you so much for thinking of it, El."

"Yes," Alice said. "It feels like exactly what I need too."

"Maybe a lot of us do," El said, her gaze far away on the horizon. "I have only told Aaron this, but I felt like Cliffside was going to kill me this year."

Robin had not heard Eloise say such a thing, and she hated that eleven months of the year had passed before she'd known this. "I'm so sorry, El."

"This month off is a test," El said, her voice definitely carrying a confessional tone. "I'm not going back until after the New Year, and Aaron and I are going to see how it goes when I'm off-site."

"I hope it goes well," Alice said.

Eloise took a deep breath and as she released it, she said, "All right, my confession came out. Now I need one from each of you."

Chapter Four

A lice Rice inhaled deeply as she stepped onto the winding path that led along the cliffs overlooking the ocean. The brisk December air filled her lungs, carrying with it the scent of salt and sunshine. She adjusted her cashmere scarf, grateful for its warmth against the chilly breeze coming over the cliffs.

Clouds filled the sky too, and she wouldn't be surprised if it rained later that day. A smile came to her soul as she thought about being in the warm swimming pool as the cooler rain came down. She'd loved that juxtaposition as a child, and she'd love to time her afternoon pool time with the rain.

Eloise and Robin fell into step beside her, their shoes crunching softly on the well-groomed gravel path. Alice glanced at her two friends, noting how El seemed ready to wait for the confessions she'd requested while Robin's eyes darted about, taking in every detail of their surroundings.

A twinge of anxiety whipped through Alice as she thought about what she might say. She'd become even closer with Robin and El in the past year, as they all lived in the same stage of life. She didn't usually love sharing her innermost thoughts, and she excelled at compartmentalizing the emotions and situations in her life, dealing with each one as she must, and then moving on to the next.

But she also knew the importance of reciprocity in friendships, and if she didn't share with them, they wouldn't truly know her. They walked in silence, the only sound the distant crash of waves against the rocky shore below. Alice steeled herself, knowing she'd have to go first.

"I think there's a lookout up here," Robin said.

"I think you're right." El glanced over to her, then to Alice.

"All right," she said, her voice a touch cross. "I'll go first, but you owe me."

"I'll go first next time," Robin said, almost over the top of Alice's last few words.

"Sure." Alice exhaled mightily and looked past the bare branches to the choppy ocean waves in the distance. The sea seemed angry today, and Alice often felt some of the same boiling, brewing unrest inside her. Especially over her daughter.

"I'm worried about Ginny," she said. "That's my confession."

"Boo," Robin said. "You can't say you're worried about one of your kids as if that's a surprise."

Alice looked at her, her eyebrows flying up. "What? Of course I can."

"I agree with Robin," El said. "I told you my inn almost killed me this year, and you think you being worried about your daughter is the same?" She gave Alice a bright smile, but that didn't mean she didn't want more than what Alice had said.

"Fine." Alice held her head high as she faced forward again. "She and Bob just met, what? A few months ago?"

"July?" Robin guessed.

"*Late* July," Alice said. "They knew each other less than a month before he moved to Boston." He attended law school there, and Alice couldn't fault him for that. "She thinks he'll propose soon, and she wants to get married in the city."

She sighed like this was the worst thing possible, and in many ways, Alice actually thought it was. "I've met him a couple of times is all, and it feels like...you know what? Full confessional: It feels like I'm losing her in a major way. Losing her to the city. Losing her to a man I don't know and who I think she barely knows. Losing her to the wealth and influence of her father."

There. She'd said it all now. Her lungs vibrated with how much she'd said. "I haven't told anyone this," she said. "Besides Arthur, so please keep it to yourself." She gave Robin a pointed look.

Her best friend had the audacity to look shocked. "Who am I going to tell?"

"Mandie," Alice fired back at her. "Who'll tell Charlie, and Charlie and Ginny are twins, Robin. They're very close and always will be. Ginny told me the other day that she hadn't seen Charlie yet that day, but something kept bothering her. When she finally got him to respond, he'd told her that he'd been pushed getting on the subway and twisted his ankle."

She looked at El and Robin, hoping they'd get it. "They *know* when something isn't right with the other, and you can't burden Charlie with this. He won't be able to keep it from Ginny, and I don't want her to know."

"Has he said anything about it?" El asked in her timid, delicate voice.

"No." Alice shook her head, a break in the trees ahead promising a great view of the water below. "I don't need solutions. We didn't give you any, El."

"True."

They arrived at the lookout, and the three of them faced the vastness of the ocean off the east side of Rocky Ridge. "This is simply incredible," Alice said. Five Island Cove was the Eastern-most land mass of the United States, and looking east, she wondered if she could see all the way to the United Kingdom.

The crashing of waves reached up the cliffs, almost

echoing off the crags and crevices the higher the sound rose.

"I love the ocean," Robin said.

"That's not your confession," El said right back.

They looked at each other, and even Alice smiled. Then all three of them laughed, and some of Alice's pent-up nerves settled. She'd always worry about her daughter, and she simply wanted the very best for her.

El stepped away from the lookout, and Robin followed, then Alice. She lined up with them again, the path the perfect width for the trio of them to walk side-by-side. Alice imagined what this place would be like in the springtime, with the leaves budding and birds singing.

It definitely possessed its own spirit in the winter too, and Alice had always loved Rocky Ridge.

"My confession is that I've got an appointment with a therapist in the New Year," Robin said.

Alice pulled in an audible breath. "Wow, Robin." Questions piled up, but that wasn't really what this walking confessional was about. So Alice kept her voice silent, and if anyone asked a question, it would be Eloise.

"What spurred that?" El finally asked.

The path curved, and Alice, Robin, and El went with it. "I need to work on things with my mom," Robin said. "And to be honest, I'm struggling with a few things with Mandie as well." She tossed a look to Alice, who once again said nothing.

She didn't worry nearly as much about Charlie as she

did Ginny. He would do whatever Mandie wanted, and Alice completely understood why Robin was experiencing some nerves with the relationship.

"I'm glad." Alice put her arm around Robin and gave her a squeeze.

"We should head back," Robin said, glancing at her watch. "We need to get to the store and get the groceries."

As they made their way back to the house, gratitude for this walk of confessions and connections with her friends filled her. Arthur did his best to support her and talk through her feelings.

But there was nothing like expressing them to other women, to moms, to her best friends, and Alice prayed she'd always be able to rely on women like Robin and Eloise.

———————————

LATER THAT EVENING, ALICE STOOD BEFORE the full-length mirror in the third-floor Andromeda Suite, assessing her outfit for dinner. She smoothed a hand over the deep burgundy silk blouse she'd paired with tailored black trousers, debating whether to add a statement necklace or keep things simple.

"You look beautiful," Arthur said, coming up behind her and sliding his hand along her hip and around to her belly. "As always." He smiled at her in the mirror, and leaned in to kiss a spot just below her ear.

"Thank you," she whispered. She decided against the necklace as Arthur continued into the en suite bathroom to brush his teeth, opting instead for a pair of small diamond studs. "Are you sure you can't stay longer than the weekend?"

Arthur sighed, adjusting his tie. "I wish I could, but with only two weeks left before the holiday break, I need to be there for the students. We have appointments to go over college scholarship applications, and I'm heading up the study sessions for finals."

Alice nodded, understanding but still disappointed. She'd cleared her entire caseload for the next three weeks, determined to fully embrace this chance to spend the holidays at a house she didn't have to clean later. But she knew Arthur's work as a guidance counselor meant a lot to a many, especially at this time of year.

"I'm glad you're here now," she said, giving his hand a squeeze as he rejoined her in the bedroom. The Andromeda Suite had deep, dark blue walls, with a bright white ceiling, baseboards, crown molding, and accessories. A white couch with starry pillows. White curtains. A stark, white bathroom. She almost felt like she'd been transported to the neighboring galaxy, where she existed in deep darkness, looking toward a bright white sun.

"I'll be here every weekend, sweetheart," he said. "And you know what? Rocky Ridge is an hour ferry ride from Diamond. I can come every evening."

"And commute to school in the morning?"

"People do it every day of the year."

She turned into his arms, feeling much younger than she was when she looked at him. "We fell in love fast, right?"

"Yes." He always smiled easier than she did, but tonight, he remained straight-faced. "Worried about Ginny?"

"She and Bob will be here next weekend," she said. "Then all through the holidays. She texted me this afternoon."

"This is good," Arthur said gently. "We'll get to meet him again. Spend more time with him. See how they are together."

"Yeah." Alice didn't want to hold this inside her tonight, so she said, "Breathe with me?"

Arthur took in an exaggerated breath, and Alice tried to fill her lungs from her belly up and up and up, through her ribcage, then her chest, all the way to her throat. Her husband held the air in his lungs, then started to push it out in a slow, controlled hiss.

Alice once again copied him, and by the time the breath ended and her chest, ribcage, lungs, and stomach felt completely devoid of air, she took a normal breath. "All right," she said. "I'm ready."

He escorted her out of their suite and down the hall to the small landing living room at the top of the steps on the third floor. With the vastness of the house, the third floor also housed a cozy library, Robin and Duke's suite, another bedroom, and two of the bunk rooms.

The rooms along the back of the house had balconies, and that included Alice and Arthur's suite. She couldn't wait to retreat there with him tonight, a glass of wine in her hand as she let the winter night and her handsome husband further soothe her.

As they made their way down to the grand dining room, a flutter of excitement wound through Alice. The Starlight Manor truly boasted the best of everything, from the tile to the carpet to the paint to the decor. Everyone had arrived throughout the afternoon, and Alice had spent an hour in the kitchen, helping Robin make guacamole and salsa for tonight's taco bar fiesta.

She simply needed an evening of good food and conversation with her closest friends—and the moment she stepped into the main part of the house, she knew she'd get it.

Someone had turned off all the main lights in the house, creating a mysterious and romantic atmosphere. Twinkling Christmas lights brightened the family room, and another string ran across the top of every window, along the underside of the dining room table, around the entire island in the kitchen, and hung like icicles from the cupboard doors.

"Wow," Alice breathed. A long, dark-oak table dominated the center of the dining room, set for twenty-four with bright white dishes, red napkins, and loose ball ornaments running down the length of it. Bowls of cheese, guacamole, salsa, and sour cream had been positioned among the Christmas decor, and Alice had never considered condiments to go so well with holiday balls.

Above, the ceiling had been painted to resemble a night sky, and Alice stared, trying to decide if the twinkling lights there were actually electrical or not. "Are those real lights?" she asked, because it sure seemed like they were.

This holiday house was made with magic, and Alice experienced a rush of joy, and joy, and more joy.

"Okay, everyone," Robin called, and the casual conversations that had broken out calmed into silence. Robin wore a black sweater dress with a clunky, bright red necklace, and she looked like the perfect picture of night sky and Christmas all in one.

"It's a taco bar tonight," she said. "There's a table in the kitchen for the teens, and they've volunteered to take the littles too. That's up to the parents. There are twenty-four spaces at the dining room table, and that's one per adult, including Lena." She smiled over to Clara and Scott's daughter.

"We can squeeze in the boosters if the parents want their kids by them." She turned and looked at the spread of food on the twelve-foot island. "There's chicken, steak, and shrimp for the tacos. There should be plenty of food, so no need to push to be first." She pinned Parker and Jamie with a look. "I'm talking to you teenagers over there."

"Okay, Mom," Jamie said, her smile huge.

Nothing could ruin Alice's mood tonight, and she

found herself smiling too. The aroma of spicy chicken and cool avocado filled the air, and her stomach growled.

"Let's eat." Robin clapped her hands, and people started to move toward the island. Alice noted they'd all dressed as nicely as she and Arthur had, even the teenagers. Billie carried Asher in her arms, and Laurel followed her with James, with Grace right behind them.

Most of the adults without children stayed out of the way for a few minutes, and that included Alice and Arthur. When she finally had her one chicken taco and her one shrimp taco, she noted that all of her friends had given up their little children to be cared for by the teens.

Lena, who had turned twenty-four this year, sat at the teen table, Heidi right at her side. Alice smiled at Parker, who took care of his baby half-sister, Daphne, and Jamie, Billie, and Grace, who'd taken on Asher and James.

She followed Arthur back into the dining room, where they found seats near the middle of the table. Alice found herself sitting next to Kelli, and she gave her friend a side-hug before she picked up a tortilla chip and brushed it through her guacamole.

"How was the trip from Pearl?" she asked. Going the length of Five Island Cove—from the southern-most island of Bell to the northern-most of Rocky Ridge—was quite the feat.

"It was fine," Kelli said. "They run the express on the weekends, so we only had to get on once, and we came straight here."

"Oh, I didn't realize they'd started up the express again." The ferry that bypassed the middle islands had been shut down after Labor Day for maintenance and repairs.

"Just last week." Kelli leaned over her plate and turned her head to take a bite of her steak taco.

"How are things at the studio?" she asked, glancing over to Shad. "With Daphne and everything. Have you found your groove?" Their daughter was only eight months old, and with every change a baby went through, her parents had to adjust too.

"Getting there," Kelli said, glancing over to her husband. AJ sat next to Shad, and she looked in Alice and AJ's direction. "Things seem to change every week."

"Sometimes every day when she wakes up," Shad said with a smile. He met Kelli's eyes, and they clearly had some sort of silent conversation Alice wasn't privvy to.

"Some days I feel like I'm barely keeping my head above water." Kelli took another bite of her taco while Alice nodded. She'd had two babies at once and a husband who worked in the city. She knew the feeling of drowning on dry ground.

"I can imagine. How's Parker adjusting to having a little sister?"

Kelli's expression softened, and she looked into the kitchen through the wide archway. "He's been amazing, actually. So helpful and patient. I was worried at first, but—"

"Patient?" AJ's voice cut in from down the table, her tone sharp. "I thought you said last week that he was acting out and giving you a hard time about babysitting."

Alice tensed and glanced between Kelli and AJ, noting the way Kelli's shoulders had stiffened and AJ's eyes had narrowed.

"He had one bad day," Kelli replied, her voice tight. "Teenagers are allowed to have mood swings, AJ. It doesn't mean he's not generally helpful."

AJ raised an eyebrow, clearly not about to let this go. The other conversations around her quieted, which only made AJ's words sound like a shout. "I'm just saying, maybe if you set clearer boundaries and expectations—"

"And as I've told you," Kelli interrupted, her cheeks flushing. "You don't have a teenager, and not every child responds well to rigid rules and constant discipline."

Alice exchanged a worried glance with Arthur, and her gaze instantly sought Robin's too. "Okay," Robin started. "El, why don't you—?"

"There's nothing wrong with having structure," AJ said.

"There's also nothing wrong with understanding and flexibility," Kelli shot back.

Alice had no idea how the conversation had spiraled so quickly. And she would've never guessed that Kelli and AJ—who'd been best friends forever—would be the two squabbling over how to raise a child. They were part of the "moms group" while Alice, Robin, Maddy, Julia, and Tessa had started having lunches and outings on their own.

Jean, Kelli, AJ, and Laurel had children under the age of three, so it made sense for them to spend more time together. And Jean had her mother and her sister-in-law in the cove, and that created a dynamic group as well.

Of them all, Eloise seemed to fit in the best, and she thankfully raised a spoon and clacked it against her wine glass. "Okay," she said loudly into the silence. "No one needs to have this conversation right now."

"I just want everyone to know I'm not too strict with Asher."

"That's not what they're saying," Matt said, and AJ rounded on her husband, her eyes flashing.

"Well, I'd rather have a well-behaved three-year-old than a rebellious teenager who thinks he can do whatever he wants."

Kelli sucked in a breath that matched Alice's. "AJ," she said. "That's just uncalled for."

"This was a bad idea," Kelli said, her taco now untouched.

"Sweetheart, it's fine," Shad said in a soothing voice. AJ and Matt had their heads bent together too, and Alice looked around the table with plenty of helplessness streaming through her. She wanted to say something to smooth all of this over, because she felt like she'd caused a problem by having a conversation with Kelli about her health and wellness studio and her children.

Nothing came to her mind, and Alice couldn't swallow. She looked at her shrimp taco, her appetite completely gone now.

As smaller, quieter conversations started up again, the lights in the room flickered erratically. The twinkling "stars" on the ceiling flashed on and off, casting eerie shadows across the faces of the stunned dinner guests.

"What on earth?" Alice murmured, her legal mind immediately cataloging the strange occurrence even as a shiver of unease coiled through her.

The flickering intensified, and for one terrible moment, total darkness covered the entire room. Several people gasped, and Arthur's hand closed protectively over hers.

Then, as abruptly as it had started, the lights stabilized, leaving everyone blinking in the sudden brightness. Well, as bright as stringed Christmas lights could be.

"Is everyone all right?" Kristen's calm voice cut through the confused murmurs.

"Probably just an old wiring issue," Robin said quickly, though Alice noted the uncertainty in her friend's eyes. "This house has been here for generations, after all."

Gradually, conversations resumed, though they didn't become as animated as before. Alice couldn't help but think that the way those lights had flickered...it almost seemed like they'd been responding to the argument, to the vibe in the house.

And she had no idea what to do with that.

Chapter Five

Eloise had no idea what to do, and as she helped Jean and Kristen clear away the taco bar, she said, "Well, at least the first fight has already happened."

Jean gave a light scoff that could have been a laugh, and Kristen simply shook her head.

"Do you think everyone will come back for our nightly meeting?" she asked.

"I'll text them," Kristen said. The reminder coming from her would probably be best, as no one wanted to disappoint Kristen, and she never took sides. Everyone felt like they could tell her things, and she would listen and agree with them.

El put the plates and silverware in the dishwasher until it was full, then she started it. Jean did the same with the second machine, while Kristen put the leftovers into plastic containers and bags.

Robin had done a great job organizing the kitchen so

that everyone had a job to do at some point throughout the next few weeks, whether that was prep, serving dinner, being in charge of the menu, or cleanup. Robin had not put herself on cleanup for tonight, yet she'd brought dishes from the dining room and cleaned up a teen table before she said, "Oh, Mandie's calling. I'll be right back."

She'd been gone for fifteen minutes, and Eloise couldn't judge her, because she had no young women living on their own in the city and didn't know how long a conversation with one might last.

Alice and Arthur had brought their own dishes over, and then Alice said she was going to go change, and they'd disappeared upstairs. The teens had gone down to the game room, which had a foosball table, a billiard table, several gaming consoles, and a big screen TV. Eloise didn't even think the TV was needed, as the home theater sat right next to the game room and could seat thirty people comfortably.

"I just can't believe it was Kelli and AJ," Jean said. "They've always gotten along so well."

"Something must have happened," Kristen said.

"You really think so?" El asked.

"I don't know." Kristen finished putting the shredded cheese, leftover lettuce, and diced tomatoes in the fridge, and turned to face Jean and Eloise. "I really don't, but it's very odd to have those two at each other's throats."

"I didn't even think AJ was that strict with Asher," Eloise said.

"She's not," Jean said. "Teenagers are hard."

"And so are babies," Kristen added.

Jean glanced into the living room where Ruben sat holding their two-year-old, Heidi. El loved holding Heidi because she had such a sweet spirit. She liked to babble to everyone, even herself, and she simply relaxed into whoever held her.

Eloise had never been pregnant and never had a child of her own, though she loved Aaron's girls unconditionally. She and Aaron had tried for a baby of their own, but it hadn't worked out, and Eloise had passed the age where it would be safe for her to get pregnant. So she simply held her friends' babies as often as she could—and tried to stay out of parenting discussions.

"Well, I want to go over the charity tomorrow," Eloise said. "Laurel's been working on it, and it would be unfair to have everyone stay away because they're mad."

"I'll text them right now," Kristen said, a slightly cooler note in her voice. She pulled out her phone, and by the time Eloise made it out of the gourmet kitchen and past the eat-in dining table to the family room, she had a text.

Kristen: *Don't forget, we're all meeting tomorrow at nine a.m. about our Christmas charity this year. Breakfast will be served right afterward.*

"Where's the meeting?" Kristen asked, her voice echoing slightly from the kitchen. She started toward them as Eloise said, "I believe Laurel has a presentation, so it's in the home theater."

"In the home theater, nine a.m.," Kristen repeated as she typed on her phone. That text came through next, and several replies started coming in. Relief washed through Eloise when she saw AJ had said she'd be there. Kelli, Alice, Robin, Clara—they all confirmed too. She added her own RSVP and tucked her phone away with a sigh.

She met her husband's eyes, and he smiled at her and patted the couch. "Come sit down, love," he said, and Eloise curled into his side. He stroked her hair and whispered, "You worry too much about how other people feel."

"I know," she murmured, because she couldn't argue with him. She did worry too much about how other people felt, and she wanted this Christmas to be joyous, relaxing, and beautiful for everyone.

With two of the better friends in the group already arguing, a sense of foreboding settled in Eloise's stomach that she couldn't quite swallow away.

"Who's on breakfast tomorrow?" Jean asked.

"I don't know," Eloise said. "Robin's binder is out in the foyer, and I'm sure we could look." But dealing with the food was not her circus, nor her monkeys. And Eloise had already spent countless hours planning this holiday retreat for everyone at The Starlight Manor.

She'd received plenty of praise and gratitude, so it wasn't that. She simply felt like she was running an inn with fifteen rooms instead of only six, and it felt like the opposite of what she wanted to accomplish this December—a relaxing, safe haven away from the stress of inn management, personnel issues, employee differences, running payroll, worrying about what they were going to feed guests the next morning, and everything else she shouldered at the Cliffside Inn.

Eloise had fought hard to get the Cliffside Inn, and she'd given up a lot to do it. She couldn't believe that now, only a few short years later, she was considering selling it. Aaron made plenty of money, and they didn't need the income that the inn generated.

It took her away from Billy and Grace during a crucial time in their lives, and while she'd tried to step back by hiring more managers, she still found herself entrenched in the daily busyness of the inn.

Even on days when she didn't physically go to Sanctuary Island, to the inn, she spent time thinking about how to improve it—which rooms needed renovation, what it would cost to keep the pool open all winter, what new breakfast options they could provide, and many more things, even when she wasn't there.

She'd only mentioned to Aaron, and now Robin and Alice, that she'd started to feel overwhelmed and run down by the inn. At the same time, her heart still pinched at the thought of putting it up for sale and walking away for good.

No one would run the inn the way she did—she knew that. She had emotional connections to that building, as her family had once owned it, and she'd reclaimed it after many years of neglect and after uncovering some treacherous secrets.

But could I still own it and simply hire someone to do what I do on a daily basis? she wondered silently.

"I need another one of me," she said, only half-joking.

Aaron chuckled and kneaded her closer. "Don't we all?"

They'd only been married for a couple of years, but Eloise felt like she had truly found her life partner in Aaron Sherman—and she wanted to be alone with him to talk through the evening, and maybe go through some options for the inn again.

She yawned as she straightened away from his side. "I think I'm going to go to bed." Eloise glanced over at him; his eyebrows went up, and Eloise smiled, hoping he'd understand that she wanted him to come with her.

They had a suite on the second floor, which only housed bedrooms and bathrooms. There were three suites and two regular bedrooms, with Eloise and Aaron's tucked away in the far corner. They had a nearly three-hundred-sixty-degree view of the property and the ocean in the distance. She might not go to bed right away, but she certainly didn't want to stay down here and be social.

She stood just as Julia came down the hall from her room. "Are you leaving?" she asked.

"Yeah," Eloise said, and she stepped over to Julia and hugged her. "I'm so glad you could come this weekend."

"Ooh, me too," Julia said as she squeezed her back. "I'm working this week, and then I'll be back the week after that, and then I have to work a couple days before Christmas."

"Right," Eloise said, as she'd been the one to shoulder all of the calendar items. She knew she could look in her binder and find out who would be at the holiday house on what days and nights, and she'd asked people to please pack up their things and either leave them in the closet or take them with them if they weren't going to be staying at the manor for more than one night.

That way, if Matt's daughter wanted to come into town, she could give Julia's bedroom to Lisa, or if Lena didn't want to sleep in the bunk room, Eloise would know where the young woman could take refuge.

She stepped away from Julia and smiled, then took Aaron's hand and led him toward the steps. They had to climb seventeen to get to the second floor, and she knew why AJ didn't want to do that with her toddler in tow.

She let Aaron pull the door closed before she turned in his arms and kissed him. He chuckled against her lips and said, "You don't want to go to bed."

"Yes, I do," she murmured. "I just want you to come with me."

She pulled away and met his eyes, somewhat shy and yet absolutely not at the same time. She loved and adored

Aaron, and she loved the way that he loved and adored her. So as his smile faded and a glint of passion entered his eyes, Eloise tipped her head back to receive a much hungrier kiss from him this time.

His phone rang, which caused him to pull away. He frowned. "I have it on silent." And that only meant one thing: the same person had called three times in the span of five minutes.

"I'll go freshen up in the bathroom," she said, assuming the call would be from the precinct on Diamond Island and that it would be extremely important. She hoped he wouldn't be too upset, or keyed up, or too long, because she wanted to make love to her husband to truly drive away her stress and worry over providing the very best holiday this Christmas.

She took her time in the bathroom, brushing her teeth and changing into a sexy nightgown she'd brought, and after several minutes, she returned to the suite to find Aaron sitting on his side of the bed, shirtless.

"It must not have been too bad," she said as she pulled back the covers on her side.

He set his phone on the nightstand and rolled toward her. "It was Carol," he said, a definite note of darkness in his voice.

His ex-wife.

"Oh," Eloise said as brightly as she could. "What did she want?"

"She's landing tomorrow in Five Island Cove," Aaron said. "She wants to see the girls."

"Well, that's not going to work," Eloise said as she ran her hand down his chest. "We're on vacation."

"I told her I'd talk to them." He sighed as he tucked her into his arms. "I like this nightgown." He pressed his lips to hers and kissed her, and as he moved his mouth down her neck, he added, "I don't want to talk about Carol."

"Okay," Eloise gasped, his hands already roaming south and touching delicate parts through the thin silk of her nightgown. He slid the spaghetti strap to the side on her shoulder, and then placed a kiss there.

"As much as I like this nightgown, it has to come off." He pressed the hard length of his cock to her thigh.

"Yes, it does." And Eloise let her husband undress her and make love to her, as a great way to forget about the fight—and the flickering lights—that had happened at dinner.

Chapter Six

L aurel Leyhe snuggled back into her husband's arms when he woke her on Sunday morning. He took a breath of her neck and placed a kiss there. "You smell good," he murmured.

She smiled, though she knew that wasn't true. Their suite sat on the second floor, and it was the nicest place Laurel had ever slept. They had a couch and two recliners in their room, which faced a TV. The bathroom housed a walk-in shower and a Jacuzzi tub in addition to the toilet room and his-and-hers sinks. Through the bathroom sat the walk-in closet, which Laurel could easily park her car in.

They'd brought a portable playpen-slash-crib for their son James to sleep in, and the sixteen-month-old had gone down easy and early last night after he'd missed his afternoon nap in favor of playing in the pool.

"Sometimes I can't believe this is my life," she whispered.

Paul simply tightened his arms around her. "Well, it is, sweetheart."

She loved lying with him. She loved talking with him. She loved being with him, and she'd never thought she'd find that sense of safety, security, and home with a man. Paul treated her like a queen and took care of her and James, especially since she'd quit the police force after becoming a mother.

His hand moved down and settled over her belly. "Are you nervous?"

"What should I be nervous about?" she asked, though she already knew.

"Your charity presentation," he whispered. "I know you're nervous about that."

"A little," she conceded. "I think I'm more nervous to tell everyone I'm pregnant."

"Why is that?" he asked. "That's happy news, and they love you."

"I know," Laurel turned in his arms. "I can't explain it."

She opened her eyes and looked into his. "I know they're not going to judge me."

"You know it," he said. "But you don't believe it." He grinned and touched his lips to hers. The way he kissed her told her that he wanted to take it further, and Laurel did love being intimate with him in the morning before he went to work.

In fact, they made love more in the morning than they did at night. When Laurel pressed eagerly into him to let him know she was willing, she pulled in a breath as he broke their kiss and gasped out, "What time is it, Paul?"

"I don't know," he murmured, clearly not caring about the time.

"I have a presentation," she said. "I have to shower. And James..."

Paul pulled away from her and rolled partway onto his back to reach for his phone. Not much light came through the blinds, so surely they had time, but Laurel didn't want to be rushed this morning.

"Six forty-five," he said, and he rolled back to her. "If we're fast, we can be done, and you can shower before James gets up in forty-five minutes."

She ran her hand down the side of his face, then his neck, and along his bare shoulder. "Okay."

He grinned at her. "I know you want to be showered before James gets up."

"I do."

He pulled her closer. "So let me have my way, baby, and I'll put you in the shower myself."

"Yes, sir, Officer," she said.

Sure enough, forty-five minutes later, Laurel toweled her hair dry as James made his first squawks of the morning. Paul finished rinsing out his mouth and said, "I'll get him."

He left the bathroom with his towel wrapped

around his waist and went to get their little boy. Laurel hadn't quite gotten dressed yet, but James could explore the suite or sit on the couch with a piece of cheese while she finished getting ready.

"Look, there she is," Paul cooed. "There's Mama."

"Ma-ma-ma-ma," James babbled, and Laurel grinned at him with every ounce of joy in her soul.

"Hey, baby." She swept a kiss across his face, loving how rumpled and sleep-worn he looked when he first woke up in the morning.

Paul smiled at her and James, kissed them both, and took him into the suite. Laurel blew out her hair and got dressed, then she took James to get him dressed for the day while Paul put on his clothes. They made their way downstairs, forty-five minutes before Laurel needed to be ready to present in the home theater.

She'd done plenty of presentations for the police department when she'd worked as a cop, and she'd sat through tons of meetings too. She'd brought her computer along and had done as much research on the charity she'd selected this year as she would have for a homicide investigation.

She put James in the front row chair while Paul set up her computer to shine on the big wall at the front of the theater.

Her stomach rumbled with nerves and the want of food, but she'd promised everyone that the presentation would only take fifteen minutes, and she vowed to stick to that. After all, Scott and Rueben had volunteered to make breakfast this morning, and they'd texted out the menu of chocolate chip pancakes and sausage rolls last night.

"You good?" Paul asked.

Laurel looked up from the notes on her phone. "Yes, thank you, sweetheart."

"I'm gonna go get coffee. I'll be right back." He picked up James and took him with him, leaving Laurel in the semi-dark, windowless home theater alone.

She didn't stay that way for long, as others started joining her by eight-thirty.

"I wanted to get a good seat," Alice said as she took a spot in the third row.

Robin and Duke arrived with Jamie. AJ and Matt came in and sat in the front row in the corner, Matt sitting on AJ's left side so that no one else would be able to sit by her. Laurel tried not to pay her too much attention, though she definitely sensed something deeper inside AJ that really had nothing to do with how she was raising Asher.

Paul returned with the coffee. Kristen, Jean, Rueben, Julia, Maddy, and Ben all arrived, and the chatter in the theater increased. Laurel sipped her coffee, bent her head over her notes, and let Paul play the social one.

Finally, when the minutes clicked to nine o'clock, she stood and faced everyone. Instant whiteness covered her vision because she hadn't addressed a group this large in a long time.

They're your friends, she reminded herself.

Once again, Laurel hardly recognized her life. She'd been a female cop for most of her life, and her friends and co-workers had mostly been men. But since meeting Alice, Robin, Eloise, AJ, and Kelli, Laurel now had more female friends than male ones. A slip of emotion caused tears to prick behind her eyes, and she drew in a breath, horrified, and calmed herself enough to speak.

"All right," she said. "I'm going to quickly go over the charity I found this year and some of the things we need to do. Some of them will be set up here in the holiday house for the duration of our stay, and you can work on them as you come and go. Others are actual events, and you can sign up to go—or not—depending on your schedule."

She swiped her fingers across the trackpad on her computer, and the presentation came up on the screen. "The charity this year is *A Very Veteran Christmas*," she said. "They have a chapter here in Five Island Cove, where, believe it or not, we have quite the contingent of men and women who have served in the Navy or the Coast Guard."

There weren't as many Marines or Army veterans from Five Island Cove, and being surrounded by water, it made sense that the population would move into the more aquatic arms of the military.

"Times are hard," Laurel said. "And they're even harder for people who are on fixed incomes or benefits that don't fluctuate with the economy. This year, *A Very Veteran Christmas* is hosting a gift-wrapping event on

December twentieth that we can sign up to help with. They're always accepting donations, of course, and they are also doing a Christmas Eve breakfast for all veterans and their families that they need a lot of hands for as well. Those are the two events.

"As for things that we can do for them here, *A Very Veteran Christmas* would like non-perishable food packages put together, Care Kits with personal care items, as well as Comfort Kits that include blankets, clothing, books to read, gift cards for streaming services, electronic devices like headphones and e-readers, and other items."

She tapped, and the slide moved to the next one, which outlined the events. "Please consult your calendar," she said. "I'm going to have a sign-up sheet here at the house, upstairs on the breakfast counter, for anyone who thinks they might be able to sign up."

She turned and faced the crowd again. She met Eloise's eyes, who gave her a bright, shining smile that buoyed Laurel's confidence and spirits. She turned to change the slide again.

"These are some single donations, outside of the kits, they'd like." The list included puzzles, card games, paperback novels, ebooks, some toiletry supplies like beard care kits, slippers, and more. The list went on, and Laurel didn't need to read every single one.

She changed the slide again. "My goal is to provide five Care Kits for veterans, five Comfort Kits for veterans, and five food packages. Paul and I will be donating some of the items, and we'd love it if others would sign up to donate as well. And anyone who's here at the house can help assemble those kits and wrap them. Then several of us will take them to *A Very Veteran Christmas,* which is located on Diamond Island."

Laurel's last slide simply said *Thank you,* and she didn't switch to it, feeling a moment of embarrassment catch her right in the chest. Her voice hurt for how much she'd said, and she just needed this to be done.

"Thanks," she said. "That's it."

She glanced at her phone and saw that she'd only been speaking for nine minutes. She looked up again and said, "Paul and I know a lot about this charity, and you can ask either one of us questions." She looked over to Rueben and said, "I believe the sign-up is upstairs?"

Rueben started nodding.

"Yep," she said, "Rueben's telling me it's upstairs, so I guess we can just head up there for breakfast."

She looked over to Eloise, who nodded. The crowd started to get up, and Laurel's energy and nerves went down.

"Great job, baby," Paul said as he swept a kiss along her cheek.

"This is a great charity," Robin said as she moved to the end of her row. "I hadn't even heard of it."

"I knew Laurel would find us something good," Alice said. Together, the ladies went upstairs, with their husbands behind them, and Laurel smiled at their compliments, though they hadn't said them directly to her.

Billie approached her, and Laurel smiled at the teen. "Hey, how are you?" Laurel asked.

"I'm good," Billie said. "I was just wondering... I have to do this project for one of my classes at school, and I was thinking that I could donate it to one of the Comfort Kits."

"Maybe," Laurel said. "What is it?"

"It's a blanket," Billie said. "I have to crochet it, and I don't even know how I'm gonna get it done, but Grace said she'd help me, and I thought maybe if we got it done in time, we could donate it to the comfort kit." She glanced over to her younger sister as she came to Billie's side.

"Sure, blankets are needed," Laurel said.

"Is there some sort of specifications on size, or if there's a lot of holes in it?" Billie became more confident with each question she asked.

"I don't think so," Laurel said, flipping through her clipboard. "But I can look. I know they'll take afghans, so crocheting shouldn't be a problem."

"Okay," Billie said. "Well, let me know. My dad said I could order all the yarn right here to the manor, and we could get started as soon as it comes."

Laurel looked at her, then Grace. "You two are still going to school, though, right?"

"Yeah," Billie said in an off-hand way. "But we don't do anything in December anyway. I can probably crochet during class."

Grace grinned. "I can *definitely* crochet during class."

Laurel giggled with them, though it had been a while since she'd been in school. "I'm definitely going to put you girls down for one of the blankets," she said.

"Great, thanks." Billie grinned as the two girls turned to leave.

The home theater had mostly emptied, and Laurel closed her computer and unhooked it from the cable that Paul had attached it to. She wasn't sure why she'd been so nervous, and then she realized she hadn't told anyone about her baby.

Her heart dropped to her stomach as she remembered why she'd put that "Thank You" slide in the presentation—because she'd made the "U" in the word *you* a stork holding a baby, with the U being the cloth part that hung down and held the infant.

She'd meant to tell everyone she was pregnant and due at the end of June as part of the presentation. Since she'd be in the spotlight anyway, she'd figured she might as well stand there for an extra slide.

"That you forgot about," she said to herself. "It's still too early to tell them anyway," she muttered as she went up the steps to the first floor. But she'd wanted to. Who needed to make a presentation with four slides to talk about veterans, events, and kits when she had everything printed out on clipboards already?

Foolishness ran through her, and she felt like crying. *That has to be the hormones too*, she thought, because

Laurel didn't just cry over nothing, and forgetting to tell her friends that she was pregnant was definitely nothing.

In the kitchen, she met Paul's eyes, and he raised his eyebrows, then got to his feet and came to her side.

"I forgot to tell them about the baby," she said.

"Oh, right." He turned around and whistled through his teeth—a piercing, shrieking sound. Several people cried out, but they all turned toward her and Paul.

Laurel's face heated, but Paul indicated her and said, "Laurel forgot to say one thing," in his really loud cop voice.

Laurel actually loved his really loud cop voice, and she smiled at him, then looked out at everyone else. In her own loud cop voice, she said, "Paul and I are going to welcome another baby to our family in June."

And as if the kitchen and dining room weren't already complete chaos, that announcement certainly did it.

Chapter Seven

K risten Shields took a moment on the third-floor
landing, which also had a sofa, a table, a lamp,
and a reading nook, to catch her breath. This floor
spanned as many square feet as the others but housed
mostly bedrooms in addition to a beautiful, brilliant, big
library.

Today had dawned frosty and cold, with not very
many people in the holiday house. She, Jean, Tessa,
Clara, and Tessa's boyfriend, Dave, were going to be
setting up the stations in the library for the charity kits.

Kristen had not requested a room on the first floor,
but Eloise had given her one anyway, and it was a good
thing. When she finally felt like she wouldn't faint, she
continued toward the library. If she had to climb all
those steps every night to go to bed or grab something
from her room that she'd forgotten, Kristen felt certain
she wouldn't last until Christmas.

And that wouldn't do, because she'd rolled two basked of Christmas gifts into the house. She wanted everyone to have something on Christmas morning, no matter what. She knew each person in the manor had someone else who cared enough about them to get them something for Christmas, but she wanted them to all know that she did too.

For a while there, right after her husband had died, Kristen thought she would lose everything. Not only had she lost the love of her life, but she'd lost the image and the person she'd believed him to be, as secrets came to light in the cove.

As her girls returned to the island community where they'd all grown up, Kristen feared they'd never speak to her again. But the opposite had been true. They'd brought her right back into their fold, as if she were one of them, and as they added new people—new women who needed the love and support of others, who needed to talk through major life decisions they were making in their forties—Kristen had found that her heart had room for each of them too.

Not only that, but she loved the men who loved her women, and she wanted them to know that she saw their good hearts and the way they took care of those around them.

She knew a tie or a wallet or a new belt didn't mean that much, but she hoped the fact that someone had thought about a person would shine through in her simple gifts.

Now, though, as she approached the library, she found the double-wide doors had been thrown open and secured with door stops. Light poured in from the back of the room as Tessa had arrived ahead of her and opened all of the curtains.

"This place is magnificent," Tessa said. She normally worked at the Five Island Cove Library on Diamond Island, but it was a part-time position, and she didn't have to go in today. Her boyfriend Dave owned a soda and cookie shop, and he said they would be fine without him for a few days.

Tessa wore her love of literature and books right on her face as she swept into Kristen's arms and hugged her. "I can't even imagine having a library like this." She stepped back and turned to it, sweeping her arm across the whole thing at once. "I mean, just *look* at it."

Kristen looked, and everything she saw caused more awe to flow through her. Floor-to-ceiling bookcases took up three of the walls, with the windows providing the fourth. Cozy couches, chairs, and bean bags lined the area in front of the windows, clearly the reading area.

Tables filled some of the space between the seating area and the door where Kristen stood. Laurel wanted the stations for the Care and Comfort Kits set up there, with the food packages being assembled in one of the three ports in the garage.

As so many people were coming and going from the house this month, Laurel figured they could bring back a few paperback books or several sticks of deodorant or a pair of slippers purchased specifically for one of the kits. And throughout the month, they would build the fifteen kits that Laurel wanted to donate to *A Very Veteran Christmas.*

Kristen had become an expert in online shopping in recent years, and she had already ordered several items from Laurel's list to be delivered straight to The Starlight Manor. She wasn't planning to return to her condo until she had to, and she hoped her continued presence would provide some sense of stability for anyone coming and going. She wasn't the only one staying the whole time, a fact for which she was grateful, for she didn't fancy staying in the manor alone at night.

But nothing too crazy had happened since the big group dinner on Saturday night, where Kelli and AJ had argued and then the lights had gone haywire.

"Have you been in here before?" Tessa asked.

"No," Kristen said. "This is the first time I've climbed all the way to the third floor." She smiled at Tessa and then Dave. "Wow, let me tell you, once you get up here, there's no going back down."

Tessa laughed with her. "It is a lot of steps."

Kristen had counted thirty-six, to be exact, and that was thirty-six more than she thought her doctor would advise her to take with her almost eighty-year-old knees.

"So, what do we have going on?" she asked, turning her attention to the tables in front of her.

"Dave just figured out how to get the printer to work," Tessa said. "So he's going to be labeling areas on each of the tables for the kits." She held her arm straight out in front of her. "There are six tables in here, so we figured we'd use five of them, straight in a row. We can do the comfort kits here, and then straight down this row—"

She stepped down several feet to the other end of the table. "—We could do care kits. That way, it's easy to see if a kit is missing, say, a blanket or a pair of slippers or a book or a gift card. The sixth table can just be used for whatever. Maybe the teens will have homework or something?"

She looked at Kristen, who nodded. "I'm sure the teens will have homework, but I'm not sure they'll come to the library to do it."

Tessa looked like Kristen had just insulted her mother, but she shook it off as Dave laid down a paper that read *Care Kit 1* in front of her.

"Laurel and Paul brought some things," Tessa said. "They're on the table way down there, and we'll organize them."

"Okay," Kristen said.

Laurel had gone with Paul to Diamond Island to drop him off at work, claiming that she had forgotten something at the house that she wanted to get and bring back for James. Kristen suspected Laurel simply wanted a few hours to herself, as she was quite introverted and might not survive at the holiday house with everyone for the next three weeks.

Kristen knew the feeling, but she took a long walk

every day, and she'd decided that she could do that with others or alone. And, of course, she had a private room where she could always escape. Even the normal-sized bedrooms had enormous king beds, and hers had a canopy with stars and constellations stuck in the upper drape that went over her head.

The library ceiling had been painted black, like her bedroom ceiling. Since Kristen had arrived early on Friday, she'd been able to check out a few of the rooms that she wasn't staying in. They had all been decorated and painted differently, and yet all matched the astronomical theme of The Starlight Manor.

She helped Dave put out the signs for each kit, while Tessa started unbagging the things Paul and Laurel had brought. There wasn't much work to be done today, and they finished in only a few minutes.

Kristen wandered over to one of the bookcases as her daughter and daughter-in-law entered the library. Jean and Clara exclaimed over the beautiful interior, but seeing so many books in one place simply reminded Kristen of Joel.

He had packed their tiny bungalow, where they'd lived near the lighthouse, with as many books, journals, notebooks, and papers as possible. She'd had quite the time going through it all after his death, and the memories streaming through her mind were bittersweet. His death and the subsequent cleanup of the bungalow had brought her girls back to her, but it had also revealed things Kristen would have rather never known.

To simply get out of her head, Kristen selected the book her fingers were touching and pulled it out of the case to find a handsome brown leather cover with gold lettering stamped into it. Just her luck that she would pull out *A Tale of Two Cities* by Charles Dickens.

She'd never liked this book, and the last time she had tried to read it, she'd hadn't finished. Still, she'd never seen this edition, and she wondered if it had been professionally recovered for whoever had owned this house.

She couldn't even imagine what it had cost to build a house like this, and she had no idea such things existed in her small island town of Five Island Cove. Her life had been so simple on Diamond Island, with a two-bedroom bungalow and the lighthouse to occupy the entirety of her days.

She opened the cover of the book and found an inscription written in the fancy cursive of the eighteenth century.

"For my darling Everleigh," she whispered aloud. Her fingers automatically went to trace the inked letters. Something old and powerful filled her heart simply by holding this book with its very human writing from long ago.

It almost felt like the book held the spirit of the person who'd written in it, and Kristen instinctively wanted to know more about them. She wanted to know who'd bought the book, how it had come to be covered this way, and who Everleigh was.

She took the book over to a wingback chair and sat

down. She wouldn't read it, but she did turn the pages, her mind revolving around the people who had lived here. Had this house always been a rental, or had a family actually lived within these walls? Had they had servants? Had they abandoned the home or sold it? And if so, why?

She wanted to know everything she could about the house. She looked up as the light changed, expecting to see clouds covering the sun, but the bright blue winter sky winked at her from beyond the glass—no clouds in sight.

Her heartbeat picked up as the filmy drapes in front of her billowed. She searched for an air duct or perhaps a window that had been opened but found none.

And yet the drape moved.

The heavier one, the one that blocked the sun and preserved the books from light damage, didn't move at all.

She glanced around and found Jean and Clara sitting at the table playing a card game. Tessa and Dave had likewise found books and had curled together on a couch, quietly talking and laughing as they looked through them.

No one had walked by. No one had caused a current that should have made that drape move, and yet it did.

"Mom," Clara called, and Kristen's attention got diverted away from the anomaly in front of her. Clara held up her cards. "Do you want to play?"

"Sure." Kristen set aside the book, pushed herself

out of the chair, and went to play cards with her loved ones. When she'd settled down, she looked back over to the window where she'd been. The drape stayed utterly still, and Kristen had no idea what to make of it.

"Do you know who owned this house?" she asked Clara.

"No idea," Clara said, shuffling the cards and beginning to deal them.

"Do you think it's been here a long time?" Kristen asked.

"Reuben and I saw a cornerstone on the pool house," Jean said. "While we were walking this morning, before he went back to the lighthouse."

"Oh?" Kristen picked up her cards, pretending not to care as much as she did.

"It had the year 1912 on it," Jean said. "So it's been here more than a century."

"The pool house must be newer than the main house," Kristen said. "I wonder if that's the year it was renovated."

Clara met her eyes, something questioning and alive there. "We used to learn about the old houses in Five Island Cove in school," she said. "I hated history, so I never paid much attention to it."

Kristen moved her cards around, organizing them by suit. Jean played first—a four of hearts—and Kristen looked at her cards to decide what to play when it was her turn. A quick glance at the pile told her that trump was clubs, and she returned her attention to her cards.

Nineteen-twelve ran through her mind, and she somehow knew that the main house was older than the pool house, which meant it had been here for perhaps as long as the lighthouse on Diamond Island. Maybe longer. She'd brought her laptop with her, and it charged in her bedroom on her nightstand. When she got a free minute, Kristen would do a little bit of research on The Starlight Manor—when it had been built and who had owned it.

Maybe then she would know why the lights seemed to turn on and off by themselves, and why the curtains drifted when there was no current.

Chapter Eight

Talk to me about the sleeping arrangements for tomorrow night. Alice sent the text to Ginny, wishing she wasn't quite so nervous about the answer.

Ginny had been dating Bob since late July, and Alice knew that relationships all progressed at different speeds. Charlie and Mandie had been together for a long time before they'd been intimate, but they'd also met and started dating in high school.

Bob was four years older than Ginny. He'd already earned his bachelor's degree and had started law school. Alice had met him twice, and he didn't seem like the pushy, pressuring type, but Alice knew better than most that relationships had a secret side that no one else knew about.

She trusted her daughter, and she knew Ginny had a good head on her shoulders, but that didn't mean she wasn't hormonal and didn't want to have sex with Bob. Alice was quite sure she did.

Whatever Eloise assigned us, Ginny texted back. *I'm sure will be fine.*

Alice had paid close attention to the room assignments for her children. Mandie and Charlie lived together, sharing a bed in an apartment in New York City. She'd expected Eloise to give them one of the smaller bedrooms here in the manor, but she hadn't. She'd split them up, putting Mandie in the female bunk room and Charlie in the male one. Ginny had also been assigned to the female bunk room, and Bob had not been assigned anything.

That doesn't help, Alice texted back to Ginny. *Eloise didn't give Bob a room.*

Eloise hadn't been sure if a twenty-four-year-old would want to share a bunk room with a fourteen-year-old—and plenty of others younger than him that he didn't know.

Parker was only fourteen, and the youngest of the teen boys in the bunk room. Liam, Coldwater's son, would be coming for Christmas, and Ian was the same age as Billie—and happened to be dating her too.

He'd stay in the male bunk room too, with Charlie and Bob. There were only four of them, while there were decidedly more on the girls' side—Billie, Grace, Jamie, Mandie, Ginny, and Lena.

But again, Lena had been given the option of staying in a different room instead of the bunk room. She'd gone back to Diamond Island with her parents on Monday, and as far as Alice knew, Scott and Clara wouldn't return to the holiday house until next weekend. Clara and Lena would then stay while Scott left to run the ferry.

They'd all be there for the Christmas Eve and Christmas Day celebrations.

Alice tapped to call Ginny, forgetting to ask her if she could take a call, which she usually did.

"Hey, Mom," Ginny said, her voice bright.

"Did I catch you at a bad time?" Alice asked. "I meant to text first."

"It's fine," Ginny said. "I'm just on my way to lunch with Evelyn and Bri."

"Oh, great," Alice said. She sighed out her breath and reminded herself that she'd had plenty of talks with her children about sex. "Ginny, I'm really asking if you're going to share a room with Bob or not. And if you are, if that means you've been intimate with him."

A beat silence went by, and then another. With each one, Alice's heart pounded harder and harder. Ginny finally said, "Sorry, there was someone right there."

"So you can't talk about this in front of other people?"

"Well, I'd rather not," Ginny hissed over the line.

"So you've slept with him." Alice wasn't asking, and she wasn't sure how she felt. Was she happy this was finally out of the way? Or was that sick feeling in her stomach a new layer of worry she'd have to carry each and every day?

"I haven't slept with him," Ginny whispered. "And I'm certainly not going to do it in a house full of forty people."

"Okay," Alice said brightly. "So I'll put you in the bunk room unless there are extra rooms. I'll talk to Eloise, because I haven't looked at the schedule or the room grid for a while. If there are extra rooms, I'm sure you could have your own room—and Bob could have one for him—or there's the bunk room, which you'll share with others."

"Will there be anyone in the male bunk room with Bob?" Ginny asked.

"Oh, that's a great question," Alice said. "I don't think Kelli and Shad are coming this weekend." Alice would be surprised if they came back at all, though Kelli hadn't said that they wouldn't.

No matter what, Parker wouldn't be there this weekend, and neither would Charlie. "I think the bunk room will actually be empty," she said. "So Bob should be fine in there."

"And I'll be with Billie, Grace, and Jamie?" Ginny asked.

"That's right," Alice said. "Mandie's not coming this weekend, and neither are Scott and Clara."

"Will there be any babies there?" Ginny asked.

Alice smiled, because Ginny did love babies and helping their moms. "Jean has Heidi here; they're staying the whole time," Alice said. "AJ and Asher will be here, and Laurel and James as well. So you'll just miss cute Daphne."

"Perfect," Ginny said. "And I should bring my swimming suit?"

"Yes, bring your suit," Alice said. "There's an indoor pool and hot tub, as well as a sauna, and the outdoor pool is heated. It's quite lovely in the afternoon. Arthur and I have been swimming when he gets here after work."

"Great," Ginny said. "Okay, Mom, I have to go."

"Okay, love you, Ginny-bug."

"Love you too, Mom."

Alice ended the call, relieved that she now knew—instead of having to guess—about Ginny and Bob's relationship. They'd be here tomorrow afternoon and all the way through Monday morning, and Alice really wanted to get to know him better.

After all, she only had one daughter, and she wanted to be part of Ginny's life. And if Ginny was going to choose Bob, Alice had better learn to like it—and him.

LATER THAT AFTERNOON, ALICE PULLED herself out of the pool when she got a text from Arthur saying he was on his way to the manor from his job at the high school. She hadn't waited for him to swim today, because he'd had an after-school meeting and had said he didn't want to swim when he got there.

I want to eat and watch a movie in that theater room, he'd said.

She loved swimming with the crisp, outdoor air against the warm water. She wrapped a towel around herself and walked across the patio and up the steps to the deck, where Kristen sat with a notebook in her lap under the heated eaves of the roof.

"This is lovely," Alice said, feeling the waves of warmth come down over her shoulders.

"Isn't it?" Kristen looked up at her as Alice took the second seat in the two-seat couch under the heater.

"What are you working on?" she asked.

"Oh, I'm just reviewing the history of this house." She passed Alice the notebook, and Alice saw a hand-sketched family tree with the last name "Everleigh" at the top.

"The Everleigh family," she said. "I feel like I should know that name. It's very familiar."

"Clara said they learned about it in school," Kristen said. "But it's been a long time since I've been to school here in the cove." She trilled out a light laugh, and Alice smiled with her.

"Me too." She handed the notebook back to Kristen. "What's got you interested in the history of the house?"

"I don't know," Kristen said thoughtfully. Several seconds passed, and Alice simply waited, because she'd known the older woman for a lot of years now, and if given enough time and space, Kristen would say what lingered on her mind.

"Have you noticed anything strange happening?" Kristen asked. "Besides the lights flashing during our first big dinner together."

Alice looked across the pool, the grounds with its neatly trimmed shrubs and the cleared flowerbeds to the trees and the walking path along the edge of the property. "Yes," she said quietly. "I've seen a few things."

Kristen turned a page in her notebook. "What kinds of things?"

Alice looked at her, unsure of how much to say. "Little things," she said. "Things that don't even matter."

Kristen nodded, and she knew Alice's game too. If she waited, Alice would talk. "Have you seen things?" Alice asked.

Kristen nodded again, and she pointed to the notebook. Alice tilted her head to look at the handwriting there, and she saw *curtains moving in library.*

AJ reported the chandelier flashing in the foyer.

Sound of whispers in one of the bedrooms when no one was present.

The house was definitely emptier during the week, and while Alice hadn't spent a lot of time exploring all of the rooms, she had poked her head in a few of them to see the unique design of each one.

"Arthur and I brought stockings," Alice said slowly. "And there's no fireplace in the room, but the TV is hung above a shelf that looks like a mantel, and we hung the stockings there. One for me and him, one for

Charlie and Ginny, and one for Bob and one for Mandie."

Alice cleared her throat. "Please don't say anything to Robin, but I wanted to have a little celebration with my core family, and right now, that includes Mandie and Bob, even though my children aren't married yet."

"That's nice, dear," Kristen said, and Alice knew she wouldn't get any judgment from her.

"Anyway," Alice said. "I came out of the bathroom the other morning, and it looked like one of the stockings was moving. Sort of like it had been touched—or there was an air current."

Kristen started writing in her notebook, and Alice almost wished she wouldn't.

"Anyway, I went over there, and it didn't seem to be swaying at all." She shrugged, though she hadn't doubted what she's seen.

"I see," Kristen said. "Anything else?"

"Oh, I don't know," Alice said. "Little things here and there. Faulty wiring. My curling iron plugged in when I thought I'd unplugged it. Things like that." She waited while Kristen wrote those things down too, and then she asked, "Do you think the house is haunted?"

"I don't know," Kristen said. "And even if it is, they don't seem menacing."

A chill stole across Alice's shoulders despite the heat from above. "The kids and I once took a trip to California," she said. "We stayed in this really old hotel that was said to be haunted. The elevator would just stop randomly on different floors."

She smiled at the memory. "The kids loved the swimming pool there."

"It could just be an old house," Kristen said.

"That plugs in curling irons when they've been unplugged?" Alice cocked her eyebrows at Kristen. "I'm far too much of a lawyer to believe that."

Kristen grinned at her. "Do lawyers believe in ghosts at all?"

Alice let out a laugh. "No, we don't." She stood. "I'm going to go shower; get warmed up."

The moment she said it, a blast of heat came down from the heater installed in the roof above. She looked up and saw the glowing, red grill, and Kristen said, "Oh, wow," somewhere outside her mind.

The heat continued to flare, flashing across Alice's ears and shoulders and down her bare arms. It went on for another few seconds, and then the redness in the coils vanished, and the heater returned to its normal function.

Alice sat back down on the patio furniture and said, "Maybe you should add that to the list."

———

THE NEXT AFTERNOON, ALICE HAD NOT SEEN nor experienced any paranormal activity in The Starlight Manor. She had found a spot on the wrap-around porch where she could watch for vehicles coming through the gate, where she could then get back into the house before Ginny or Bob would know she'd been loitering.

She had Ginny's pin on her maps, and she knew they had arrived on the Nantucket Steamer twenty minutes ago. Without checking her app, she suspected her daughter and her boyfriend would be here any minute.

Tears choked in Alice's throat. She was so excited to see her daughter. Just then, movement caught her eye as the gate rumbled open and a dark-colored SUV rolled through it.

Alice jumped to her feet and hurried toward the front corner of the house. She didn't want to seem overeager, though she suspected Ginny would know how Alice felt the moment Alice grabbed her and held her tight.

Dinner sat a couple of hours away, and Alice hoped to simply sit and visit with Bob and Ginny—ask them about school, ask them about their finals, get to know Bob better, and maybe even get a little hint as to what Bob and Ginny were thinking for their future.

You will not be pushy, she told herself as she gained the front door and hurried inside. She took a deep breath in the foyer, glanced up at the chandelier that AJ had said had flickered, noticed nothing, and continued into the back of the house.

Alice had lived in big houses throughout her life, but this one was so much more compared to the monstrosity she'd owned in the Hamptons, nor the vacation house she and Frank had owned right here on Rocky Ridge.

Alice had never seen anything like The Starlight Manor, unless it had been a hotel or another commercial enterprise.

It seemed to take forever for the SUV to arrive and for Ginny and Bob to get their things out before the door opened and Ginny called, "We're here."

Alice spun from where she stood and started walking back the way she'd come. "You're here," she echoed back to Ginny, and she moved right into her daughter's arms and hugged her tight. "Oh, it's so good to see you."

Thankfully, the tears she'd experienced earlier stayed dormant, and only a rush of happiness poured through her as she held her daughter. Ginny stepped back, and Alice moved right over to Bob.

"How are you, dear?" She hugged him too, glad when he didn't seem to mind the invasion of his personal space.

"Just fine, Alice," he said.

"How was the Steamer?" She stepped back and looked from him to Ginny.

"I love taking the Steamer," he said.

"Oh, did you come to Five Island Cove before you knew Ginny?"

Alice flicked a look over to Ginny, who reached for Bob's hand. The touch between them seemed easy and casual, and Alice sure did like it. Bob stood a few inches taller than Ginny, and together, they made a handsome couple—her with her blonde hair and him with his dark looks.

Bob said he'd once been on the rowing team, and he had the chest and shoulders to prove it, but that law school had started to soften him.

Alice knew there was nothing soft about law school.

She wanted to know how things were going for Bob in his second year, but she told herself there was plenty of time to ask more questions. Instead, she gestured for the younger couple to head into the house. "Come on," she said. "Come take a tour of this place."

"It's enormous," Ginny said, looking around.

"Yes," Alice said. "There are four levels of this, with every type of room you can imagine."

She didn't want to be a helicopter mom, hovering around her daughter and her boyfriend, so she let Ginny and Bob go around by the house themselves, enjoying the way they exclaimed over this room or that one, or how big the home theater was in the basement.

Once they'd concluded their tour, they joined Alice in the living room, where Ginny sank onto the couch and pulled Bob down next to her.

Alice got to her feet. "Would either of you like a drink? I can make mocktails."

"You'll love my mom's mocktails," Ginny said. She turned to Alice with a bright look on her face. "Can you make the cranberry-lime one?"

"I can make whatever you want." Alice traced her fingertips across Ginny's face as she passed her. "What do you like, Bob? Citrus, lime? Something more fruity?"

"Oh, I don't know, Alice," he said, and Alice liked

how he called her by her first name and not something more formal like *ma'am*. "Whatever you've got is fine."

"He likes fruity stuff, Mom," Ginny called as Alice moved into the kitchen.

Alice quickly put together three mocktails, wondering where AJ and Jean had gotten to this afternoon. Their kids took naps in the afternoon, and Alice had learned that they often retreated during that time as well. Since they had suites, they had sitting areas, televisions, and walls of windows in their own rooms.

"Cranberry-lime," Alice said, giving the fizzy drink to Ginny.

"I made you a raspberry lemonade," she said, handing another glass to Bob. "With mint."

"This is beautiful," Bob said about the bright pink liquid with the green leaves in it.

Alice returned to the kitchen to get her own drink. She loved something with a lot of orange and a lot of lime. When she returned to the living room, she smiled at Ginny and Bob. After taking a delicate sip of her mocktail, she asked, "What does your family do for Christmas, Bob?"

He finished sipping his drink, his smile returning quickly. "They're going on a cruise this year," he said. "That's why Ginny and I decided to come here."

"You didn't want to go on the cruise?" Alice looked between Ginny and Bob, and Ginny shook her head, something flashing through her eyes that Alice would have to find out more about later.

"Not this year," Bob said brightly, clearly concealing private conversations between the two of them.

The nosy part of Alice wanted to know everything they talked about, and yet, a quieter part told her that such a thing simply wasn't possible. That Ginny was going to start living her own life, and that she *should* have a relationship with Bob that Alice didn't know anything about.

They *should* have private conversations. They *should* be sharing parts of themselves with each other and no one else.

While that made part of her heart sing with sadness, it also made her realize that her daughter had grown into a beautiful young woman who knew how to have a healthy relationship with a man.

And dang it, tears stung Alice's throat and eyes with such a realization.

Chapter Nine

Ginny Kelton couldn't stop smiling as she sank onto one of the plush couches in the game room. "I can't believe I hit the Bullseye."

Bob grinned at her and pulled her closer, as if she needed any encouragement to snuggle into his side. He chuckled and shook his head. "I think you actually closed your eyes when you threw."

"Shh." She giggled into his chest. "I think it sort of upset Ian." She glanced over to the other couch, where Billie and Ian had parked themselves after Ginny's come-from-behind win at darts. She showed him something on her phone, their heads bent close together. Then Ian smiled, so maybe he wasn't mad about losing.

"What's next?" Jamie asked. "We can't waste this amazing game room by sitting on our phones." She looked over to Grace, who'd indeed sunk into an armchair and had her device in front of her face.

"I'm not on my phone," Lena said in a loud, blunt voice.

Jamie turned a kind smile on her. "No, you're not. Should we play pool?"

"Let's do teams," Ian said, standing up. "Because Jamie's right—this place is insane."

"My mom killed it by finding the manor," Billie said. She got to her feet too and moved to Ian's side. "Can I be on your team?"

"Of course." He grinned at her, and Ginny recognized how much they liked each other, though they didn't touch, hadn't kissed in front of anyone, and probably wouldn't do anything inappropriate at all.

Ginny simply wanted to stay under Bob's arm, where his body heat melted into hers, making her comfortable, cozy, and warm.

"Bob? You in?" Ian pointed a pool cue toward Ginny and Bob, who laughed.

"All in," Bob said, and he had to pull his arm from Ginny's shoulders to stand. "Come on, Ginny-baby. You can be on my team."

She groaned as she allowed Bob to pull her to her feet. "I'm no good at pool."

"Yeah, that's what you said about darts," Ian said dryly.

"I don't have a partner," Grace said.

"You can be on our team," Jamie said. "Me, you, and Lena."

Grace moved over to them, and Ginny waited for

Bob to get her a pool cue and the others to decide what game they'd play. She loved how easily Bob fit in with her friends and family, how he seemed to genuinely enjoy being here at the manor with her.

Of course, they'd only been here for a couple of hours, and they'd opted to come down to the basement game room instead of spending time in the pool. They'd be here through Monday morning, so they still had plenty of time for swimming.

She loved how he called her "Ginny-baby," almost like that was her name. The way it rolled off his tongue sounded so natural, and she glanced over to him as he laughed with Ian. She feared she'd fallen in love with him the moment she'd met him, though she'd never told anyone that.

Not even Charlie, though he wouldn't tease her or judge her.

Ginny felt old in some ways and entirely too young to fall in love and get married in others. But she sure enjoyed spending time with Bob, talking to him, learning more about him, and dreaming of a future with him.

"Your turn, Ginny," he said as he came over to her.

"What am I doing?"

He gave a knowing look that accused her of not listening—and he wouldn't be wrong. But his eyes only held kindness and warmth among that bright edge he always had, and he nodded to the pool table. "Try to get that solid blue two-ball in the corner pocket."

She very nearly rolled her eyes. "You talk like you've spent a lot of time in pool bars."

"Maybe I have." He grinned at her, and Ginny did roll her eyes then. He so hadn't, though he did seem to be good at everything he did.

She moved over to the table, the pool cue in her hand awkward and too long. "I don't know how to do this."

Bob came up behind her, his wider stance and long arms easily enveloping her inside them. "Hold it like this, baby." He positioned her hands where they should be, his breath washing softly along her ear. She fought a shiver and instead, looked over to Billie.

The teen watched her and Bob with an edge in her eyes, and Ginny's face heated.

"Then, you just give it a little tap," Bob said quietly as he backed up. "A little tap, Ginny. It doesn't take much."

"It sure doesn't," Billie said, her eyebrows now lifted.

Ginny gave her a grin, because she didn't have anything to be embarrassed about. So she and Bob liked each other. He was twenty-four; she was twenty. She wasn't in high school, wasn't a teenager, and had nothing to hide from anyone.

She focused on the solid blue ball, moved the cue the way Bob had, and thrust it out in a short, tight movement. The tip hit the ball, and Ginny stayed leaned over the table, watching as the ball rolled toward the pocket. Excitement zinged through her when it dropped into the leather bag, and she straightened quickly, lifting her cue straight up as she said, "Yes! I got it!"

The tip of her pool cue hit the ceiling, and Ginny quickly pulled it back. Looking up, she saw a slight blue smudge on the ceiling, and a new kind of humiliation filled her. "Oops."

"Let me have that before you decapitate someone." Bob laughed as he took the cue from her. Then he pulled her to his side, his arm around her waist as they watched Grace take her turn.

Turned out, she'd just experienced a bit of beginner's luck, because she missed every shot after that. She didn't care at all, and she pulled her phone out to check the time. "I have to go babysit soon," she said, noticing she'd missed some texts from her twin.

Charlie had texted: *How's the fancy house? Mom driving you crazy yet?*

Ginny smiled and quickly typed back a response. *It's amazing, Charlie. You and Mandie are totally missing out. And Mom's been surprisingly chill so far.*

She hasn't asked you five thousand questions about Bob? I'm shocked.

She called yesterday, Ginny said, though she didn't tell Charlie what she'd talked with her mother about. Just because they were twins, lived together, and were very close didn't mean she wanted to discuss her sex life with her brother.

We'll be there next weekend. Can't wait to see the house and get out of the city.

Miss you, Charlie.

Love you, Ginny.

"Everything okay?" Bob asked, coming up beside her.

Ginny nodded, tucking her phone away. "Just Charlie. I think New York is suffocating him."

"It's the finals," Bob said, and he would know. He'd already earned a bachelor's degree and had moved on to law school. Ginny still hadn't declared a major, and she really needed to pick something as she was running out of general-ed classes to take.

"Did you tell him I've promised to have you home by curfew?" Bob's dark eyes twinkled like a night sky, which so fit with all the decor of this manor.

"You two are ridiculous." Ginny grinned and shook her head. She loved how well Bob and Charlie got along, how they'd formed their own friendship independent of her. It made her relationship with him feel...grown-up.

Her phone chimed, and she hurried to silence it. "I have to go meet Jean."

"I'll come find you later," Bob said, his attention over on the foosball table. "I think Lena needs a partner to go up against the Sherman sisters."

Billie actually stretched her arms up as if she'd be going into a boxing ring instead of playing foosball with friends. Ginny loved her in that moment, because Billie had become a good friend, and she'd grown up into a pretty amazing young adult.

Ginny said, "I have to go, everyone. See you later."

Calls of "Bye, Ginny," and "See you later," filled the air as she left the game room. She'd just reached the bottom of the steps when Jean did. "Oh." She carried Heidi in her arms, and she quickly side-stepped out of the way.

"I was just on the way up." Ginny reached to take Heidi from her mother. She smiled at the little girl, then took in Jean's pretty black dress. "You look so amazing."

Jean smiled and ran her hands down the front of her body. "Thanks. I just got this in the mail, and I haven't even worn it yet."

"You're wearing it well right now." Ginny smiled at Jean and started up the stairs.

"Reuben and I haven't had date night in a while," Jean said from behind her. "Thank you so much for taking her tonight."

"Of course."

"She's eaten already," Jean continued. "I've put her pajamas on our bed in the Celestial Room. It's on the second floor."

Ginny emerged onto the first floor, where several adults sat at the table in the eat-in kitchen, a game of Scrabble in front of them. "What time do you want me to put her down?"

"Eight," Jean said. "It's only a couple of hours."

Ginny turned back to her, catching the nervousness on Jean's face. "We'll be fine." She grinned at Heidi. "Won't we, Heidi-ho?" The little girl smiled at her, and Ginny's heart expanded another size.

Jean took a diaper bag from Reuben, who wore a classic pair of black slacks and a dark green sweater fitting for the season. "There are diapers, wipes, a change of clothes, and some snacks in here. Oh, and her favorite stuffed animal is in there too—she can't sleep without it."

Ginny nodded, mentally cataloging the information. "Got it. Don't worry about a thing, you guys." She nodded over to the table. "It's not like I'm here alone or anything."

Jean hesitated for a moment, then leaned in to kiss Heidi's cheek. "Be good for Ginny, okay, baby doll? Mommy and Daddy will be back soon."

Ginny took Heidi's chubby hand and waved for her as Jean and Reuben went down the hall toward the front door. Once it clicked closed, Ginny looked at Heidi, then around the living room. Her mother played Scrabble with Arthur, Robin, Duke, and AJ, but Ginny didn't want to sit in here with them.

She didn't see Asher, and she wondered if AJ had already put him to bed. She'd taken a self-guided tour of the manor when she and Bob had arrived a few hours ago, and she turned back to the staircase. And just like that, she slipped away from the busyness on the first floor and made her way up two flights to the top level.

The library seemed to be calling her name, and she entered the semi-dark room to see the sun had just started to set. "Wow," she said, magnetically drawn across the vast space to the wall of windows. "Look at that, Heidi."

Every corner of this house seemed to hold some new wonder, from the intricate moldings to the celestial-themed artwork that adorned the walls.

She dropped the diaper bag and sank onto one of the window seats, settling Heidi on her lap. The little girl simply leaned back into her like she had soft spaghetti noodles for bones. "The sun is going down," she said to Heidi. "See how the sky looks like it's starting to bruise?"

Of course a two-year-old wouldn't know what a bruise was, but Ginny wasn't expecting to have a conversation with the little girl.

In the winter, sunsets happened quickly, and before Ginny knew it, the last of the light faded, leaving the sky a dark navy blue that continued to sink into blackness.

And that meant the stars would be coming out.

A sense of peace settled over her. She'd only lived in the cove for four years before leaving for college, but the quiet moments here, the natural beauty, the feeling of being part of something bigger than herself—those things had always been present here.

"Home," she whispered, as Five Island Cove had definitely become home to Ginny.

Pricks of light started to appear in the black drape the sky had become, and Ginny noted how utterly dark it had become. New York City never got dark like this, and Ginny had forgotten what a Five Island Cove night was like.

Did she want to move back here after she finished school? She loved her mom and step-dad, and it wasn't the worst thought in the world.

"There you are," Bob said, and Ginny nearly jumped out of her skin. She emitted a yelp, her arms tightening around Heidi.

"It's just me," Bob added. "Sorry, I didn't mean to scare you."

"I was just..." Ginny looked out the window again as Bob settled beside her. "Stargazing."

He took Heidi from her, saying, "Hey there, little lady." He grinned at her and tried to fake-gobble up her fingers. Heidi shrieked with delight and laughed, which was about the cutest sound in the whole world.

Ginny's heart swelled as she watched them interact. Bob was so good with kids, so natural and patient. It made her think about the future—their future—in a way that both excited and terrified her.

"The stars have stolen you from us," Bob said.

"Not true." She leaned into his shoulder and watched the night sky again. "I'm right here."

"Thinking about what?" he asked.

"Us," she said honestly.

"Mm." Bob didn't say more, and they sat in comfortable silence for a while, more and more stars appearing as they watched. Heidi eventually began to yawn, her little head drooping against Bob's chest.

"I should probably put her to bed," Ginny said,

checking her phone. "It's not quite eight, but I need to change her and put on her pjs."

Bob stood up with her, keeping Heidi in his arms. "I'll come with you." He didn't say he wanted to talk more about the "us" she'd said, but Ginny saw it in his eyes all the same.

She nodded and led the way to the second floor. As luck would have it, Kelli and Shad's suite on this floor was available, and Ginny had decided to stay in it instead of the bunk room. Bob would be staying in the third-floor bunk room on his own, as none of the other single males were at the manor this weekend.

In the Celestial Room, Ginny quickly changed Heidi's diaper, giving her a raspberry on her belly to keep her laughing and happy. She changed her into her pajamas and then tucked the toddler into the portable crib in the corner of the room.

Lastly, she dug out the stuffed lion and handed it to Heidi. She hugged it to her neck and closed her eyes, and Ginny could only pray for a baby as good as Heidi. "Sweet dreams, baby doll," Ginny whispered, brushing a soft kiss against Heidi's forehead.

Then she picked up the baby monitor and made sure Heidi's part had been switched on before she and Bob headed for the hallway. Once there, she took his hand and led him further into the depths of the second floor —to the suite where she'd be staying for the next three nights.

"And to think I got the bunk room," he said as he entered the suite.

Ginny could only smile. "El picked a great place."

"It's incredible."

She set the baby monitor on the nightstand and flopped onto the bed. "It's like sleeping on clouds."

Bob went around to the other side of the king-sized bed and lay on top of the comforter as well. "Anything is going to be better than your couch-mattress-bed."

"Right?" Ginny rolled toward him, her sleeping arrangements in the city not going to ruin her good mood. "I won't have to sleep there forever."

He gathered her into his arms, the two of them settling in the middle of the giant bed. "I want you with me," he whispered.

Ginny tensed, though she wanted to have this talk with him. This one, and plenty more. "Do you really?"

"Yes." He pressed his lips to her temple, then moved his kiss down to her cheekbone. "I have a real bed."

She smiled and turned her head so she could kiss him. He kept the union slow and sweet, and he broke the kiss far sooner than she'd have liked. "Come to Boston after Christmas." He kept his voice low and soft, and that only made Ginny feel closer to him.

"Boston?" she asked.

"I don't have to be back to work until the winter semester starts."

"I thought you were going to Kansas City to see your parents."

"I can cancel." He opened his eyes and looked into hers. "I want to spend a few days with you in my city."

She'd been to Boston before, but no, she had not stayed with him. "I have to work."

He ran the tip of his nose down her cheek and kissed her neck. She pulled in a sharp breath, stars shooting across her skin, emanating from where he touched. "You can call in," he said. "I want to spend some time with you, Ginny-baby. Just us."

The implication of his words hung in the air between them. They hadn't been intimate yet, both agreeing to take things slow. But lately, the tension between them had been building, the desire to take that next step growing stronger.

"I love you, Ginny." He lifted his head and offered her that boyish smile she loved so much. "I'd marry you tomorrow if you'd let me."

"We haven't even known each other for six months," she said. "There's no way you're proposing before then."

He reached up and played with a strand of her hair. "Do you love me, baby?"

"Yes," she whispered. "I—I—yes, I think I'm in love with you." She buried her face in his chest and took a deep breath. "My mother is going to kill me."

"You don't need her permission."

"She's my mom."

"I know she is." Bob kissed her again, his lips strong and yet tender as he showed her he loved her. Ginny kissed him back, hoping her feelings went through in her motions too.

He pulled away and brushed her hair off her forehead. "Your mom doesn't have to know all the details." A hint of mischief entered his eyes. "We're adults, Ginny. We can make our own decisions."

Part of her wanted to say yes immediately, to throw caution to the wind and dive headfirst into this next phase of their relationship. But another part—the practical, cautious part that sounded annoyingly like her mother—held her back.

"Can I think about it?" she asked finally. "It's not a no, Bobby."

He grinned at her. "I like it when you call me Bobby." He brought her hand to his lips and kissed her knuckles. "Of course. Take all the time you need, love."

Ginny leaned in, pressing her forehead against his. "Thank you," she whispered. "For understanding. For being patient with me."

"Always," Bob murmured back.

They stayed like that for a long moment while Ginny felt like she stood on the edge of something huge, something life-changing.

As she lay there and thought about Boston post-Christmas, in that brief week between the holidays and New Year's Day, Ginny realized that she was ready to take the next step. Ready for whatever came next, ready to take that leap with Bob.

Tomorrow, she decided. She could tell him she'd stay in Boston with him tomorrow—and he'd spoken true... her mom didn't need to know anything about it.

Chapter Ten

Saturday morning dawned as the perfect December day, the kind that invited a person to step outside, even if the cold bit at their skin, just to feel alive. Eloise wrapped her scarf tighter around her neck as she rode the ferry with Aaron at her side and the girls in the row in front of them.

It seemed everyone wanted to get from Rocky Ridge to Diamond Island this morning, and they'd barely gotten seats inside on the ferry. The few that had remained had been near the open door, and the wind that came in certainly caused a chill to run through Eloise's blood.

"You okay?" Aaron draped his arm around her shoulders and pulled her tightly against his body. His brown eyes softened, and the corners of his mouth lifted in the faintest of smiles.

Eloise nodded, though a quiet weight settled in her

chest. The events of the past few days had left her feeling more untethered than usual, as if something just beneath the surface of her normally well-ordered life had been knocked slightly off-kilter. The lights flickering at The Starlight Manor, the small oddities she couldn't quite explain, the bickering, the fact that Kelli and Shad hadn't been back to the manor since—none of it sat well with her.

"I'm fine," she said, managing a small smile in return. "Just a little tired."

Aaron chuckled softly. "I think that's the understatement of the year." He leaned in, his voice dropping to a playful whisper. "You've been running yourself ragged trying to make this holiday perfect, El. It's okay to let go of the reins a little."

Eloise sighed, the weight of his words pressing gently against her pulse. She couldn't even argue with him, because he always knew when she was trying to make something square go in a round hole. And lately, it seemed like that was all she did.

She hadn't been able to shake the feeling that if she didn't hold everything together—The Starlight Manor plans, the Christmas festivities, the balance between her work at the Cliffside Inn and her family—everything would disintegrate into dust.

But as she drew in a deep breath, she knew today would be different. Today was about giving back to the veterans in Five Island Cove.

Stepping foot back on Diamond Island made her

smile, though she'd enjoyed her time away from the home she and her family shared. She let Aaron navigate them toward the RideShare line, and they got in an SUV to get to the community center, where the breakfast would take place.

She moved back into the wind when they arrived at the brick building, which bustled with activity, as it often did during the holidays. Volunteers streamed in, and the scent of bacon and maple syrup hung in the air as she followed Aaron inside. People moved about, setting up tables, unfolding chairs, and bringing out trays of food.

Aaron stood beside her, his hands tucked into his jacket pockets. He looked at ease, his posture relaxed, though Eloise could sense the hum of energy just beneath his calm exterior—always alert, always ready to help wherever needed. Billie and Grace walked a few paces ahead, stopping to chat with Robin and Jamie, their laughter carrying across the gymnasium.

She glanced over her shoulder and found a check-in table. "I'm going to go check us in," she said to Aaron, who said, "All right, sweetheart."

Kristen stood near the check-in table, talking with Alice and Arthur, and the three of them turned toward Eloise and welcomed her into their trio. "Good morning, dear." Kristen hugged her, and Eloise did the same with Alice and Arthur.

"You're lucky you took the ferry back last night," Eloise said. "It was packed this morning."

"I bet." Alice tucked her hair behind her ear and glanced over to Robin and the girls. "Where's Duke this morning?"

"Fishing," Eloise said. "Who else is coming?"

"Laurel and Paul are in the back, helping with the cooking," Kristen said. She leaned closer and wore a dazzling, sparkly look on her face as she added, "And they brought Liam and Ian with them, so Julia's on her way now."

"I didn't think she'd signed up," Eloise said. "Oh."

Alice grinned at her and shook her head.

"All volunteers over here, please," someone called, and Eloise's pulse blipped through her veins. She still needed to check-in, but she didn't want to miss any directions. "We'll be going over a few food safety items."

Kristen turned and gave her name, then Eloise's, and Alice and Arthur's. It only took a few seconds to get their names checked off, and the woman looked up at them, pushed her glasses up higher on her nose, and said, "Thank you so much for being a large-group sponsor this year. You can head on over to Tracey, who's going over a few things."

Eloise smiled at the woman and went with her friends into the fray of tables and chairs. They joined the other volunteers as Tracey said, "Everyone has to wear gloves if you're going to be on the food line. We need people to help clear plates and wipe tables too, and a group to man the check-in tables. Veterans didn't have to register for this, but they do have to show their ID to prove they're a veteran, and they can bring in their families as well."

"Luke here will take a group and do a quick orientation on greeting. I'm taking the bulk of you back to the food tables for service, and Martha here—" She indicated a woman on her right-hand side. "Is over the dining room and clean-up. If you have a preferred area, you can congregate there, but we may need to shuffle you around."

Eloise slipped her arm through Aaron's. "Food service?" she asked as people began to move and talk. "We'll be able to stay together that way."

"Yep." He looked over to Billie and Grace with Robin and Jamie. "Girls, over here."

Everyone came over, and Eloise stayed with Tracey. She took them back behind the serving tables and started issuing directions for serving scrambled eggs, pancakes, bacon, sausage—patties and links—hash browns, and how to deal with the condiment station.

She needed runners to take away empty trays and bring out new ones, and she added, "We still need people to keep cooking throughout the two-hour event."

Eloise found herself standing between Grace and Aaron, scooping fruit salad for anyone who wanted it. She'd first put it in small, clear plastic cups, and she'd fill those and replace them as needed. Aaron got scrambled egg duty, and Grace and Billie were in charge of the pastry basket.

The first wave of veterans and their families began to

arrive. Eloise's heart warmed as she watched the familiar faces of Five Island Cove's older generation—the men and women who had served in the Navy and Coast Guard, who had weathered storms, both literal and metaphorical, with quiet resilience. Some walked with canes or leaned on family members for support, while others moved with surprising energy and vigor despite their years. There were fathers and grandfathers, mothers and grandmothers, and even younger veterans who had served more recently, their faces lined with experiences she could only imagine.

She heard a familiar laugh and glanced over to find Kelli restocking cups at the coffee station. Her heartbeat leapfrogged in her chest, and she turned to her husband. "Kelli and Shad are here."

Aaron looked in the direction Eloise did. "See? They're adults, and they'll come back."

"Can I get some fruit, please?" a tiny voice asked, and Eloise startled. She hadn't even realized all of the cups had been taken, and a darling girl with dark hair stood in front of her, two chocolate croissants on her plate and nothing else. "Maybe just the strawberries?"

"Karla," her mom said. "You can't just—"

"I can get just the strawberries for you," Eloise said, and she used her oversized spoon to fish out the berries the little girl wanted. Her face shone with the brightness of the sun and moon combined, and Eloise let her happiness and joy seep way down deep into her soul.

When she got close to running out of fruit, another

volunteer brought her another bowl of strawberries, cantaloupe, and pineapple. She scooped and chatted with people as they moved through the line, but she would never be able to keep up with Aaron.

She heard, "Thanks, Chief," at least a hundred times, and since everyone knew him, they all had something to say to him. He could be broody and silent as a cop, but today, he'd turned on his extroverted personality, and he laughed, talked, and even took pictures with the citizens in the cove.

Eloise simply smiled at him, her heart filling drop by drop with more love for her good husband.

"Can I take several of these?" Kristen asked. "I've got a family who needs it."

"Take them," Eloise said, though she already had. Kristen gave her a warm smile and turned to take the fruit to who needed it. Several other people did similar things, and Eloise was suddenly glad she'd gotten a stationary position.

"Hey, Billie."

Eloise turned her attention to two people down, where Ian had just arrived, an empty plate in his hand. Billie smiled at Ian, who'd been at the manor last night with his dad. Billie had gone out with him a few times now, and Eloise actually liked him.

"Let's see," he said. "I need a blueberry muffin and two cream cheese danishes."

"You got it." Billie gave him the danishes while Grace plucked the muffin from the bunch and put it on the plate. Ian should've then moved down the line, but he didn't.

"What are you doing later?" he asked.

"I don't know," Billie said. "I think we're going home to do some laundry, and then we'll go back to the manor tonight." She glanced down to Eloise and then her dad, but Aaron currently talked with someone.

"Maybe while your clothes dry, we can go to a movie."

"I'll—let me talk to my mom and dad." Billie gave him a smile, and Ian nodded.

"Fair enough," he said. He smiled at Grace and then moved down the line. He blinked rapidly when he saw Eloise, and she couldn't believe how narrow his tunnel-vision had been. Then again, when it came to Billie, Ian couldn't seem to see much besides her.

"Good morning, Ian," she said diplomatically.

"Hey, El." He cleared his throat and looked at his phone. "I, uh, don't need any fruit."

"Great." She nodded to Billie's father. "Aaron's got scrambled eggs."

Ian swallowed and moved down the line. "Hey, Chief," he said.

"Ian," Aaron said in a big, jovial voice. "You need eggs?"

"Yes, sir." Ian held out his plate, his eyes still a little too wide. "Thank you, sir."

"Ian," Eloise said before he could move down to the

bacon. "I'm sure Billie can spare a couple of hours for a movie this afternoon."

Aaron whipped his attention to her. "We're going to the movies this afternoon?"

"You know what?" An amazing idea formed in her head. "I think you should go on a double-date to the movies. You and Grace, and Billie and Ian."

"What is going on?" Billie asked, her voice pitching up into almost a squeak.

"I think I'd like a couple of hours to myself this afternoon," Eloise said. "I'll take a really long bubble bath and order my favorite cookies from Baked Bliss." She smiled at the girls. "And you guys can all go to the movies."

The five of them stood there, berries and baked goods between them. Then Billie said, "I'd do that."

"Can I pick the movie?" Grace asked.

"Absolutely not," Aaron said. "If I'm paying for a double-date at the movies, I'm picking what we see." He grinned at Eloise and then Ian. "You in, Mister Coldwater?"

Ian glanced down to Billie and then back to Aaron. "Yes, sir."

Aaron smiled at him as people piled up in line behind him. "Great, now get on down the line and get your people their food."

Ian nodded and did that, and the buffet line continued as normal.

"This will be fun," she said to Aaron out of the side of her mouth. "She won't be around forever."

"I'm more concerned about you needing a couple of hours to yourself." He gave a bright smile to the woman in line, then chatted with her husband for a quick couple of seconds. "You said you were okay."

"I am," she said. "There's a lot of people at the manor, and a quiet house to myself—for just a couple of hours—sounds nice."

"Okay," he said. "I'll bring back a bucket of popcorn for you."

"Yes, do that." Eloise grinned at him. "With extra butter."

"You know, we don't have to go back to the manor tonight," he said. "If you need a break, let's just stay home."

"Do *you* need a break?" she asked.

"Not really," Aaron said. "The room at the manor is huge, and the girls are getting along." He shrugged and kept scooping eggs. "You tell me, El."

"I just want the house to myself this afternoon. Maybe I'll take Prince for a walk."

Aaron cocked his eyebrows. "So you're going to go get him from Mike?"

"No." Eloise shook her head. "I forgot he wasn't at home." Of course their dog wasn't home; they'd moved their family to the manor for just over three weeks, and Aaron had asked one of his cops to dog-sit Prince.

"So maybe just a walk on the beach."

"Yes." Eloise grinned at him.

"All right," Aaron said. "I'll look up what's playing and we'll go this afternoon."

Eloise turned back to her bowl of fruit, ready to dive into her own task of filling cups, but before she could begin again, she noticed an older man sitting alone in a wheelchair at the end of the line.

He'd combed back his silver hair neatly, and he wore a navy-blue sweater over a collared shirt. His hands rested on the wheels of his chair, and his gaze moved slowly over the food as if trying to decide what to put on his plate. For a moment, Eloise hesitated, unsure if he wanted help, but then she stepped forward, her decision made.

"Grace, take over with the fruit, would you?" Then she rounded Billie and the pastry table and smiled at the man. "Good morning," she said brightly. "May I help get your plate for you?"

She glanced over to the check-in table, and sure enough, they'd run out of volunteers to help with this kind of thing.

The man looked up at her, his blue eyes sharp despite his years. He smiled, the lines around his eyes crinkling as he nodded. "I'd appreciate that."

Eloise picked up a plate and moved beside him, holding it steady as he pointed out what he wanted. A cinnamon twist from the pastry basket, a cup of fruit, scrambled eggs, and bacon—all of it came together on the plate.

"Are you from Five Island Cove?" she asked as they moved through the line.

"Yes, I'm from Pearl," he said, his voice gravelly but not unpleasant. "Used to live on Diamond, though. Retired to Pearl a few years back. Name's Mark Daniels, by the way."

Eloise smiled. "I'm Eloise Sherman. It's nice to meet you, Mark."

Mark nodded, then gestured toward the stack of pancakes near the end of the buffet tables. "One of those, if you don't mind. Can't say no to a good pancake."

Eloise placed one on his plate, and they moved to the end of the line, where she grabbed a small container of syrup and a foil-wrapped pat of butter for him. As they made their way to one of the tables where his wheelchair would fit, Mark glanced over at her, his eyes sharp with curiosity.

"Are you spending the holidays here in the cove?" he asked.

Eloise nodded, setting the plate down in front of him. "Yes, my family and I are staying at The Starlight Manor on Rocky Ridge for the next few weeks. It's a big house, so we're having a Christmas retreat with some of our friends and their families."

At the mention of the house, Mark's gaze shifted slightly, his expression darkening just a fraction before he looked back at his plate. "The Starlight Manor, eh? That's quite the place."

Eloise tilted her head, surprised. She'd been living in the cove for a handful of years and had never heard of The Starlight Manor. "Have you been there before?"

Mark shook his head slowly. "No, never been inside. But I've heard stories about that place—some good, some...not so good."

Eloise frowned, her memories suddenly flooding with all the strange occurrences at the manor. "What kind of stories?" She slid his plate in front of him and pulled up the chair beside him.

Mark paused, his fork hovering over his plate. He seemed to weigh his answer, as if deciding how much to share. Finally, he said, "My grandfather was a firefighter here in the cove. He was called in when The Starlight Manor caught fire one Christmas...sometime in the early nineteen hundreds."

A shiver ran down Eloise's spine, and she thought of Kristen's interest in the history of the house, the way she'd been piecing together the story of the Everleighs, the original owners. Eloise had only skimmed some of the details, distracted as usual by the chaos at the manor, but now, sitting here with Mark, a strange pull—a need to know more—nagged at her.

"The manor caught fire?" She kept her voice steady despite the unease creeping into her thoughts.

Mark nodded, his gaze distant as if he could see something long past. "Yes. It was during a grand

Christmas party, or so the story goes. My father didn't like to talk about it much, but from what I gathered, the fire was bad. It destroyed most of the house, took the lives of a few guests too. One of them was the lady of the house—Elizabeth Everleigh."

Eloise's breath caught, her mind spinning with the implications. Elizabeth Everleigh. The woman Kristen had been researching. The woman whose name seemed to be woven into the very fabric of the manor itself.

"What caused the fire?" she asked quietly, her heart racing.

Mark finished his bite of cinnamon twist. "No one really knows for sure. Some say it was faulty wiring or a candle that got knocked over. Others say...well, that it was something more."

Eloise swallowed, the weight of his words pressing down on her. "More?"

Mark glanced up at her, his blue eyes sharp once again. "Rumors, mostly. People said Elizabeth and her husband had been fighting. Something about money, or the way they were running their charitable work. My father used to say that places have a way of holding on to things—memories, emotions, even anger."

Eloise's pulse quickened, her thoughts racing back to the flickering lights at the manor, the strange occurrences that had seemed like nothing more than quirks of an old house. But now, standing here with Mark, she couldn't help but wonder if something lurked beneath the surface, waiting to be uncovered.

"Do you think the house is...haunted?" Eloise asked, her voice barely a whisper.

Mark chuckled softly, shaking his head as he picked up his fork. "I don't know about that, ma'am. But I do know that some places hold on to their history more than others." He popped a bite of bacon into his mouth. "I used to do safety checks on ships, and I'd be the only one on-board to do it. Some places... They can maintain the vibe of what happened there, that's all I'm saying. A spirit, if you will."

Eloise sat there for a moment, his words settling over her like a weighted blanket. The Starlight Manor—a place filled with history, with memories, with secrets.

A place that held on to its past.

She forced herself to smile as she said, "Enjoy your breakfast, Mark." She excused herself to return to the fruit station in the buffet line, but as she walked through the bustling community center, the hum of conversation and the clatter of dishes fading into the background, her thoughts remained fixed on the house.

As she navigated through the patrons enjoying breakfast, she caught sight of Kristen. Eloise met her gaze, and in that moment, she knew she wasn't the only one who felt it—the weight of The Starlight Manor's secrets pressing down on them, waiting to be uncovered.

This holiday was supposed to be about rest, about reconnecting with her loved ones and friends. But now, Eloise couldn't shake the feeling that something much larger, much older, was at play.

Something that refused to stay buried.

And as she moved through people laughing and sharing stories over breakfast, Eloise knew one thing for certain: The Starlight Manor still had secrets to tell, and she found she wanted to hear them.

Chapter Eleven

K elli Webb inhaled deeply, centering herself as she did. She only had a few more minutes of her intermediate yoga class, and then Kelli would take Daphne home to the townhome on Pearl Island, shower, and try to figure out how to answer the multiple texts from her friends.

"Inhale deeply to lift your chest, and exhale as you come back to Tabletop. Now, move into Child's Pose—bring your big toes together, widen your knees, and sit your hips back onto your heels. Stretch your arms forward, forehead to the mat. Let this be a moment of grounding. Feel the earth beneath you and soften your breath."

Kelli worked through the movements too, needing these moments of grounding in her own life.

"Slowly walk your hands back, coming to a seated position. We'll finish with a few minutes in Savasana. Lie down on your back, arms resting by your sides, palms facing up. Close your eyes. Allow your body to become heavy, letting go of any tension you might still be holding. Soften your face...your shoulders...your fingers. Let your breath flow naturally. Take these final moments for yourself."

She did the same thing, truly enjoying just being with herself. She hadn't always been her favorite person, but the more experiences she had, and the older she got, the more comfortable with herself she became.

"When you're ready, start to wiggle your fingers and toes, slowly bringing awareness back to your body. Roll onto your right side, and when you're ready, come to a seated position."

Kelli went through the motions with her students, a rush of satisfaction and contentment filling her. "Bring your hands to your heart center. Thank yourself for showing up today, for taking the time to nourish your mind and body. Namaste."

She smiled at her students as they rolled up their mats and gathered their belongings, the peaceful energy of the class still lingering in the air. "Thank you all for coming," she said, her voice soft but carrying easily across the room. "Remember to take this sense of calm with you throughout your day."

As the last of her students filed out, Kelli turned her attention to the corner of the room where her nine-month-old daughter, Daphne, lay contentedly in her playpen. The baby gurgled happily, reaching out with chubby hands as Kelli approached.

"Hey there, Daphne-doll," Kelli cooed, lifting Daphne into her arms. She pressed a kiss to her daughter's forehead, inhaling the sweet baby scent that never failed to soothe her frazzled nerves. "Ready to help Mommy with some paperwork?"

Balancing Daphne on her hip, Kelli made her way to her small office at the back of Whole Soul, her yoga and wellness studio on Bell Island. She'd opened the studio after moving back to Five Island Cove, after her divorce, and after she'd met and married Shad, determined to build something for herself after years of feeling lost and untethered.

As she settled Daphne into the bouncy seat she kept in the office, Kelli's thoughts drifted to her son, Parker. Shad had taken him to school on Diamond Island this morning, as usual. At fourteen, Parker's moods had been swinging wildly between sullen silence and explosive outbursts. Kelli's heart ached, remembering the sweet, curious boy he'd once been.

She'd just sat down at her desk, ready to tackle the mountain of invoices and schedules waiting for her attention, when a knock at the door made her look up. Her breath caught in her throat as she saw AJ standing in the doorway, an uncertain smile on her face.

"Hey, Kelli," AJ said softly.

"AJ." Kelli's heart flopped around in her chest, as if it had no idea how to perform its proper function.

She couldn't speak, so Kelli nodded, gesturing for AJ to come in. The tension that simmered between them since their argument at The Starlight Manor filled the small office, making the air feel thick and heavy.

AJ stepped inside, closing the door behind her. She'd dressed well in a cute denim skirt and an understated Christmas sweater. She'd blown her hair out so it flowed straight and shiny over her shoulders, and she'd come alone.

She looked different somehow, more vulnerable than Kelli had seen her since she'd returned to the cove. The AJ who'd come back had been the usually confident, sometimes brash woman Kelli had known since childhood. In the past year or so, as their friend group had grown and smaller splinters had started branching off, AJ had been more sullen and angry.

But now, in her place stood someone who looked... lost.

"I owe you an apology," AJ said, her words coming out in a rush. "I was way out of line the other night, and I'm so sorry, Kel. I never meant to hurt you or imply that you're not a good mother."

Kelli's carefully constructed walls started to crumble. She and AJ had been best friends for so long, weathering countless storms together, both physically and figuratively. The idea of losing that friendship over a stupid argument was almost unbearable.

She nodded, tears already flowing out of the corners of her eyes. "I shouldn't have gotten so defensive."

"No, you were right." AJ wiped at her own tears. "I don't have teenagers, and it's not my job to give advice. I can't believe I...I mansplained parenting to you when you just needed someone to vent to."

Before she could think too hard, Kelli rushed at AJ and hugged her, years of shared history and understanding flowing between them.

"I've been such an idiot," AJ mumbled into Kelli's shoulder. "I don't even know why I got so worked up about it all." She stepped back and sniffled, then moved over to the bouncy seat and picked up Daphne. "Hey, Daph." She swept a kiss across the baby's cheek, and Daphne squealed in delight.

Kelli didn't know what to say, but she'd been taught that it was always okay to apologize. "I didn't need to come back at you either," she said. "I'm sorry."

"Will you come back to the holiday house?" AJ sank down into one of the chairs in front of Kelli's desk. "Everyone is really worried about you. *I'm* really worried about you."

Kelli returned to her seat at her desk, and she sighed as she sat down. "I was going to text everyone today."

"Okay," AJ said. "I know you teach here and all that, but you could come, and I'll tend to Daphne so you can rest. Then, you could be back in Rocky Ridge for our luncheon, and I...need you, Kel."

"Jean's at the house," Kelli said quietly.

"Jean is not you," she said simply.

Kelli hadn't known how much she needed to hear

that until AJ said it. Emotions surged through her again, a sudden tidal wave of water that threatened to break down everything Kelli had built to protect herself.

AJ took a shaky breath, her gaze falling to Daphne's reddish hair. She stroked the baby's hair back. "I guess... I've been feeling so insecure lately. About everything. Being a mom, my relationship with Matt, my place in the group. Sometimes I look at you, or Robin, or Alice— even Jean—and you all seem to have it so together. And then there's me, constantly feeling like I'm one step away from screwing it all up."

Kelli couldn't help but laugh, the sound tinged with a hint of bitterness. "I am so far from being together it's not even funny." She smiled at her baby daughter. "I love my children more than anything in this world, but being a mom is the hardest thing I've ever done. Some days, I feel like I'm drowning, especially with Parker."

"I know," AJ said softly. "I'm sorry I added to that."

"We're both doing the best we can."

"I can't seem to do anything without you." AJ gave her a rueful smile. "Have you been keeping up with the group text about all the weird stuff at the manor?"

"I read the texts," Kelli said. "Has anything else happened?"

"Not really, other than El called a group meeting last night, and she and Kristen literally presented to us in theater room." AJ's tone took on a dryer quality and she almost rolled her eyes. "They want to do a top-to-bottom exploration of the house, and I need you there."

Kelli tilted her head. "Why?"

"Because I saw the lights flicker in that ridiculously huge chandelier in the foyer, and no one else has." She hugged Daphne close as her eyes took on a harder quality. "I think there's definitely something going on in that house, and Robin is acting like the rest of us are going mad."

"Maybe you are."

"Alice has seen some things," AJ said. "And she's the most practical out of any of us."

"So this is just one more thing for us to argue over." Kelli leaned back in her chair, the mess on her desk still there, so she couldn't just rush off to the manor even if she wanted to.

"No," AJ said. "It's a way for us to come together."

"To solve a mystery?" Kelli shook her head. "Those haven't historically helped us."

"Sure they have," AJ said. "They're the reason we're all still friends, because we realize that it doesn't matter if you're right or I'm right—we want to be friends no matter what."

Kelli couldn't really argue with her, so she didn't. "Tomorrow?"

"Can you maybe rearrange your classes, so you can come?" AJ looked so hopeful, and Kelli did miss her friends. She could easily come to Rocky Ridge and The Starlight Manor tomorrow, because she didn't teach on Tuesdays.

"Wait," AJ said before Kelli could answer. "You

don't teach on Tuesdays. You and Daphne could come tonight." She grinned at Kelli. "Please?"

Kelli looked into her friend's pleading eyes, then glanced down at Daphne, who'd fallen asleep in her best friend's arms. She thought of Parker, of Shad, of the life they'd built here in Five Island Cove. Part of her wanted to say no, to retreat into the safety of her daily routine.

But another part of her, a part that had been dormant for far too long, yearned for adventure, for connection, for something more than the endless cycle of diapers and yoga classes and teenage mood swings.

"Okay," Kelli said finally, surprising herself with the certainty in her voice. "Daphne and I will come tonight and go through the holiday house with everyone."

KELLI'S STOMACH VIBRATED AS HER RIDESHARE driver pulled up to the holiday house. Or maybe that was because she didn't even have another couple of minutes to get Daphne and herself out of the car with their bags as Robin, Eloise, AJ, and Alice all waited for her on the front steps.

Only AJ got to her feet, and she stayed at the top of the porch, leaning against the pillar there as if she held back the tide of their other friends.

Kelli hated walking into a situation like this. A situation where everyone had been talking about her while she'd been gone. A situation where she wasn't sure who to watch, what to say, or how things would go. She employed the same yoga breathing she taught at her studio, and reached to pay for her ride.

"Thank you," she said to the driver. "Come on, Daph." She smiled at her daughter and unbuckled her from the carseat. Part of her wanted to put her baby in the bath immediately, as she hadn't brought her own seat from Pearl Island, and the other part of her told herself it was good for Daphne to be exposed to germs so her body could fight them off.

The house seemed bigger than it had last weekend, or perhaps it had taken a big breath and was holding it, waiting for something to happen.

Kelli started up the walkway with Daphne in her arms, the diaper bag strap cutting into her shoulder, and towing their suitcase behind them. "Hey," she said as AJ finally pushed away from the pillar and came down the steps.

"Give me that baby," AJ said, smiling. She took Daphne, which relieved Kelli of a big burden. She hitched the diaper bag up, feeling too old to have and be responsible for a baby.

Her eyes landed on Eloise, and Kelli absolutely would not complain about having Daphne. She knew El would've liked a baby of her own, and she hadn't been able to have one. And with Jean and Reuben going through all they had before they'd been able to adopt Heidi?

No, Kelli would hitch her smile in place and say

nothing but good things about being a new mom at age forty-eight.

Once AJ had stepped away from the pillar, the others came toward her too, and Kelli found herself encircled in the arms of the women who'd always loved her, no matter what.

She didn't want to cry, but Kelli sure was glad she could feel something again. The past week had been days and nights of her trying to numb away the very public argument she'd had with her best friend. She'd dove into her work, into cooking after work, baking cookies for Parker, drinking too much wine with Shad in the evenings. Anything to keep from thinking about why AJ had been so snippy with her, and why Kelli had felt the need to bite back at her.

"I'm so glad you're here," El said, and the words couldn't have been said in a more sincere way. "Let's go inside; it's so windy today."

"You guys didn't have to wait outside."

"It's great to see you," Alice said as she took the diaper bag from Kelli.

Robin tugged the suitcase handle away from Kelli, her bright blue eyes vibrating with life. "You look good, Kel."

"Thanks," she said, following them up the steps while they took her things with them. She barely knew what to do with her hands without something to carry and someone to be in charge of. She'd gotten Parker to school this morning, told Robbie she wouldn't be into the studio for the next couple of days, and boarded a ferry to come here.

Eloise opened the door and held it while they all filed past her, smiling at each person as they did.

"How was the breakfast yesterday?" Kelli asked as she passed El.

"Great," El said. "They had a big turnout, and it was nice to do something for someone else."

"I don't do that enough either," Robin said. "I'll have Jamie take this stuff up to your room." She parked the suitcase at the bottom of the staircase.

"I can take it."

"No, it's fine." Alice put the diaper bag on top of the suitcase and continued into the large family room. Kelli didn't want to argue with anyone tonight, but her stomach did an unexpected flip.

"Wait, Alice, Ginny was staying in my suite."

"It's fine." Alice waved her hand in the air. "She and Bob went back to the city yesterday." She flashed Kelli a smile that strained around the edges. She turned then, concealing her expression from Kelli.

But she met Robin's eyes, and she shook her head. So Kelli wouldn't press this issue right now. She couldn't even begin to understand what it would be like to try to parent young adults like Ginny, Charlie, and Mandie. So she couldn't offer Alice any advice anyway.

She'd do what she'd wanted from AJ last weekend— love and support. Nothing more.

"All right, everyone," El said, her voice carrying easily

through the open space at the back of the house. "Kristen and I have put together some information about the Everleigh family and the history of this house. We've also created checklists for each team to use during their investigations."

Kelli glanced around the room, taking in the familiar faces of her friends. Robin and Alice stood with Laurel, who had one hand placed protectively on her belly. With a flash of realization, she remembered reading a text from Robin that had said Laurel was pregnant again.

A smile stole across Kelli's face even as she looked over to AJ, who still held Daphne. She stood close to Kelli, but further from everyone else, her eyes darting around the room as if expecting something to jump out at any moment. Kelli felt a surge of protectiveness towards her friend, remembering their conversation from the day before.

"We'll be dividing into pairs," El continued, pulling Kelli's attention back to the present. "Each pair will be responsible for investigating a different area of the house. Look for anything unusual, anything that might give us clues about what happened here all those years ago."

Kristen stepped forward, her silver hair glinting in the sunlight streaming through the windows and almost glowing white. "Remember," she said, her voice gentle but firm. "This is a rental. Don't break anything. If a door or cabinet doesn't open, don't try to force it."

"Right," El said. "Okay, pair up and come get a checklist."

Kelli looked over to AJ. "Want to be my partner?"

"Absolutely."

Kelli backtracked to her diaper bag and pulled out the sling. "I can bring Daphne with us in this." She started to put it on, glad when AJ helped with the straps and Daphne settled against Kelli's chest. Then AJ handed Kelli the checklist. "We got the east wing of the second floor."

Kelli looked at the items on the list. *Check outlets, light switches, and fixtures*

Open all doors and inspect contents of closets, cupboards, and drawers

Open all curtains and blinds

She scoffed out loud. "What are we looking for?" she asked, because she felt like she'd missed something important.

AJ looked at her with wide eyes, a lingering tension between them, a fragile peace that could easily shatter if Kelli wasn't careful. "I'm not sure. Kristen swears she saw the curtains move in the library when there wasn't a fan or any windows open. I guess we're just...looking."

"Okay." Kelli let AJ go toward the grand staircase first, the plush carpeting muffling her footsteps. The second floor waited in eerie quiet, the thick walls seeming to absorb any sound from the rest of the house.

"Alice swore the outdoor heater flared up when she shivered," AJ said. "So we've talked about just making notes of anything out of the ordinary. Cold spots, strange noises, objects that seem to move on their own.

And we're supposed to document the layout of each room, noting any areas that feel...off."

Kelli raised an eyebrow. "Off? That's pretty vague."

AJ shrugged, a hint of her old spark returning. "I guess we'll know it when we feel it."

The east wing on the second floor had three rooms: two suites and the art studio, and AJ led them into the first room, which was the the Gemini Suite—and the room Kelli had stayed in with Shad and Daphne when they'd been here that first weekend.

The beautifully appointed space held a large four-poster bed with a deep, dark midnight black comforter. The dark bed was offset by soft blues, pale yellows, and creamy whites in the wall color, the twin couches in the sitting area, and the artwork on the walls.

Everything came in pairs, as the astrological sign of Gemini was symbolized by "the twins."

Two mirrors in the bathroom, one above each sink. Two couches in the sitting area. Two pillows on each side of the bed. Two tall, slim pieces of artwork depicting boats on the sea.

Kelli found herself drawn to the window, gazing out at the sprawling grounds of the estate. "It's beautiful here," she murmured, more to herself than to AJ.

"Yeah," AJ agreed, coming to stand beside her. "Hard to imagine anything bad happening in a place like this."

Before Kelli could respond, a loud crash came from

the hallway. Both women jumped, and Daphne let out a startled wail.

"What was that?" Kelli whispered, clutching her daughter close.

AJ moved toward the door, peering out into the hall-way. "It's Robin," she said in a gaspy voice, and without further explanation, AJ darted out into the hall. As their voices echoed back to Kelli, she decided she couldn't simply hide out in this bedroom if her friends needed her.

So she went to see what had caused that crash and caused AJ to speak in such strained tone.

Chapter Twelve

R obin's heartbeat pounded and then skipped as she stared at the seemingly solid wall where Alice had vanished moments ago. She wiped her hands on her jeans before banging on the wall again. "Alice!" she called, her voice echoing down the empty hallway. "Alice, can you hear me?"

Silence answered her, and Robin's mind raced with possibilities, each one more terrifying than the last. She and Alice had been exploring the second floor, following the checklist Eloise and Kristen had given them, when Alice had noticed something odd about the wall paneling at the top of the steps.

The landing of the second floor was nothing, just a place to catch a breath before turning left and going into one of the bedrooms, or moving right and doing the same thing. Two suites sat to the right, with one on the left.

She could still hear Alice's voice. "Look at this, Robin," Alice had said, running her hand along a barely perceptible seam in the wood. "Doesn't this look out of place to you?"

Robin had agreed, and they'd spent the next few minutes examining the wall, looking for any clue as to what might be hidden behind it. Then, with a soft click, a section of the wall had swung inward, revealing a dark passageway.

Alice, ever the adventurous one, had stepped forward without hesitation. "I'm just going to take a quick look," she'd said, pointing her phone's flashlight into the darkness.

Before Robin could protest, the wall had swung shut behind Alice, slamming closed in a very final way, eating Alice whole and leaving Robin alone in the hallway.

"What's going on?" AJ asked, and Robin turned to see her hurrying toward her, concern etched on her face.

"Alice went into the wall." Robin knew how that sounded, and she didn't care. Panic rose through her, because this house that was supposed to be the magical place they could bond and spend Christmas together had just swallowed her best friend. Literally.

"Alice went into the wall?" AJ repeated.

"The wall?" Kelli asked, joining them. "Robin, where's Alice?"

She gestured angrily toward the wall. "She noticed something off with the paneling, and the wall opened." She saw the way her friends looked at her, and she seriously didn't have the patience or time for this. She banged on the wall again. "Alice! Can you open it from the other side?"

"She went into the wall," Kelli said slowly, as if trying to piece together each word and have it make sense.

"Yes," Robin said. "And I can't get it open again, and she's trapped in there, and I don't know what to do." She pushed her hands through her hair, trying to think. *Think, think, think.*

"Where?" AJ asked. "Where did she touch to open the wall?"

"Right here." Robin ran her fingertips down the seam between the panels. "I can feel it, but I don't know what she did to get it open."

Kelli stepped forward to examine the wall where Robin had indicated. "This is crazy," she murmured. "You can barely see it."

"I didn't until Alice pointed it out," Robin said, trying to keep the frustration out of her voice. She took a deep breath, forcing herself to think logically. "Okay, let's all take a step back and look at this carefully. There has to be a way to get it open again." She physically took a step back, trying to see something she hadn't before.

"Yeah, an axe," AJ said darkly.

Robin ignored her and moved her hand over a panel, searching for any irregularity that might indicate a hidden latch or mechanism. Kelli and AJ did the same, and Robin could only imagine how the three of them looked, rubbing down the wall here on the second floor landing.

"Wait," AJ said suddenly. "I think I found something." She pressed the butt of her palm against the wall, and with a noticeable click, the whole thing swung open again.

Sort of. The wall moved halfway into the wall cavity and halfway out onto the landing, and a dank smell filled Robin's nose as she stepped over to the opening, already calling, "Alice?"

She shrieked and jumped back when she saw the illuminated face of her best friend. Immediately following that, relief flooded through her.

"Come on, you guys," Alice said, her eyes shining in the light of her phone's flashlight. "You're not going to *believe* what I found. There's a whole secret room back here."

A mix of emotions washed over Robin—adrenaline, fear, relief, excitement, anxiety. No matter what, she did not want this wall to close again, and she quickly kicked off her shoes and positioned them so they'd block the wall from being able to trap them in—or out.

"Are you okay?" Robin asked, stepping right into the wall and hugging Alice. "I started panicking when I couldn't get the door open again."

Alice nodded, still grinning. "I'm fine. Come see this."

Robin exchanged glances with Kelli and AJ, seeing

her own curiosity and apprehension mirrored in their faces. Then, taking a deep breath, she followed Alice

The narrow corridor was dark and musty, the air heavy with the scent of old wood and dust. Robin's footsteps echoed softly as she walked, her hand trailing along the rough wall for balance. After what felt like an eternity but was probably only a few yards, the passageway opened up into a larger space.

Alice raised her phone, casting light around the room, and Robin gasped. They now stood in what appeared to be an old office, complete with a massive mahogany desk that looked like it belonged in the early nineteen hundreds. Bookcases lined the walls, their shelves sagging under the weight of ancient-looking tomes, folders, and dusty knickknacks.

"What is happening?" Kelli whispered, her eyes wide as she took in the scene.

Robin moved further into the room, her gaze drawn to a large oil painting hanging on the far wall. It depicted a stately couple—a man with a neatly trimmed beard and a woman with piercing eyes and an elaborate updo. Something about their faces seemed familiar, though Robin couldn't quite place why, where, or when she'd have seen them.

"Look at this," AJ called from near the desk. She pointed to a stack of yellowed newspapers, their headlines barely legible in the dim light.

Robin moved closer, squinting to read the faded print. Her breath caught in her throat as she made out the words: "Tragedy Strikes The Starlight Manor: Christmas Fire Claims Lives."

"Oh my goodness," she murmured, leaning over the newspapers with AJ. "This must be the fire El and Kristen were talking about."

Alice joined them, her flashlight illuminating more items on the desk. Stacks of letters, old ledgers and journals, and a collection of black and white photographs took up the space. Robin picked up one of the photos, her heart racing as she recognized the exterior of The Starlight Manor, though it looked different—smaller, for sure, without the elaborate porch and turret.

"These must be the original owners," Kelli said, peering over Robin's shoulder at the photo. "The Everleighs, right?"

Robin nodded, her mind whirling with the implications of what they'd found. "This is incredible," she said, setting the photo down and picking up one of the letters. "We need to show this to the others. Maybe it can help us figure out what's been going on in this house."

As she unfolded the letter, a small object fell from between the pages, clattering to the floor. AJ bent to pick it up, holding it up to the light.

"It's a locket," she said, turning it over in her hands. "There's an inscription on the back."

Robin leaned closer, reading the tiny engraved words aloud: "To Elizabeth, my guiding star. All my love, Edward."

A shiver ran down Robin's spine as she looked back

at the painting on the wall. "That must be them," she said, gesturing to the couple in the portrait. "Edward and Elizabeth Everleigh."

Alice nodded, her expression thoughtful. "This is amazing, but why was all of this hidden away?"

"How do you even hide a room behind a wall?" Kelli asked.

Robin shook her head, feeling overwhelmed by the questions swirling in her mind. "I don't know, but I think we need to get the others. We should document everything in here before we start moving things around."

"Good idea," Kelli said.

"I'll go get the others," AJ volunteered.

Robin met Alice's eye. "Let's start cataloguing what we see here."

Kelli moved over to the far wall, and she said, "You guys, there's a window here." She pulled on a cord, and the drapes started sliding open with an irritating grating sound. Natural light poured into the room, and Robin blinked into it.

"This room did not exist on the floor plans," Robin said. And she knew, because she'd looked at them when El had sent them out. Multiple times.

"That helps so much." Alice switched off her phone flashlight and tucked her device away. Robin turned back to the desk, her hands hovering over the scattered papers and photographs. A strange mix of excitement and trepidation filtered through her, as if they were on the verge of uncovering something monumental.

"Where should we start?" Alice asked.

Robin took a deep breath, forcing herself to approach the task methodically the way she would taking a nebulous event and turning it into the wedding of the century. "Let's start with the newspapers." She reached for the top one. "Maybe they can give us a time-line of events."

As they began sorting through the yellowed pages, typing in the dates at the top of them, and then a couple of the headlines, Robin couldn't shake the feeling that they were being watched. She glanced up at the portrait of Edward and Elizabeth Everleigh, their painted eyes seeming to follow her every move.

"This is so strange," Kelli said as she returned to the desk. She patted her baby's bottom and rocked from foot to foot, clearly trying to get the little girl to go to sleep. "Why would someone go to such lengths to hide all of this?"

"Great question," Alice said, echoing Robin's thoughts.

"When do you think this room was walled off?" Kelli asked next.

"I have no idea," Robin said.

"I'm going to write down all these questions," Alice said. "Because I feel like they should have answers."

"Do you think a hidden room with books and letters

and even a window—" Robin turned and gestured toward the glass. "Has anything to do with why we've been experiencing all those odd occurrences in the house?"

And how could it?

They were old newspapers, not ghosts flipping switches or rats gnawing through wires.

She picked up another newspaper, this one dated a week after the fire. The headline read: "Questions Surround Starlight Manor Fire: Foul Play Suspected."

"Look at this," Robin said, her voice hushed. She pointed to a paragraph halfway down the page. "It says here that there were rumors of financial troubles and marital discord between Edward and Elizabeth Everleigh in the weeks leading up to the fire."

Alice leaned in, her eyes scanning the text. "That's interesting. That could explain why this room—and all of this—got hidden behind a solid wall."

Voices came down the hall, and the three of them turned toward the entrance to the hidden office. Moments later, Eloise appeared in the doorway, her eyes wide with disbelief.

She sucked at the air as she took in the scene before her. "AJ wasn't exaggerating. This is..."

"A hidden room," Robin said.

"Edward's office," Alice said. "At least, I think it's his."

"It's not on the floor plan," El said as she joined

them at the desk. "I wonder what other secret rooms and passageways this place has."

AJ returned, with Kristen moving slowly behind her. Her breath came in labored spurts, and Laurel brought up the rear, saying, "Maybe there will be a chair here, and you can sit."

"There's a chair," Robin said, pulling it out from the desk. "Come sit down, Kristen."

But the older woman and Robin's mentor and beloved friend didn't continue forward to the chair. Her eyes widened as she too drank in the office. "I don't know if my old heart can take this." She pressed one hand to her heartbeat, her fingers almost at her throat.

The room suddenly felt a bit claustrophobic with all seven of them in it, but she pushed the suffocating feelings down until they went away.

"Okay, everyone," she said, raising her voice slightly to be heard over the chatter. "We need to document everything in here carefully before we start moving things around. Can we split into teams?"

"Let's take pictures," El said, her phone already out and ready. "We don't even know what will be a clue."

Robin nodded along with Alice, and Kristen finally did come sit in the chair. "Looks like newspapers, photographs, journals, books..." Her gaze swept the office. "Look, they've got a filing cabinet."

She pushed herself up with a groan and walked over to the cabinet positioned next to the bookcase. "These had to be very new at the time." Kristen depressed the button, and the top drawer popped out so she could pull it open.

She turned back to the group. "It's empty."

"Less to go through," Alice said. "Robin and I have started on the newspapers, and we can take this stack of journals here."

"Kel and I will work on this bookcase," AJ said.

"Laurel, Kristen, and I will do the photographs and ledgers," El said.

The newspapers all came from a single month, and Robin invented a story about Edward as she and Alice catalogued them, took pictures, and leafed through their thin pages. Edward got the newspaper everyday, and he kept them until the end of the month, when the recycling went out.

These all came from the days and weeks immediately before the fire—from the last week of November through nearly Christmas.

"Look," Alice said softly as she tipped an open journal toward Robin. "It's Elizabeth Everleigh's diary."

Robin leaned in, her heart racing as she read the elegant script on the first page. "My dearest Edward," it began. "If you are reading this, then I fear the worst has come to pass..."

As she continued reading, a chill ran down Robin's spine. The diary entry spoke of Elizabeth's fears – fears of financial ruin, of scandal, of losing everything they had built together. But more than that, it spoke of a deep, unresolved conflict between her and Edward.

I cannot bear the thought of facing our friends and neighbors, knowing the truth of what we've done. Edward insists we can weather this storm, but I fear the price will be too high. How can we continue our charitable work, and maintain our social standing, when everything is built on such a fragile foundation of lies?

She looked up at Alice. "It sounds like they were hiding something big."

Alice pointed to another entry.

Edward will not listen to me, and I'm tired of pressing my ear to the door of his office while he meets with the constable, a lawyer, and his father. He insists we host our annual Christmas Eve party, but I don't even know if the servants will be here by then. How does he expect me to pay a staff and put on a party when he won't tell me everything and when our finances are so up in the air?

Robin looked at Alice. "What could've gone wrong in Nineteen-Twelve?"

"The Great Depression wasn't for another couple of decades," Alice said. "I don't know."

Robin felt like they were assembling a complex puzzle, but the final picture remained frustratingly out of reach. Across the room, she could hear snippets of conversation from the others as they made their own discoveries.

"Look at this photo," Eloise was saying. "This room doesn't exist in the current floor plan."

"Maybe it's behind a wall," Laurel said dryly.

"I found an article about Edward Everleigh's business dealings," AJ called out. "It mentions some questionable investments and potential fraud."

Robin's head spun with all the new information. She turned back to the diary, flipping through the pages until she reached an entry dated just days before the fire. As she read, her breath caught in her throat.

"You guys," she said urgently. "I think I found something important." She waited until they'd all gathered around the desk once more, then she began to read out loud.

"December 20, 1912

My dearest Edward,

I fear this may be my final entry, for I can no longer bear the weight of our secrets. The walls of The Starlight Manor, once a symbol of our outlandish and out-of-this-world dreams and aspirations, now feel like a prison. The whispers grow louder with each passing day, and I know it is only a matter of time before the truth comes to light.

You say we can weather this storm, that our love and our reputation will see us through. But at what cost, my love? The thought of facing our friends, our benefactors, knowing the truth of what we've done...it is more than I can bear.

I have made a decision, one that I pray you will understand in time. By the time you read these words, I will have taken steps to ensure that our legacy, tarnished though it may be, will endure. The fire that burns within me now will soon consume all evidence of our transgressions.

Forgive me, Edward. Know that my love for you has never wavered, even in these darkest of hours.

Forever yours,

Elizabeth"

As Robin finished reading, a heavy silence fell over the room. She looked up to find everyone with the same round eyes her's had become.

Alice cleared her throat, her face pale. "Are you saying that Elizabeth started the fire here at her own house intentionally?"

Robin nodded slowly, the weight of the revelation settling over her. "It seems that way. But why? What were they hiding that was so terrible?"

El held up a weathered filing folder. It had no shapely tab, but looked like a buff piece of cardstock folded right in half. "I think I might have an idea." She flipped open the folder. "These are financial records, and they have handwritten notes on them. To me, it looks like Edward and Elizabeth were using their charitable foundation as a front to funnel money into their own pockets."

She handed the folder to Alice. "I mean, I'm no expert, so."

Alice said nothing as she opened the folder and started examining the documents inside.

"Okay," AJ said in a near-shout. "But that doesn't explain the strange occurrences we've been experiencing." She looked around at all of them, and Robin folded her arms, hugging herself to try to keep warm.

"Are we seriously saying the ghosts of Edward and Elizabeth are haunting the house now, after all this time?"

"We don't even know if they died here," Laurel said.

Kristen sighed as she gained her feet again. "Perhaps they're not haunting the house," she said. "Perhaps they're trying to make amends."

Robin considered this, her mind racing. "The flickering lights, the moving objects...what if it's not about scaring us away, but about leading us here? To this room, to these documents?"

A thoughtful silence fell over the group as they considered this possibility. Robin looked around at her friends, seeing her own mix of excitement and trepidation reflected in their faces. She couldn't shake the question—but why? Why did they need to be here, see these things? What could they do more than a century later?

But as she gazed at the portrait of Edward and Elizabeth Everleigh, their painted eyes seeming to follow her every move, Robin couldn't shake the feeling that they had only scratched the surface of the mystery. What other secrets lay hidden within the walls of The Starlight Manor? And how would uncovering them affect their own lives and relationships?

As if in answer to her unspoken questions, a cold breeze swept through the office, causing the papers on the desk to rustle. Kelli cried out, and AJ sucked in a breath.

Truth be told, Robin did as well. Goosebumps

pricked her arms, flowed over her shoulders, and made her shiver.

The lights flickered once, twice, and then steadied.

"Okay," she said loudly. "Time to vacate this office. Who needs a drink?" She looked around at her friends. "I need a drink—and not a mocktail."

Chapter Thirteen

K risten's fingers trembled as she lifted the delicate china teacup to her lips. Steam curled from the deep amber liquid, carrying the comforting scent of Earl Grey. She inhaled deeply, willing the familiar aroma to calm her still-racing heart.

The rhythmic lapping of water against the pool's edge provided a soothing backdrop to the tense atmosphere. Kristen's gaze swept over the faces of her friends gathered around the outdoor patio. Eloise, Robin, Alice, AJ, Kelli, Laurel, and Jean—women she'd known for years, some for decades. Women she considered family.

And yet, as they sat in silence, each lost in their own thoughts after the shocking discovery of a hidden office, a chasm seemed to be growing between them.

She set her cup down with a soft clink. "Well," she

said, her voice cutting through the otherwise lazy afternoon. "I think it's time we had a proper talk."

Seven pairs of eyes turned to her, a mix of relief and apprehension reflected in their depths.

"What kind of talk?" Robin asked, her fingers tapping an anxious rhythm against her glass of wine. Only her first, because her daughter and husband would be at the manor soon, and Kristen had never seen Robin over-drink anyway.

Kristen smiled, though it didn't quite reach into her soul. "A Tell All."

"Oh, here we go." Alice put her elbows up on the side of the pool, her face the only one wearing a smile. "I'll second it."

"Alice," Robin said crossly, and she punctuated the name with a sigh.

Kristen sat up straighter. "Everyone takes a turn to share what's truly bothering them. No judgment, no interruptions, no follow-up questions. Just honesty."

El looked like she might throw up, but she said, "This is a good idea. I want to know if anyone is considering setting this holiday house on fire."

A beat of silence carried across the pool and patio, and then Kristen burst out laughing. Several others joined her, and that drove the last of the suffocating silence away.

"I'll go first," Kelli volunteered as they quieted, her voice barely above a whisper. She cradled her mug of hot chocolate, staring into its depths as if it held the answers to life's greatest mysteries. "Sometimes the world moves too fast, you know?"

She looked up, her smile the firmest Kristen had ever seen. "Between the studio, and Daphne, and trying to figure out how to parent a teenager... I feel like I just need to slow down."

"This was supposed to be that for people," El said.

Kelli reached across the table and covered El's hand. "Now that I'm here, I'm sure it will be." She nodded, her gaze coming back to Kristen. "I'm done."

AJ cleared her throat. "I'll go next." She set down her cocktail, twisting her wedding ring nervously. "I'm...lost. I used to know exactly who I was and what I wanted. Sports journalist, career woman, independent. And now?" She laughed, but it was a hollow sound. "Now I'm 'Asher's mom' or 'Matt's wife.' Don't get me wrong, I love them both more than anything. But sometimes I look in the mirror and I don't recognize the woman staring back at me."

She paused, taking a shaky breath. "I'm trying to figure out who I am in the midst of everything else. And I'm terrified that I'll never find that confident, ambitious woman again."

Kristen nodded, her heart aching for AJ's struggle. She remembered all too well the challenges of balancing motherhood with one's own identity.

"It comes," Alice said quietly. "And soon enough, your kids will be gone." She took a deep breath. "I don't think anyone will be surprised that I'm worried about

Ginny." She didn't elaborate further, but she didn't need to. Alice had opened up a lot in the past few years, and she simply wanted the best for her kids.

And she thought Ginny was moving too fast with her boyfriend, Bob.

Alice ran a hand through her hair and pushed herself out of the pool. Water dripped everywhere as she walked over to the table and picked up a towel. She buried her face in it, then wrapped it around herself and looked at Robin. "Is there more of that red?"

"Absolutely," Robin said, and she turned over another wine glass. "It's on AJ's table."

Alice turned to get the wine, and Kristen let the group listen to the sound of the lapping pool water. Robin took a sip of her wine, her eyes darting around the group. "I... I'm not sure what to say," she admitted. "Everything's fine, really. The wedding planning business is booming, Duke and I are great, the girls are doing well."

"Dig deep," Alice said as she poured herself a glass of wine.

Kristen caught the sharp look on Robin's face, but it only stayed for a moment. "I guess...I'd like a me-day," she said finally, surprise coloring her tone. "I'm always taking care of everyone else, always planning and organizing something for everyone but me. And I love it, I do. But—" She looked around at everyone. "I need a me-day."

"Let's plan one for here at the holiday house," El

said, her voice rising with excitement. "And you know what? You don't even need to plan it. Let's just *do it*."

"Yeah, I'm sick of planning things," Robin said, her own smile growing.

Kristen ducked her head to hide her own smile, because she knew Robin would have a very, very hard time letting go like that.

"You're up, El," Robin said, and the familiar fear struck across Eloise's darker features.

"Okay." El took a deep breath, her hands clasped tightly in her lap, her own cup of tea untouched. "I'm thinking of selling the Cliffside Inn." The words hung in the air like a deep, thick, dark thundercloud, threatening to ruin everything beneath it.

A collective gasp went up from the group. Even Kristen leaned forward, her eyes wide. "Eloise, are you sure?"

"What?" AJ asked. "After everything you went through to get it?"

"This is unbelievable," Jean said.

Laurel exchanged a glance with Alice and then her eyes flitted over to Kristen. But Kristen couldn't control this narrative, and she'd had no idea Eloise wanted to sell the inn that had brought her back to Five Island Cove.

She did notice that Alice and Robin didn't look as surprised as the others, and she hoped no one else would see that. She cut a look over to AJ, who had taken the micro-groups in their bigger group of friends the hardest, and she still blinked at El like she'd sprouted a third eye in the middle of her forehead.

A mixture of relief and fear played across El's features. "I've been considering it for a while now. It's just—it's too much. I'm stretched so thin, trying to manage everything. The inn, my family, this holiday—I feel like I'm drowning in responsibilities."

She gestured to Robin. "There is no time for me-anything, and I'm starting to resent the inn."

"Have you talked to Aaron about it?" Kristen asked.

El nodded. "He said it's up to me, and I haven't fully decided yet." She finally reached for her tea and took a sip. "Ew, that's cold." She set the cup back down, a small smile spreading her lips.

An afternoon breeze came across the pool, and Kristen squinted into the sky. "Looks like it might rain again this afternoon."

"Mm," Alice nodded.

"I'll go next," Laurel said. "I'm not sure I'm ready to start all over again with a newborn, when James can't even talk." She nodded, and she'd never been one to go on and on, delving into the deeper parts of her psyche. And during a Tell All, she didn't have to.

Kristen looked around the group, realizing she might have to say something in all this. She met Jean's eye, wondering what her wonderful daughter-in-law would say.

Jean smiled softly, though her eyes held a hint of

sadness. "I'm not sure what to say," she admitted. "Everything's good, really. Heidi's growing so fast, Reuben and I are happy."

"The Seafaring Girls love you," Kelli said. "Parker does too."

"You should bring him by more often," Jean said. "I love having him at the lighthouse."

Kelli nodded, her throat working as she swallowed.

"Okay." Kristen drew in a breath and blew it out. "I guess it's just me."

Seven pairs of eyes turned to her, a mix of curiosity and concern reflected in their depths. Oh, how she loved her girls. Those she'd led so long ago, and those who'd come to their group in recent years. They'd all brought something amazing and awesome to her life, and she hoped they knew it.

"I'm afraid," Kristen admitted, the words feeling foreign on her tongue. "Not just of the strange occurrences in this house, though those certainly aren't helping. I'm afraid of becoming irrelevant."

She paused, gathering her thoughts. "For so long, I've been the one you all come to with your problems. The wise old woman with all the answers." A wry smile twisted her lips. "But lately, I've been feeling...obsolete. The world is changing so fast, and I worry that my advice, my experiences, aren't useful anymore."

Kristen looked around at the women she'd watched grow from girls into strong, capable women. "You're all so accomplished, so smart, and doing such good things —whether you know it or not. And I'm proud of you, more than you could ever know. But sometimes I wonder...do you still need me?"

It was such an interesting question, and as Kristen looked around the group, she knew most of the struggles each of them each had stemmed from the root of such a question. Did they feel needed? What would happen if she simply got in her car and started driving? Would anyone notice, and how long would it take them?

"I think I'll always need you," Robin said. "You've been like my mother figure for a long time."

"Mine too," Alice said.

"Same," AJ said.

"Thank you," Kristen said softly. "But that's not why I shared this. I didn't say it to fish for compliments or reassurance. I said it because it's the truth, and because I think it's important for you all to know that even I have doubts sometimes."

She straightened in her chair, her gaze sweeping over the group. "Okay, that's everyone." Kristen paused, choosing her next words carefully. "Now, I think it's time we address the elephant in the room. Or rather, the ghost in the manor."

A collective shiver ran through the group at her words. Kristen continued, her voice steady and sure. "We've uncovered some troubling things about the history of this house and the Everleigh family. And I believe it's our responsibility to learn what we can, even if that's just that this place is really old so the lights flicker sometimes."

Alice and Robin nodded, then El and AJ and Kelli, until they'd all agreed.

She leaned forward, her eyes bright with determination. "I don't want this to take over our holidays. Some of us have little children, and some have jobs they need to keep up with, at least a little bit."

"Right," Eloise said. "And if someone doesn't want to hear more about it, or do anything, that's fine. That's not what this holiday house is about."

"I agree with that," Robin said. "This vacation should be whatever people want it to be."

Alice stood and tightened her towel around herself. "We know the fire happened in Nineteen-Twelve, but we need to look at the years leading up to it. What changed for the Everleighs? What led to their financial troubles?" She poured herself another glass of wine and met Kristen's eye. "This is my last one."

"Okay," Kristen said.

Alice settled back at the table with El and Kelli. "I can dig deeper into the financial records we found. There might be clues there about Edward's embezzlement and Elizabeth's attempts to cover it up."

"Excellent," Kristen said. "AJ, you have a background in journalism. Could you research local newspapers from that time? See if there were any reports about the Everleighs or their charitable foundation?"

AJ nodded, a spark of her old enthusiasm lighting up her eyes. "Absolutely. I'll start first thing in the morning."

"I love reading the diaries," El said. "I can light a fire in my suite and spend all day doing that." She grinned around at everyone. "That actually sounds like a vacation to me." She laughed lightly, and a few others joined in.

"I'm really good at Internet searches," Jean said. "I can see what I can dig up."

"We're here," someone called from inside the house, drawing their attention, and then Jamie, Billie, Grace, and Parker came filing out onto the deck from the house.

"How was school?" Kelli asked as she rose to her feet. "You guys want something to eat?"

The group started to disperse, with mothers of teens going off to put together something for their children in the kitchen. Kristen wasn't on dinner duty until tomorrow night, and she determined she simply wanted to relax in this beautiful place for the next couple of hours.

A renewed sense of purpose coursed through her veins, and while she might not ever admit it out loud, she was excited about the mystery of the holiday house, as it felt like it simply wanted to be understood.

"Oh, Asher's up," AJ said as a squeal came through her baby monitor, and she hurried into the house too.

"That was a good Tell-All," Lauren said. "I might go take a little nap while James is still down." She stood and leaned over Kristen. "I feel irrelevant all the time, Kristen. Thank you for making me feel less alone." She gave her a tight, closed-mouth smile and headed up the steps to the deck.

That left Kristen with Alice and Jean, and neither of them said anything or made a move to leave. The pool continued to lap restlessly, and the storm rolled through the sky but didn't drop any rain.

And life felt...easy. She'd lived in Five Island Cove her whole life, and she'd known plenty of people over the eighty years of her life. Good people.

"Some secrets too," she said aloud, and that drew Alice's attention.

"We're *so* good at uncovering secrets," Alice said, a smile on her face as she lifted the last of her wine to her lips. She too looked over the backyard. "And none of them have broken us yet."

She stood and gave Kristen a healthy smile now. "I love you, Kristen." She put her hand on Kristen's shoulder as she went by.

Kristen covered it with her own. "I love you too, Alice."

"Arthur and I are on dinner tonight," she said. "And he's almost here with all the groceries, so I better go meet him."

"You better." Kristen finished her tea and got to her feet, reaching for Jean as she said, "I'm so glad you're happy, dear." Jean and Reuben had certainly been through their fair share of heartache in the past.

She took one more look at the immaculate grounds. "And no matter what happens, this is going to be an amazing Christmas, in this amazing house."

Now all she needed was for what she'd said to come true.

Chapter Fourteen

E loise watched the morning light filter through the
filmy curtains of the Cassiopeia Suite. For a
moment, she lay still, listening to the gentle rhythm of
Aaron's breathing beside her. The tranquility of the
manor at dawn was a stark contrast to the whirlwind of
thoughts spinning in her mind.

She rolled toward her husband and gazed at him.
He'd been getting up and getting the girls and other
teens on the ferry to school, so she could sleep in and
have a slower start to the morning. He'd brought his
laptop, and he did a few things for the police department
before lunchtime, and then he only wanted to spend
time with her.

He breathed evenly, but his eyelashes fluttered.

Eloise smiled. "I think I'll ask my mom if she wants
to stay over on Saturday," she whispered.

Aaron opened his eyes and it only took a moment for him to focus on her. "El."

This weekend, The Starlight Manor would once again be filled to the brim. Charlie and Mandie would be here later today, as they came in on the New York ferry.

Spouses and children would gather after work and school, and Eloise had planned two big meals—one tonight, and one tomorrow night.

The house would come alive with laughter and chaos —just the way it should be during the holidays. Eloise had planned a few activities she hoped would entertain teenagers and adults alike. Sugar cookie decorating in the grand kitchen, a crafty stocking stuffer workshop for the kids so they'd have something to give their parents on Christmas morning, and a festive pool party complete with an array of holiday-themed floaties she'd ordered through her connections at Cliffside.

"I want her to be here if she wants to be here," Eloise said.

"There's nowhere for her to sleep," Aaron whispered. "Where are you going to put her? In the bunk room with the boys?"

The only empty bed this weekend would be a single twin in the boys' bunk room on the third floor, and Eloise grinned at her handsome husband. "Maybe I'll put you in there and let my mom sleep in here with me."

Aaron scoffed, but he searched her face as if she might be serious. Eloise giggled and took his face in her hands to kiss him. He matched her stroke for stroke, and then pulled back. "You're joking, right?"

"Yes," she whispered.

"I know you want everything to be perfect," he said. "But your mom won't want to stay here anyway."

"No, probably not." Eloise sighed as she rolled over.

"What are you doing this morning?" Aaron asked. "More sleuthing?"

She slipped out of bed and padded over to the window. Pulling back the curtain, she gazed out at the estate. The gardens were covered with frost, each blade of grass shimmering like it had been sprinkled with diamond dust. They stood in leafless contrast against the pale sky, and in the distance, she could just make out the ocean's horizon blending into the morning mist.

Eloise hugged her arms around herself. "Yeah, we've been looking through all the items from the office, and we're going to meet this morning." She gave him a glancing smile and looked back outside. "I promise I'll be waiting at the ferry when you get off, and we'll go to lunch."

"Just the two of us?" He got up and came around the bed to where she stood, wrapping her in his arms. The warmth from his chest kissed her back, and Eloise leaned into his strength.

"Yes," she murmured. "Just me and you."

"Who's on dinner tonight?" he asked, rocking her slightly.

"Jean and Reuben," Eloise said. "And Clara and Scott."

"So dessert will be delicious." He stepped back and moved toward the bathroom.

"They know how to cook too," she said.

"I'll eat a lot at lunch," Aaron called. "And bring home leftovers."

Eloise didn't care what he did for food, as Aaron had more tact cells in his body than most people, and he wouldn't say anything about the food. In fact, he'd load his plate with it and eat it anyway, and Eloise didn't worry about him when it came to getting enough to eat.

The girls, yes. But not Aaron.

So Eloise stayed at the window for another few moments, drinking the beauty of this place. Something else lingered too—a feeling she couldn't quite name. The discovery of the hidden office and the tragic story of the Everleighs weighed on her. Elizabeth Everleigh had tried so desperately to maintain control, to preserve her world even as it crumbled around her.

Was she so different?

Eloise wasn't sure, but she did feel like she'd been trying to climb a mountain and was coming away with handfuls of dirt as she did. She dressed without showering, and once Aaron was ready, they went downstairs together. At least a half-dozen boxes of cereal had been lined up on the counter, and Eloise smiled at Grace as she poured herself a bowl of Lucky Charms.

"Morning, my beautiful girls." Aaron pulled Billie to

his chest despite her protests, and he did the same to Grace as she continued to try to put milk on her breakfast.

Eloise usually only drank coffee for breakfast, and she set about making herself a cappuccino from the fancy coffee maker in the manor. Once she had that, she joined those who had to leave and go somewhere that morning at the eat-in table in the kitchen.

Soon enough, Aaron bustled everyone out of the manor who needed to get on the ferry, and that left Eloise in the house with only women and children under the age of three. She went up to the third floor and made up all the beds in the bunk room, as Ian and Charlie would be coming in that afternoon. She checked on the Cosmic Bunk Room too, as Tessa and Dave would be staying there.

"My mom could sleep in here with them," she mused, smiling to herself as such a prospect. Of course, she would never do that to her mother—or Tessa and Dave.

Down the hall, she checked on the Shooting Star Room, where Ben and Maddy would be tonight. Maddy would be gone for dinner service at The Glass Dolphin, a high-end restaurant she managed on Diamond Island, for tomorrow's dinner, but she'd be here tonight.

With the third floor ready for its weekend guests, Eloise returned to the second floor. She paused on the landing, seeing the creases in the wall now that she knew it opened. Part of her wanted to open up the office and let it air out, but she hadn't been in the room alone since they'd found it, and she wasn't keen to do so now.

Then she continued downstairs, because all of the bedrooms on the second floor had been lived in for a couple of weeks now by women or couples who'd been here, and Eloise wasn't going to go make up Jean's room. She wouldn't even make her own bed.

Back downstairs, she found Kristen coming up from the basement. "Clara and Scott's room is ready," she said.

They had the only bedroom in the basement beside the female bunk room, and Eloise nodded. "Thank you, Kristen. Do you think Lena will be okay in the bunk room?"

"I told her she could some sleep with me if she's not." Kristen smiled and patted Eloise's arm. "She'll be fine. We're not worrying about the sleeping arrangements, remember?"

"I'm not, you're right," Eloise said.

"I found something I think you should see." Kristen moved into the kitchen, where someone had put away the cereal boxes. Laurel stood there with James on her hip, a squeezable applesauce at the boy's mouth. "I'll make tea."

"It requires tea?" Eloise asked as she took a barstool at the island.

Kristen opened a drawer and pulled something out of it. Eloise had spent plenty of time in this kitchen in the past week, and she knew that drawer to hold rolls of plastic wrap and aluminum foil. But Kristen plucked a leather-bound book out of it and put it on the island in front of Eloise.

"What is this?" Eloise reached for it, already reading the gold lettering on the front. *JOURNAL* in all caps. "Another one of Elizabeth's diaries?"

"I believe so," Kristen said as she busied herself with the kettle. "But this one is different. More personal, perhaps."

Opening the journal carefully, Eloise began to read. The script boasted an elegance no one printed with anymore, the ink faded with time. As she skimmed the pages, fragments of Elizabeth's thoughts emerged—her fears about the mounting debts, her desperation to keep up appearances, her obsession with controlling every aspect of their lives to prevent scandal.

Eloise's throat tightened. The parallels were unsettling. She only read one entry, then looked up as Kristen put a cup of tea in front f her. "She was so consumed by her need to manage everything. Even when it was all falling apart."

Kristen sat beside her, her fingers curled around her cup, which had to be scalding hot. "Holding on too tightly can sometimes cause everything to slip through our fingers."

Eloise let the words sink in, feeling like they'd been ordered just for her. She closed the journal, unwilling to read it right this moment. She would leaf through it later. "Thank you for showing me this," she said. "It gives me a lot to think about."

Kristen placed her hand over Eloise's. "You're not alone in this, you know. We're all here to help."

Eloise squeezed her hand gratefully. "I know. I think I've done a pretty good job the past few days just letting people help."

"You have."

"I think so, too, El," Laurel said as she went behind them. She'd just strapped James into a booster seat, and he shrieked as he slapped the tray with both hands. "I'm getting it, buddy." Laurel laughed as she re-entered the kitchen. "He is so demanding."

She started cracking eggs, glancing past Kristen and Eloise as someone else entered the main part of the house. "Morning, Kel," she said. "Do you want any scrambled eggs?"

"Sure," Kelli said. Daphne perched on her hip, her pretty strawberry blonde hair thick and still tousled from sleep.

"Can I take her?" Eloise got to her feet and reached for the baby.

"Of course," Kelli said, sliding Daphne into Eloise's arms.

Eloise instantly felt everything and anything that had been pent up release. Nothing compared to holding a baby and the peace that came with it. She walked away with Daphne as Kristen asked, "Tea?" of Kelli.

"Tea would be lovely," Kelli said.

Eloise took a rocking recliner in the family room and tucked Daphne against her chest. The little girl simply melted into her as if she had no bones in her body, and Eloise toed them back and forth, back and forth.

She thought about the waves that came in from the sea, and how they seemed to move in the same way, perpetually coming ashore and then washing back out again. Life mirrored that sometimes, with each new day simply a repeat of the wave of activities from the previous day.

She closed her eyes and simply enjoyed this new, different thing she didn't get to do everyday. Soon enough, Kelli came to get Daphne so she could feed her, and Laurel put James on the floor in the living room to play. Kristen took a seat too, and Eloise's heart felt over-full as she surveyed all of them.

"Kelli," she said. "I'd love it if you could take charge of the cookie decorating tomorrow. You're so creative, and the older kids adore you."

Kelli blinked a couple of times. "I'm sure that's not true."

"If you don't want to do it, because of Parker, I'll ask Jean." The fact that Eloise was asking anyone didn't feel like her at all.

"I can do it," Kelli said.

"Good," Eloise said. "Because I've already asked Jean to run the stocking stuffer craft." She grinned around to everyone. "Alice is going to run the pool party, because she's the best at mocktails, and she loves that pool."

"That she does," Kristen said.

"Speaking of which," Kelli said, stifling a yawn. "I heard you ordered some over-the-top floaties?"

Eloise grinned mischievously. "Perhaps. There's a reindeer you can ride, a gigantic Santa-shaped doughnut, and a candy cane raft that fits four people."

Kelli laughed and shook her head. "The kids are going to go nuts."

"Who says it's just for the kids?" Eloise asked innocently. "Alice has already called dibs on the raft for her and Arthur."

They laughed, and the tightness in Eloise's chest eased. This weekend, only nine days away from Christmas, was going to be fun on many levels.

Her phone buzzed, and Eloise pulled it from her pocket to find a message from Maggie, the assistant manager at the Cliffside Inn.

Good morning, Eloise! Just wanted to update you—the new reservation system is up and running smoothly. No issues so far. Enjoy your holiday!

Eloise stared at the screen. Normally, she would have been the one triple-checking every detail on a busy holiday weekend before check-in. But she'd left it in Maggie's capable hands, albeit with a lengthy list of instructions.

And nothing had fallen apart.

"Everything okay?" AJ asked, appearing at her side with a mug of coffee.

She slipped the phone back into her pocket. "Yes. Maggie was just updating me on the inn." She flashed her friend a smile. AJ wore a pair of black, flowing pants and a pale purple pajama shirt. Her hair sprouted in an unruly way from her head, but she still exuded beauty and charm.

Asher now crouched down in front of James, and he asked, "I play? I play?" while holding up one of the toy cars James had been playing with.

"You can play, buddy," Laurel said for her son. She nodded and smiled at Asher as he straightened.

"Vroom!" he said, lifting the car up into the air as if flying vehicles existed. In his world, they obviously did.

Robin came in the front door, calling, "Duke's got lobster for tomorrow night!" She hurried into the living room, a triumphant look on her face. "He just texted me. Fresh lobster to add to our barbecue."

"Good job, Robin," Eloise said.

"I'm going to put it in the binder." She started for the kitchen, and Eloise laughed at her as she did.

She once again picked up Elizabeth's diary. As the women around her chatted, and children played, Eloise traced her fingertips down the side of the aged paper.

The pages whispered as she turned them, Elizabeth's voice emerging from the past.

December 18, 1912

Everything teeters on the edge of ruin. Edward insists that we host the Christmas gala, but I fear our charade is unsustainable. The debts mount, and whispers of impropriety have begun to circulate. Control slips through my fingers like sand, no matter how tightly I grasp.

"What are you reading?" Kelli asked, and Eloise looked up.

"Kristen found a new diary," she said, holding it up.

Kelli perched on the armrest of the recliner, jostling Eloise slightly. "I found something too." She held out a folded piece of parchment.

Eloise took it gently. "What is it?"

"I found it tucked inside one of the books in that office yesterday," Kelli said. "It's a letter from Edward to Elizabeth. It's interesting."

Eloise unfolded the letter carefully. The handwriting was bold, the strokes heavy, so unlike the careful, controlled, frilly strokes in the diary.

My dearest Elizabeth,

I know not how to bridge the chasm that has grown between us. The pressures weigh heavily, and I fear I have become a man you no longer recognize. But believe me when I say that all I have done was in hopes of preserving our legacy.

Please, let us not fall to ruin apart. Together, we can withstand any storm.

I must confess, in the quiet of these words, what I dared not speak aloud. The decisions I have made in the past months—no, years—have led us to this precipice. What began as small compromises to our values quickly became something far greater. I thought I could manage it all, conceal the cracks forming beneath the surface, but the walls are beginning to close in.

They watch more closely now. My name is no longer

spoken with respect in the circles we once held dominion over. Questions are asked. Deals, once hidden, now hang on fragile threads.

I never intended for the business with Haversham to go this far. I thought it was a mere transaction, a loan we could repay without issue. But he's ensnared me in something darker, Elizabeth. I have wagered more than money, and in doing so, I fear I have wagered our future. If they discover what I've done—if they learn of the false investments and the accounts I created in your name—it will not just be our reputation that falls. We could lose everything. You could lose everything.

But you must believe me when I tell you, there is a way out. Haversham is a dangerous man, but not an infallible one. I've learned of his dealings with the Banksworth family, and it is far worse than anything we've done. He won't dare expose us for fear of his own ruin. He thinks I'm ignorant, but I've gathered enough to ensure his silence. We can use this against him, Elizabeth.

If I can pull this final thread, we will be free. No one will suspect anything. Our standing will be restored, and you will never again need to worry about maintaining the life we've built here.

I ask for your forgiveness for the lies I've told, and the burden I've placed upon you without your knowledge. But I ask, too, for your trust. If you stand beside me, I will not let this destroy us. There is still time to turn this around. I just need to make one final move.

Tell no one of this. Not even those closest to you. The less they know, the safer we will be.

Forever yours,

Edward

Eloise swallowed hard. "Wow," she said. "This says so much more than anything else I've seen."

"I thought so too," Kelli said. "But I found it in the afternoon, and you and Aaron had already gone on your winer walk." She smiled at Eloise, who returned the gesture.

She had time this morning to look up some of these names, and she got up to go get Aaron's laptop. Alice hadn't come downstairs yet, and she had the financial information she'd been working on to share with everyone.

So Eloise had a few minutes to search the Internet for these new names. As she went up to the second floor, she thought of Edward. He'd tried to salvage what he could, but perhaps too late.

Was she making the same mistake? Waiting too long to give up the Cliffside Inn, to acknowledge that it didn't make her as happy as it once had?

Aaron's laptop sat plugged in on his nightstand, and Eloise unplugged it and picked it up just as a shadow covered the light coming in through the window.

A chill ran down her arms, making the fine hairs stand up tall. Eloise stepped over to the window and peeled the curtains back. Clouds had come in, and the sudden tension that had come into Eloise's muscles bled away.

A story below, near the pool, Dave worked with a string of multicolored lights, already prepping for the pool party tomorrow afternoon.

The clouds shifted again, and sunlight poured into the room once more. Nothing supernatural about that. Eloise turned away from the window, the laptop tucked securely under her arm. She wondered about the people who'd lived here in the past. She couldn't help feeling some strange connection to them, as if they'd left a piece of themselves behind.

Anticipation blossomed as she went downstairs and found Alice spreading out a sheaf of papers on the table. Yes, there were still mysteries to unravel, both within these walls and within herself, and for the first time in a long while, Eloise felt ready to embrace them.

Chapter Fifteen

A lice's fingers trailed over the stack of papers spread before her on the dining room table. Each document represented hours of painstaking research, piecing together fragments of a century-old financial puzzle. She'd barely slept the night before, her mind racing with numbers and names, trying to make sense of the Everleighs' tangled web of investments and debts.

The sound of footsteps on the stairs drew her attention. Eloise appeared, Aaron's laptop tucked under her arm. Their eyes met, and Alice saw her own mix of excitement and trepidation mirrored in her friend's face.

"Ready?" El asked, setting the laptop down on the table.

Alice nodded, taking a deep breath. "As I'll ever be." She nodded to the laptop. "Why do you have that?"

"Kelli found a letter that had some names in it, and I wasn't sure when you'd be ready."

"Almost there." Alice picked up her coffee mug and took a sip. "I suppose I should text everyone who wants to come." Her stomach vibrated with nerves, and she wasn't even sure why.

"I can," El said. "I can't wait to hear what you've found. These people knew how to keep their secrets."

"Don't they always?" Alice murmured, more to herself than to El. She thought of her own past, the carefully cultivated image she'd maintained for years in the Hamptons. How easily it had all come crashing down.

Beeps and chimes filled the room as El's text went through, and Robin poked her head up from the binder she'd been bent over on the kitchen island. "You're ready?"

"Yep." Alice waited while everyone gathered at the table—AJ, Kelli, Laurel, and Kristen coming from the living room; El pulled out a chair and sat; Robin wrote one more thing in her binder, slapped it closed, and took the seat at the end of the table.

Maddy, Julia, and Tessa were not here during the day, though they'd be here for dinner tonight. Clara and Scott and Lena would arrive this afternoon, probably about the same time as Mandie and Charlie. Alice's pulse sped at the thought of seeing her son that evening.

"Where's Jean?" she asked, glancing around at the others.

"She had to go get a diaper for Heidi," Kristen said. "She'll be right back."

Sure enough, Jean bustled into the room, her dark-haired daughter on her hip, only a few moments later. "Sorry," she said as she lowered Heidi into the living room where Daphne, James, and Asher had been contained by baby gates and furniture.

Once everyone had settled, the scraping of chairs and murmur of conversation faded into expectant silence. Alice cleared her throat, suddenly aware of the weight of their collective gaze.

"All right," she began, her voice steady despite the flutter of nerves in her stomach. "I've spent the past few days combing through every scrap of financial information I could find on Edward and Elizabeth Everleigh. It's...well, it's a mess, to put it mildly."

She picked up a yellowed newspaper clipping, holding it up for the group to see. "This is from 1910, two years before the fire. The Everleighs were at the height of their social and financial power. They'd just made a substantial donation to the local hospital, and there was talk of Edward running for mayor."

"They sound like pillars of the community," Robin said, leaning forward to get a better look at the clipping.

Alice nodded. "On the surface, absolutely. But underneath..." She spread out a series of bank statements and ledgers. "I found evidence of some very creative accounting. Edward was moving money around, creating what we'd call shell companies today, taking out loans under false pretenses and under different names. It started small, but by 1912, he was in over his head."

"What about Elizabeth?" AJ asked. "Was she involved?"

Alice hesitated, thinking of the diary entries El had sent her, the growing desperation in Elizabeth's elegant script. "I don't think she knew the full extent of it, at least not at first. But some of the accounts were in her name—well, women couldn't have bank accounts, but they were opened with a version of her name. Ben was the most common one, with some of the writing making that N look like a TH. So Ben or Beth." Alice shrugged, because she couldn't say for certain what had happened over a hundred years ago.

"Whether she was aware of that or not, I can't say for certain."

"So what happened?" Kelli asked, getting up as baby Daphne began to fuss in the other room. "How did it all fall apart?"

Alice took a deep breath, steeling herself for the next part. "From what I can piece together, it was a perfect storm of bad luck and worse decisions. The economy took a downturn, some of Edward's investments went south, and then there was this man named Haversham."

She saw Eloise perk up at the name, and Alice tilted her head at her. El simply shook her head though, and Alice looked down at her notes. "Haversham was some sort of business associate of Edward's. I couldn't find much concrete information on him, but it seems he was involved in some shady dealings. Edward borrowed heavily from him, thinking he could turn things around quickly."

"But he couldn't," Kristen said softly, her eyes sad.

Alice shook her head. "No, he couldn't. By December 1912, just before the fire, the Everleighs were on the brink of bankruptcy. There were whispers of fraud, of misused charitable donations. Edward was desperately trying to keep it all from crumbling, but..." She trailed off, not wanting to be the one to make accusations of people who'd long been gone.

"The fire changed everything," Alice continued after a moment. "In the aftermath, all of the Everleighs' financial misdeeds came to light, but there were no records of the shell accounts, the multiple loans, and it seems that most of their debt was went up in smoke too."

"Wow," Robin said, her voice tinged with awe.

"That's one way to wipe out debt," AJ said.

"The scandal was enormous," Alice said. "Several investigations, and Elizabeth was forced to leave the house. She left the cove completely, and I lost track of her in Maryland."

A heavy silence fell over the room. Alice looked around at her friends, seeing the weight of the Everleighs' tragedy reflected in their faces. She thought of her own past, the careful facade she'd maintained in the Hamptons, how close she'd come to losing everything that truly mattered.

"What happened to the house after that?" Laurel asked, breaking the silence.

"I want to know if Edward died in the fire," El said.

"Sadly, he did," Alice said. She then looked at Laurel. "The house stood empty for decades. A reminder of tragedy and scandal that no one wanted to touch. Then, during World War Two, a wealthy family from Connecticut bought it."

"Really?" Robin's eyebrows shot up. "Who were they?"

"The Astors," Alice replied, shuffling through her notes. "Richard and Margaret Astor. They were...well, frankly, they were a bit eccentric. They became fascinated with the history of the house, especially after finding some of Elizabeth's old journals detailing her love of astronomy and astrology."

"No wonder the manor is themed as such," Kelli said.

"The Astors decided to take her love of the stars and space when they renovated. They're the ones responsible for most of the celestial decor and naming conventions we see now."

"So the house we're staying in isn't really the same one the Everleighs lived in," AJ said.

"Not entirely, no," Alice agreed. "But some of the inner bones are the same. And who knows? Maybe some of the Everleighs' secrets are still hidden within these walls."

As if on cue, a sudden gust of winter wind rattled the windows, making them all jump. A chill ran across

Alice's shoulders, and she caught Kristen's eye and saw her own unease mirrored there.

No one else said anything, and Alice's phone rang, the shriek breaking the silence.

"Hello, hello, hello!" Asher called from the living room, and Alice smiled in his direction.

"It's Charlie," she said, lifting her device. "I'm done here anyway. I'll be right back." She turned away from the group and stepped out onto the deck, leaving the others to talk without her. "Hey, you," she said.

"Mom," he said, and he sounded a bit out of breath. "My card isn't going through at the ticket kiosk."

And he wanted her to do what about it? "Okay," she said. "Have you got your emergency card?"

"Can I use it?"

"Is it an emergency?"

"Yes," Mandie practically yelled. "If we miss this ferry, Charlie, we'll be getting there at almost midnight."

"RideShare doesn't run past ten on Rocky Ridge," Alice said.

"We have to get on this ferry," Charlie said. "So yes, it's an emergency." Scuffling came through the line, and he said, "Use that, Mandie. Hurry up."

Alice blinked at the briskness in his tone, but Mandie didn't argue with him.

"Okay, Mom, I think we'll get on."

"See you in a few hours then."

"Yep, see you then." He hung up as he started to say something else to Mandie, and Alice lowered her phone.

She stood outside in the windy weather, the clouds shifting and moving across the horizon. She thought of Edward and Elizabeth, their desperate attempts to maintain the illusion of perfection even as everything crumbled around them.

How different was she, really? Hadn't she done the same thing in the Hamptons, presenting a flawless facade to the world while her marriage disintegrated behind closed doors? While her life fell apart one piece at a time until they'd avalanched, she'd sold the house, and moved her and the children to the cove.

"Alice," Robin said, and she turned back to her friend. "I just wanted to check and see if you needed help with the pool party tomorrow."

"Uh, I think I'm good," she said. "Mocktails, floaties, Christmas lights." She gestured to the pool. "The pool." She smiled as Robin joined her outside. "How hard can it be?"

"Not that hard," Robin said. "I just want El to see that everything she's done is worth it."

Alice laced her arm through Robin's and leaned her head against her shoulder. "I want that too."

"Mandie just texted that they got tickets on the twelve-fifteen ferry."

"Charlie called and had to use his emergency card."

Robin turned to look at her, and Alice lifted her head. "He did?"

"He must have a problem with his."

They fell into silence again, and then Robin said, "You're not them, you know."

She nodded, but the knot in her stomach didn't ease. "I know, but I can't help but see the parallels. The desperate need to maintain an image, to keep up appearances no matter the cost."

"But you chose a different path," Robin reminded her gently. "You walked away from all that. You built a new life here, with people who love you for who you are, not for some carefully crafted persona."

Alice smiled and leaned into Robin again as some of the tension left her body. "You're right. Of course you're right. It's just... sometimes I wonder if I've really changed as much as I think I have."

"You want to know what I think?"

Alice thought about it for a moment. "Yes, of course." If anyone would tell her the truth, it was Robin. She'd never pulled punches in the past, and they hadn't always agreed either. But Alice loved her unconditionally, because she knew Robin loved her the same way.

"The very fact that you're questioning it, that you're so determined not to repeat past mistakes—that shows how much you've grown. You're not perfect, none of us are. But you're trying, every day, to be better. That's what matters."

"Thank you," she whispered.

Robin took a big breath and then blew it out noisily. "El's going to lunch with Aaron," she said. "She told us we're not invited, but Laurel wants to try that new fried chicken place near the ferry dock. Do you want to go?"

Lunch here, possibly alone, or fried chicken with her friends? This choice wasn't even hard, and she said, "Yes, I'd love to go to lunch."

They turned back to the house, and Alice half-expected some sort of flare-up in the overhead heater. Or for the lights to flash, or for something to happen.

Nothing did, but in the back of her mind, a small voice whispered: *What other secrets are hiding within these walls? And how far are we willing to go to uncover them?*

Chapter Sixteen

The ferry cut through the waves, the sunlight casting reflections across the dark water ahead. Mandie Grover stared out over the railing, her fingers gripping the cold metal so tightly that her knuckles had turned white. The frigid air bit against her cheeks, but it didn't compare to the chill that had settled between her and Charlie.

He stood a few feet away, his arms crossed over his chest as he leaned against the side of the ferry, staring out at the horizon like it might offer him some kind of escape. His shaggy blond hair caught the wind, whipping around his face, but he didn't seem to care. He hadn't spoken to her for at least the past fifteen minutes.

Oh, and that was after he'd barked at her to buy the tickets for this fast-track ferry to Five Island Cove. She had not appreciated his tone, and she'd told him as much.

Mandie pressed her teeth together, trying to swallow the words that bubbled up inside her. But they wouldn't stay down. They hadn't stayed down for the past couple of days, and they certainly weren't about to now. She turned toward him, wanting this out before they arrived on Rocky Ridge.

"So that's it, then? You're just going to quit school? Just like that?"

He flicked his gaze toward her, his dark blue eyes unreadable. The wind picked up, tugging at her hair, and she pulled her coat tighter around her body.

"I never said I'm quitting," Charlie finally muttered, his voice low but edged with frustration. "I said I'm thinking about it. There's a difference."

Mandie stared at him, disbelief flooding through her. "It's the same thing, Charlie, and you know it. 'Thinking about it' is just a way of putting it off. You've already made up your mind."

He pushed off the railing, his hands flexing as if he wanted to grab something—or maybe break something. "I haven't made up my mind, Mandie." He sounded tired, and Mandie could see the dark circles under his eyes, a testament to their sleepless nights and endless arguments. "But I'm drowning. I can't keep up with everything—classes, work, rent—any of it. It's just too much."

"It's too much for me, too," she shot back, her voice rising with the sting of his words. "But I'm not quitting.

222

I'm still going to my classes. I'm still working. You can't just walk away when things get hard."

Charlie let out a bitter laugh, the sound carrying over the wind. "I'm not walking away. I'm trying to find a path I can *keep* walking on."

Mandie's heart clenched as she looked at him, really *looked* at him. He did look exhausted. He was wearing a coat that was too thin for the winter chill, and his jeans had a rip at the knee that wasn't fashionable—it just showed how worn down everything had become. Including him.

Her heart softened toward him, because he did get up every morning and go to work, to class, keep up with his homework, and heck, sometimes he came back to the tiny apartment they shared with Ginny and made dinner.

But that didn't change the fact that she couldn't let him give up on his college education.

"Surviving isn't the answer," she said, her voice shaking as she didn't really like conflict. "You have to think about the future, Charlie. What happens if you quit school? What are you going to do? Work construction for the rest of your life?"

"And what's wrong with that?" he asked, his frustration boiling over. "At least I'd have a paycheck that would stretch further. At least I wouldn't feel like I'm constantly falling behind. Do you know what it's like to sit in class and not understand anything? To spend every night trying to catch up, only to get knocked back down again?"

His words hit her like a punch to the gut, and for a moment, Mandie didn't know how to respond. She did know what it was like to struggle. She wasn't exactly acing all her classes either, and they both knew living in New York wasn't cheap. But they had a plan. Or at least, she'd thought they had a plan.

"I get it," she said, her voice softer now, but still tense. "I know it's hard. I know everything feels impossible right now. But you can't just give up. I believe in you, Charlie. You're smart. You can do this."

He shook his head, his expression hardening. "Maybe you believe in me more than I believe in myself."

The silence that followed deafened her. The ferry's horn blared as they neared the dock on Rocky Ridge, but Mandie barely heard it. She could only focus on the sinking feeling in her chest, the growing distance between her and Charlie.

She wanted to reach out, to bridge the gap between them, but she wasn't sure how. Every time they talked about the future, it turned into a fight. And now, with Christmas approaching and their families waiting at The Starlight Manor, the tension hovered above her like a dark cloud.

"We're almost there," Mandie said quietly, glancing toward the island that was coming into view. "I don't want to fight with you this weekend."

He didn't say anything, just shoved his hands into

his pockets and stared at the approaching dock. Mandie moved over to him and linked her arm through his. "I love you, Charlie. I can see you in a few years, done with school, taking on the world as the best pharmacist in the world."

"It's so far away, Mandie," he grumbled. "Not a few years. Like *six* more years. Six."

The ferry bumped against the dock, and people began to gather their belongings. Mandie grabbed her bag, slinging it over her shoulder before turning back to Charlie. "You're the smartest person I know."

"That's the dumbest thing I've ever heard." Charlie's eyes flicked toward her, and for a moment, she thought she saw something soften in his gaze. But then he looked away again, his jaw tightening. "I didn't mean that."

Mandie nodded, though it felt like a weight on her chest. She didn't know what else to say, or if there was anything left to say. She just hoped that being home, away from the stress of the city, away from the busyness of work and finals, might help cool things down between them. Maybe some time with their families would remind him of what he really wanted for his future.

And Mandie knew it wasn't construction work.

Yes, pharmacy school would be several more years. Mandie didn't care. She'd be at his side if he wanted her there. But she couldn't let him give up on school just because this semester had kicked him around a little bit.

They stepped off the ferry, the cold wind whipping around them as they made their way toward the line for a

RideShare. When it was their turn, the driver gave them a polite nod as they climbed in, but Mandie barely noticed. Her mind stormed with thoughts, running over every argument, every conversation, every moment where things between her and Charlie had started to unravel.

As they drove through the semi-familiar streets on Rocky Ridge, Mandie's heart ached with the weight of everything unsaid. She didn't want to lose Charlie. Not like this. Not because of something as stupid as money or school.

But she didn't know how to fix it either.

The ride to The Starlight Manor was quiet, the tension between them thick and heavy. Charlie stared out the window, his arms crossed over his chest, while Mandie sat with her hands clasped tightly in her lap, her mind racing. What if he really did quit school? What if he decided that living paycheck to paycheck, working some dead-end job, was enough for him?

What if he stopped dreaming about a future with her?

The thought twisted her insides in knots. She didn't want to live paycheck to paycheck and send her husband out into the winter weather day after day, just because one semester had been hard. She wanted more.

What if Charlie can't give you more?

The car pulled to a stop in front of the manor, and Mandie's breath caught in her throat. The grand Victorian architecture stood tall against the backdrop of the gray sky. Twinkling Christmas lights lined the porch railing and every inch of the eaves, casting a warm glow over the ground, and the scent of pine and saltwater filled the air.

For a moment, Mandie allowed herself to believe that everything might be okay. That maybe, just maybe, the magic of the holidays and the comfort of home would be enough to mend the cracks in her relationship with Charlie.

But as they stepped out of the car, the front door of the manor swung open, and Mandie's heart sank as she saw Alice standing on the porch, her sharp eyes immediately zooming in on them. She smiled from ear-to-ear, and Mandie just wished she could whisk Charlie away until they'd ironed everything flat.

As she came down the steps, her smile faltering the longer she looked at Charlie. Great. She knew something was wrong. She always did.

"You made it." She half-jogged the last few steps to Charlie and hugged him tightly. "I'm glad you made it. We were starting to wonder if you'd missed the ferry after all."

"No, we made it," Mandie said, forcing a smile that felt brittle against her lips. "Just ran into some trouble with the ticket kiosk." She moved into Alice and hugged her lightly while Charlie got their bags out of the trunk of the car.

"Well, I'm so glad you're here." She smiled at Mandie and smoothed her hair off her face. Mandie dang near burst into tears, because Alice was so kind to her. "Need any help with anything?"

"I got it, Mom," Charlie said, and he didn't even try to hide his surliness. Alice flicked him a look as he went by her, and then she walked after him.

Mandie followed her up the steps, her stomach tightening with every step. Inside the manor, the warmth and smell of a roasting turkey wrapped around her like a comforting blanket. The soft hum of conversation from the dining room wafted back to her in the lobby, the laughter of tiny kids playing in the living room, and the warmth of house enveloped her. It should have felt like home, but instead, all Mandie could think about was the growing pit in her stomach.

Charlie had barely said a word since they left the ferry, and as they stepped into the grand foyer, he still wasn't looking at her.

"You can leave the bags," Alice said. "You're in the basement, Mandie, and Charlie, you're up on the third floor."

"I'll take them," he said, his voice clipped as he grabbed his duffel and headed for the stairs without so much as a glance in Mandie's direction.

Mandie wasn't sure if she should retreat to the basement, and her face heated as her eyes filled with tears. Before she could move, her mom came around the corner.

"Mandie," she said.

And just like that, the tears overflowed, and Mandie rushed into her mom's arms.

"Oh, my baby." Mom wrapped her up in her arms, and while Mandie stood a couple of inches taller than her mother, she felt very small within the circle of her embrace.

"Mandie's here," her dad said.

"She's crying," Mom whispered, but Dad wrapped them both up, further anchoring Mandie to her core, to herself, to her family. Mom stroked her hand down Mandie's hair, and Dad started to hum in the back of his throat.

Mandie calmed herself quickly, and she absolutely did not want to betray Charlie's confidence.

"What's wrong?"

Mandie pulled away. "Nothing," she said, wiping her eyes. "I've just had a rough semester, and it's so great to be here." Beyond them, the twinkling white lights of the Christmas tree winked in the next room, and Mandie simply wanted to sink into the holidays and keep the real world out for a while.

Well, a weekend.

She had to go to work on Monday morning, and they'd come back next weekend for the Christmas festivities. She ducked away and looked at her bag. "I'll take this down to the bunk room."

"I've got it," Dad said, and he swooped down and picked up her suitcase. He disappeared down the stairs, and her exit narrowed to nothing.

Mom tilted her head, her bright blue eyes studying Mandie with the intensity only a mother could have. "Mandie, don't lie to me. What's going on?" She glanced over to Alice, who hadn't gone very far. They stood in the narrow neck of the hallway between the foyer and the rest of the house, the steps going up and down to her right.

"It's..." She couldn't do it. "Charlie and I are working through something, that's all."

Mom and Alice—her best friend—looked at one another, and Mandie didn't know what she'd do if they pressed her for answers. She'd taken a marriage and family relations class at the end of last year, and one thing she'd vowed to do was forge her own relationship with her husband.

She wanted that person to be Charlie, and that meant she couldn't go running to her mom every time something happened between them.

"I'm not going to talk about it," she said before either of them could ask a question. "It's something we're working through together."

Footsteps sounded on the stairs, and Charlie slowed as he saw the three of them standing there. His expression tightened, and he sighed as he continued down to the main level. Then he looked at her, and everything changed. "You've been crying."

"Just happy to see my mom," Mandie said as lightly as she could.

"Why is Mandie crying?" Alice asked, her lawyer voice in full force.

Charlie glared at his mother. "She just said she's happy to see her mother." He looked over to Mom, his expression changing once again. "Hi, Robin." He stepped into her and hugged her, and that made Mandie's heart melt all over again.

She loved Charlie, and she'd told her parents she thought they'd probably get married in the spring. She hated the feeling of having so many balls up in the air, especially because she'd never been very good at sports, and catching things as they got pulled down by gravity felt impossible to her.

Charlie laced his fingers through hers when he returned to her side. "I took a peek out the window, and the grounds are amazing. Do we have time to walk for a bit before dinner?"

"Of course," Mom said diplomatically.

Alice turned and moved into the back of the manor. "Dinner's not until six-thirty. You have a couple of hours." She twisted and looked over her shoulder at them. "Then, I want to hear how everything's going in the city." She wore her eagle-eyes, and that meant she'd dig at them until she learned what she wanted to know.

Charlie looked at Mandie and said, "Will you walk with me?"

"Yes," she whispered, and she ducked her head as she moved by her mom and toward the back sliding glass door. The grandeur of the house stole her breath, and she couldn't look from one magnificent thing—the huge table in the eat-in kitchen, the stockings hung over the fireplace, which flickered with yellow-orange light, the ornate carpet and wallpaper and artwork—fast enough.

Charlie slid open the door and let Mandie exit the manor first. They walked across the deck and past the pool, their feet finally landing on the immaculately graveled path before he said, "I'm sorry, Mandie."

She wanted to ask him for what, but she'd learned that if she waited, he'd explain more. Sometimes, he just needed more time to order the words right.

"I didn't mean to snap at you at the ticket kiosk, and I don't mean to make you second-guess everything."

"You are my favorite person," she whispered. "I know you can conquer college and pharmacy school, and I want to be at your side as you do." She took a couple more steps, then another. "But if you don't want me there, that's okay. I mean, it's not okay, but I'll—I honestly don't know what I'll do."

Her heart would be broken, she knew that much.

"I want you with me," he murmured. "I just want to give you the world, and right now, it feels like I'm carrying it instead of standing on top of it."

"It was one class."

"I have dozens more like it."

She squeezed his hand. "I know you do." She didn't want to diminish how he felt, something she could admit she'd done in the past. They walked toward the trees bordering the back of the lawn, and the path went in two directions. Mandie could see both ways, but she still didn't know which one to take.

In the end, it didn't matter. If she walked at Charlie's side, it didn't matter if they went left or right. Not on this path, and not in their lives.

"I love you," he whispered. "I'm sorry I've been short with you lately. I'm sorry you have to see me at my worst, filled with this self-doubt."

He took her left, and Mandie simply went with him, thinking about what he'd said. "I don't need you to give me the world," she said slowly. "I know you want to, and that's good enough. But what I really want is for us to *discover* the life we want to have together."

"That does sound nice."

"And I don't think that includes you working construction and having a broken body in a decade. And you get to tell me when I'm being irrational or high-strung, so I'll calm down." She paused, glad when he turned toward her and stopped too. "I really really *really* don't think you should quit school."

"Okay," he said, like everything could be so easy. "I won't."

"Charlie," she said. "You can't just give in to me on everything."

"I'm not," he said. "I'm leaning on you about this, just like you'll lean on me for some things."

"Okay."

"I'm trusting you when you say I'm smart enough to do this."

"You are."

"I'm choosing to believe you." He leaned closer and touched his forehead to hers. "I'm choosing you, because I think this is so important to you that I might lose you over it, and I'm not willing to do that."

She closed her eyes and stood in the presence of the man she loved. "Thank you, Charlie," she whispered. "You *can* do this."

"I hope you're right," he murmured just before he kissed her, and finally—finally—Mandie thought she might be able to enjoy this weekend away from the city.

Then, a cry rose into the air from the direction of the house, breaking their kiss and causing them both to turn back to the manor. Everything that had been lit up before now sat in darkness.

"The power went out," Mandie said, hardly daring to move amidst so much blackness.

Chapter Seventeen

A scream echoed through the house, its sharpness slicing through the sudden stillness left in the wake of the power outage. Robin's heartbeat skipped and leaped and hopped, her body instinctively freezing in place as her ears strained to locate the source of the cry.

She'd been standing at the kitchen island, wiping down the counter and mentally ticking off the final items for tonight's big dinner. *Gravy, rolls, put the desserts out to thaw.*

The lights had flickered once, twice, and then—nothing. The hum of the refrigerator went silent, the overhead lights blinked out, the Christmas tree had gone dark, and the only illumination now came from the dim shafts of early evening sunlight filtering through the windows.

Another cry pierced the air, this one closer, more frantic.

Her pulse quickened as she turned toward the sound, her hands still clutching the damp dishcloth. "Jamie?" She called out, the name tumbling from her lips before she could even process where it came from, instinct guiding her thoughts.

Robin tossed the dishcloth aside, hurrying across the kitchen and into the foyer, where shadows lengthened and distorted the familiar grandeur of the space. The once-warm glow of the Christmas lights and the roaring fire in the hearth had been swallowed by the growing darkness, and with it, an unsettling feeling began to take root in her gut.

"Mom." Jamie's voice trembled as she came barreling down the stairs. She clutched her phone in one hand, the screen casting an eerie blue light over her pale face. "It's so dark up there, and—" She broke off, her wide eyes searching Robin's face. "What's happening? Why did the power go out?"

Robin pulled her daughter close, wrapping her arms around Jamie's slender shoulders, trying to lend her strength. "I don't know yet," she said, forcing calm into her voice even though her mind raced with possibilities. "But I'm sure it's nothing serious. Just a breaker or something."

A flashlight beam moved toward her, and Duke said, "I'll see what I can find." He turned toward the basement and started down the steps, Aaron and Paul on his heels.

"We'll find the breaker box," Aaron said. "Have things back on in no time."

"Do you know if it's downstairs?" Robin asked.

"They usually are," Paul said, and he too disappeared into the darkness leading into the basement.

"There's no outages on Rocky Ridge," Alice said from the living room. The fire crackled in the hearth, putting out light for the manor too. She lowered her phone, but Robin could still see her eerie, grim expression as she said, "So it's just the manor."

Of course it was just the manor.

Robin's gaze flicked toward the windows that lined the back of the house. The sky outside had turned a dull slate-gray as thick clouds had rolled across the horizon. Winter storms weren't unusual this time of year, especially on Rocky Ridge, but this felt different. More ominous.

And Mandie and Charlie had gone out in that. Robin shivered as she pulled her phone from her pocket to text her oldest daughter.

Another cry rose into the air, this one from the living room where the younger children had been playing, and drew her attention. Robin exchanged a quick glance with Jamie before hurrying toward the sound, her daughter trailing close behind.

In the living room, Kelli knelt on the floor, cradling Daphne in her arms while Asher and James toddled around, their cute little faces seemingly nonplussed about the disappearance of the electricity.

"It's okay, sweetheart," Kelli murmured to Daphne, her voice soothing even as her eyes darted toward Robin with a mixture of concern and frustration.

Robin reached for Asher, who blinked up at her with wide, inquisitive eyes, his toy car clutched in one hand. "It's okay, buddy," she said softly, picking him up and ruffling his hair. "We'll have the lights back on soon."

But even as she said it, the unease in her chest grew.

Where were Duke, Aaron, and Paul? They should've had this figured out by now. They were smart men—resourceful. If the power was out because of a blown fuse or a tripped breaker, surely they'd have fixed it by now.

"Mom?" Jamie's voice wavered from behind her.

Robin turned to face her daughter again. "Yes, sweetheart?"

Jamie hesitated, her phone still casting that ghostly glow over her features. "Do you think—do you think this is because of the, you know, the house?" Her words hung in the air, as heavy as the thickening shadows.

Robin swallowed hard, hating that she couldn't give Jamie the immediate reassurance she so clearly needed. She didn't believe in ghosts, not really. Nothing about a few flickering lights and fluttering curtains had convinced her that this house was haunted.

But she couldn't deny that something about this

place had been off since they'd arrived. The manor was physically magnificent, yes—opulent, sprawling, with its celestial-themed decor and rich history. But ever since they'd uncovered that hidden office, whispers of the Everleigh's tragic past had seemed to weave themselves into the very fabric of the house.

It was just a house. Bricks and mortar and wood. A house couldn't hurt them.

"I'm sure it's nothing," Robin said, injecting as much confidence as she could into the words. "It's probably just the weather. We'll get it sorted out."

Before Jamie could respond, voices came up the steps from the basement, and Duke appeared, saying something over his shoulder. Robin hugged Jamie to her side as they faced him, and she didn't like the grim look in his expression when he reached the first floor.

"Only one of the breaker boxes is downstairs," he said. "And they're all working."

"How do you know there's more than one?"

"For a house this big?" Aaron asked as he rejoined everyone in the living room. "There should be three times the breakers we saw down there." He turned in a full circle, pausing on El for a moment. "There might be one on every floor."

"Have you guys seen a breaker box in your search of the house?" Paul asked, moving to Laurel's side.

She shook her head, and Robin couldn't recall seeing anything electrical besides light switches and outlets as she'd gone through the manor.

Robin's stomach tightened as she searched their expressions for reassurance, only to find none. "Great," she said. "We've got dozens of people in this house, and no power right before dinner."

"Could just be an outage," Arthur said. "For the island."

"I just said there are no reported outages on Rocky Ridge," Alice said, her phone lighting her face. "I'm looking right at it." She glanced up. "No outages, so it has to be just this house."

"Let's check the bathrooms and laundry room," Duke said.

Robin closed her eyes for a moment, taking a deep breath to steady herself. She couldn't afford to panic. They had plenty of food, even if it wasn't the roast turkey dinner she'd planned and worked on. She thought of all electricity did, and they'd need hot water to shower, to use the pool, and so much more than just dinner.

She opened her eyes, half-hoping the lights would flare back to life. They didn't. "I guess we'll just have to make do, won't we?"

She glanced around the room, taking in the mix of worried faces, young and old. Kelli still cradled Daphne, her expression pinched with concern. Kristen stood near the doorway, her hands clasped tightly together as if in prayer.

"Mom," Lena said. "It's getting dark."

"It sure is," Clara murmured, her eyes stuck on

Robin.

In fact, everyone looked at her. Her, of all people.

El moved to her side. "Okay," she said, and Robin squared her shoulders and plastered on the most confident smile she could muster. "Candles, maybe?"

"Candles." Robin clapped her hands, her mind working again. Duh—she didn't need electricity to cook. "Here's the plan. We've got a big dinner planned, and we're not going to let a little thing like a power outage ruin it. The stove and oven is gas, so I can finish dinner, and I'm sure we have enough candles to light up the whole manor. We'll make it work."

For a moment, no one moved. Then Jamie stepped forward, her eyes bright with determination. "I'll help get the candles."

Robin's heart swelled with pride as she nodded. "Good girl. Check the kitchen drawers. I'm sure we can find some matches in there too."

Jamie strode into the kitchen, her duty clear, and slowly, the others began to fall into action. Alice tucked her phone in her pocket and went after Jamie to help with the candles. Kelli passed Daphne to Robin for a moment, so she could get to her feet, and Kristen, AJ, and Jean turned on their phone flashlights and pointed their phones at the ceiling to illuminate the area where the kids continued to play.

Duke, Aaron, and Paul moved down the hall, and Robin hoped they'd find another breaker box. She believed in her husband, and she passed Daphne back to

Kelli and went to help the others find anything they could use for light.

As she went past the table, the sliding door opened, and Mandie and Charlie stepped inside, their faces flushed from the cold. Robin's gaze immediately flew to her daughter, searching for any sign of distress or unease. Mandie's eyes met hers for a brief moment, and Robin's heart clenched at the sight of the raw emotion there.

Something was definitely going on with Mandie and Charlie, but she hoped they'd learn to work things out between them. "Hey," she said, making a quick detour. "The power is out, but we have a gas stove, so dinner is still on. We're looking for candles and flashlights right now."

"Okay," Mandie said, and she cut a look at Charlie. He gave her a smile, and that made Robin's heart sing. She wanted to fix everything for her daughter—and Charlie—to swoop in and make it all better, the way she always had when Mandie was a little girl.

She couldn't do that anymore, not without pushing her daughter away.

Instead, Robin forced a smile and moved into the kitchen again. "Okay," she said as Jamie set two jarred candles on the countertop. "I'm going to check on where we are with the food. It's going to be an adventure— cooking by candlelight."

A few scattered chuckles rippled through the group, and a small surge of relief moved through Robin. If she could keep them laughing, keep them focused on the task at hand, maybe—just maybe—they wouldn't dwell on the strange, creeping sense of unease settling over the manor.

The shadows lengthened as the sun dipped lower in the sky, casting the house in deep twilight, but Robin paused to take stock of where she'd been with the dinner prep. She had no idea if she could pull this off in the dark, but she was determined to get through the night no matter what.

Chapter Eighteen

T he cold metal of the staircase railing pressed into Laurel's palm as she ascended the steps two at a time, her breath steady, her mind racing. The dim light from the few remaining candles downstairs cast long shadows that danced across the walls, but up here—the second and third floors of The Starlight Manor—darkness reigned.

She hadn't been scared of the dark since she was a little girl. Not when she had the kind of training that came with years on the police force. But now, with the power out and the house seemingly conspiring against them, a strange tension hummed in her bones. Each step felt heavier than the last, as if the air itself had thickened.

She reached the second-floor landing and paused briefly outside her suite, her portable charger plugged in near the bed, waiting for her. She reached for the doorknob, but her eyes drifted up the stairwell that led to the third floor, where the darkness deepened into an impenetrable void.

Then she saw a flicker of light.

Laurel's muscles froze, but her heartbeat raced forward, spiked now with adrenaline. It wasn't like the candlelight below, or even the faint orange glow of the fire from the living room. This light was different. Sharper. More deliberate.

She blinked, waiting to see if it would happen again, the way she did when the smoke alarm battery was going out and it would beep every minute. The seconds stretched out, long and quiet, until once more the flicker appeared, casting strange shadows down the stairwell.

"Almost like there's a fire upstairs," she said, panic gripping her now. Could the manor be on fire?

Laurel's fingers tightened into fists, her instincts kicking in. No one was supposed to be up there. As far as she knew, everyone had gathered in the kitchen or in the living room, trying to keep the children calm and the adults from panicking.

She hadn't worn a badge in over a year, but some things she didn't forget. Like how to keep her breathing steady, how to move quietly, and how to assess a situation without jumping to conclusions.

Laurel had no intentions of jumping to conclusions, but she wasn't about to ignore flickering firelight in a house that had been full of peculiarities since the moment they'd arrived. Oh, and that had been engulfed in flames before.

She took the first step toward the third floor.

The wooden stairs creaked beneath her weight, the sound unnaturally loud in the silence. She crouched slightly, her hand trailing along the bannister as she continued upward, her eyes fixed on the darkened hallway above.

When she reached the top, she paused again, listening. From her vantage point, she could just make out the faint outline of the library door, left slightly ajar. The flickering light shone bluely through the narrow gap, casting thin slivers of barely-there light across the floor.

Laurel's heartbeat quickened as she moved forward, her steps careful and measured. She reached for the door, nudging it open just enough to peer inside.

The library sat still and quiet, the familiar scent of old books and polished wood filling the room. The kits she'd been working on with her friends waited, assembled, on the tables, and Laurel would take them to the *A Very Veteran Christmas* office.

But something wasn't right. The large, floor-to-ceiling windows that lined the far wall had always provided a stunning view of the estate's gardens below, but now—

"The pool lights," Laurel breathed out. She hurried toward the far wall, where sure enough, one look below showed her the dazzling, blue pool lights rippling across the grass, the deck, and up to the library's floor-to-ceiling windows. For a moment, it looked like the water itself was alive, shimmering under some kind of otherworldly influence.

As she stood there and watched the lights below, she realized the gauzy curtains to her left were drifting. Lazily moving an inch forward, then back, as if caught by a light breeze.

Kristen had seen this exact thing, over a week ago.

She'd seen these very curtains moving when there was no wind. Laurel had brushed it off at the time—drafts existed in old, large houses, after all. But now, standing here, watching the way the curtains seemed to sway ever so slightly, she couldn't shake the uneasy feeling crawling up her spine.

Laurel scanned the room, her eyes narrowing as she surveyed the space. Something didn't feel right. Something more than just the pool lights and the curtains. She moved closer to the wall of bookshelves, tapped on the flashlight on her phone, and trailed her fingers along the spines of the books at eye-level. The flickering lights from outside cast long, wavering shadows across the volumes, leaving parts of the room in near darkness.

Her fingers bumped from one panel of shelves to another, and she sucked in a breath. "That wasn't even." She immediately retraced the touch, noting that the wood felt different here, almost as if it had been worn down by years of use.

Without thinking, she pressed against the abnormality, and to her great surprise, the shelf moved without much pressure at all.

Lauren then used two fingers to slide it easily to the side, revealing a humming, hot, control room.

Her pulse quickened as she stepped back, her eyes widening in disbelief. She hadn't expected to find another hidden room. They'd searched this house top to bottom, inside and out, and while they'd found that hidden office, no one had mentioned anything about a secret doorway in the most obvious room.

But she stared right at it.

The bookcase had slid to the side, as if it were on tracks, the way the ladder was. Hot air flowed out of the gap now that it had been widened, setting the curtains aflutter—just like Lauren's pulse. She shined her flashlight into the space, noting the dozens and dozens of cables and wires.

"No wonder the electricity here flickers." She wasn't an electrician by any means, but this did not look up to any sort of code. Extension cords lay wadded up on the floor, with other cords actually plugged into them.

"Paul," she called, though she didn't think her husband would hear her up here on the third floor. She moved into the opening and snapped a picture, still stunned by the tall wall with cables running through it. This room seriously looked like the technical hub for an office building, which would have dozens of computers, modems, routers, and users attached to it.

She quickly sent the photo to the whole group, with the words, *Come to the library and see what I found.*

An electrical hum buzzed in the air, and Laurel

cautiously entered the room, wondering how long it would take for someone to see her text. She turned to shine her light on the wall to her left, sucking in a breath when the beam landed on a metal box mounted against the wall—an ancient electrical panel, its switches and dials worn with age.

"What a mess," she murmured just as she heard a shout from somewhere below her.

So someone had seen her text. Laurel backed out of the control room and stood with her flashlight aimed toward the newly found control room.

Arthur entered the library first, Charlie right on his heels. "What...?" He trailed off as he came to stand next to Laurel. "Just...wow."

Duke, and Aaron, and thankfully, Paul arrived next, followed by Alice, Matt, and AJ. She'd left Asher downstairs, and Laurel's stomach swooped when she thought of her son. "Is James okay?" she asked Paul.

"Kristen has him," Paul said, and then he exchanged a glance with Aaron. "Let's go see what we've got."

"We're going to get electrocuted," Duke said, going with them. "Look at this. It's a disaster."

Old wiring tangled like a nest of snakes, some of the connections frayed and exposed. Laurel followed them, and with the wall of wiring, and the old desk with various small appliances on it, including an old rotary phone. With her in the room, it was full, and she added her flashlight beam to those of the men.

"Look at this one," she said, toeing one of the cords

that had frayed. A spark shot out of it, and she yelped and stepped back.

"I'm going to call Kevin," Aaron said, turning his phone to dial. "I'm honestly not sure it's safe to stay here like this. The whole place could go up in flames."

"Again," Laurel said.

Paul swung his attention to her. "Don't say that."

"Aaron said it," she said. She also didn't want to pack up everything she'd been living with here for the past couple of weeks and go home. They only had another week here, and she'd so enjoyed the getaway, even with the mystery and history and strange occurrences.

Eloise arrived, and she sucked in a breath. "Oh, this is not okay," she said. "I'm calling the host." She too stepped out of the room, her phone hard at work.

Laurel met her husband's eyes. "Could this make the lights in the chandelier flicker?"

"Absolutely." He nodded at the clunky electrical box. "Look. This is labeled foyer." He touched the switch, and it wobbled. "It shouldn't move like that. It's either on or off, not both at the same time."

"And the air from the fans on the electrical equipment in here was seeping out and causing the curtains to move."

"Strange that the pool lights are on," Duke said, peering into the box too. "I mean, the breaker is right, but why isn't the rest of the house on too?"

"Great question," Paul said.

"Kevin's on his way," Aaron said, joining them at the box. "If he says we can't stay, you guys..."

"My wife is going to lose her mind," Duke muttered.

Laurel found her lips tipping up into a smile, though she didn't want to leave the manor either.

"The ferries are still running," Paul said. "We might-should get out while we can."

"Paul," Laurel said quietly. "We've been working hard on dinner for hours." She didn't want all of the plans that Robin and Eloise had spent so long making and executing to be for nothing. She also wasn't sure how she could put her son to bed on the floor below with full confidence that they were all safe.

As she stood there while the men talked about how upset their wives and children would be, one of the breakers snapped off. Laurel jumped. "What was that?"

"The pool," Duke said, pointing to the now-off switch. "Oh, except it's kind of still on."

"This could be why the heaters in the overhang flared," Laurel said.

"I think all of the things happening here are because of this room, yes," Aaron said. "I'm going to go talk to El. Wish me luck."

"Good luck, brother," Duke said, and Paul echoed it while Aaron pressed past Laurel and went back into the library.

A sense of pure, unadulterated relief flowed through Laurel. For now she knew the reason for the flickering lights. The reason the pool lights were flashing outside. The reason for Kristen's mysterious moving curtains.

It wasn't ghosts. It wasn't some supernatural occurrence.

It was faulty wiring.

Some mega faulty wiring, but wiring nonetheless.

"Fran says she's sending an electrician." Eloise joined Laurel, Paul, and Duke in the control room, sans Aaron. "I just can't believe this." She picked up the receiver on the yellowed phone. "Like, what is this?"

"Where did Aaron go?" Duke asked. "He said he was going to find you."

"He got a call." El looked at everything with the widest eyes Laurel had ever seen.

She met her gaze, feeling nothing but sympathy for El. "Can an electrician even fix this?" Even she knew the wiring went through all the walls, and that this wasn't a job that could be done in a few minutes on a Friday evening.

She linked her arm through El's and said, "Come on. We have gas still, and that means dinner can be cooked and served as normal." Laurel started to lead El out of the room.

"Will we be able to stay in the manor, though?" El asked.

"I don't know," Laurel said. "But we're not leaving right now, so let's go see if Robin needs any help."

Chapter Nineteen

Eloise followed Laurel out of the control room and into the library. She paused in front of the sliding bookcase, because it truly was a marvel. "I can't believe we missed this."

Laurel gave a breathy laugh. "I know. It's so obvious."

"Well, not really," Eloise said.

"It's a hidden room behind a bookcase," Laurel said. "They're in every spy movie made." She grinned at Eloise and shrugged. "I only found it, though, because I felt the air moving."

Eloise squeezed her forearm, though she wasn't sure what would happen next. "I'm glad you found it."

Aaron came back into the library and held up his phone. "Kevin is here."

"Already?" Eloise hurried to go with him, because

night had fallen while they'd been getting out candles and running up stairs to see secret rooms.

"He lives here on Rocky Ridge," Aaron said.

Eloise was glad she could accompany him downstairs to face the others. They'd want answers, and she didn't have any. She only had more questions, one of which was really loud and really pressing.

Could they stay in the manor tonight?

The doorbell rang as she reached the bottom of the stairs, and she nearly stumbled over her own feet. Aaron did touch her to steady her, and she exchanged a worried look with him.

"I'll go see where we are with dinner," she said, slipping her hand into his. "Come tell me everything the moment you know anything."

His dark eyes searched hers, and Eloise could get lost in his gaze. "Of course I will."

She knew he'd follow her anywhere, and that he'd protect her from anything and anyone he could. She nodded and ducked her head, because she didn't want him to see her nerves. "Okay."

He leaned in and pressed a kiss to her temple, which sent a shiver racing down her arm. "It's going to be okay, El," he whispered.

She wanted to ask how he knew that, because she knew Aaron didn't say things idly. But she didn't ask, and he separated from her to go get the door while Eloise continued into the kitchen and living room, where everyone had gathered.

Robin stood at the stove, candles flickering as the only source of light in the kitchen. Someone had placed a row of flashlights down the middle of the dining table in the kitchen, and the fire gave off light in the living room.

"The electrician is here, and he'll get things fixed right up," Eloise said, because she couldn't think of anything else to say. The moment she did, the overhead lights blazed back to life. The refrigerator hummed, the fan in the vent above the stove started to turn, and someone started to clap.

"Oh, wow," Robin said with her trademark smile. "He must work fast." She turned to Alice, and the two women laughed and embraced each other.

The lights flickered again, and then went off.

A groan moved through the crowd, and Eloise wanted to be the strong and powerful one making the decision that the lights—or lack thereof—wouldn't affect her. She reached for Robin and Alice, and the three of them hugged. Robin broke the circle first and said, "Okay, let's get dinner on the table. We don't need electricity to do that."

Eloise knew there was a huge green salad in the fridge, and she went to get it. She tried not to look at the rest of the food in the fridge, because if the power didn't come back on, they'd lose it all.

Or have to eat a lot, really fast.

She set about opening bags of lettuce, croutons, and shaved parmesan cheese, totally inside her mind. She heard talking around her, but she didn't bother to try to make what they said into something coherent.

The doorbell rang again as Laurel and Kristen started to set out plates and utensils on the island, and Eloise hoped the electrician, or electricians, could fix the problem quickly, so they'd have power and wouldn't have to leave.

So many people had spent time packing and traveling here, and she wasn't even sure where they'd all go if they couldn't stay here tonight. Her mind wandered to the Cliffside Inn, but she only had six rooms—nowhere near enough for everyone here, and the inn was booked out for the holidays.

She'd looked at several rentals for this holiday, and she wondered if she could perhaps book two of them, they could split in half, and...somehow they'd be able to get into the new houses in the next couple of hours.

That is so not happening, she told herself, because she currently stirred a mega-bowl of Ceasar salad with tongs, and she wouldn't be able to access the Internet without power.

Suddenly, everything felt too heavy, and she couldn't smile or stir it away. She left the bowl of salad on the island and ducked into the mudroom, her nose now running as she fought tears.

She wasn't sure how long she paced in the mudroom, taking three steps toward a door that led onto the back deck, and then returning to the wide doorway that led to the rest of the house. She'd just reached the back door and turned when someone came in from the garage.

"Excuse me?" a man called. "Chief?"

Eloise met him in the doorway. "Are you looking for Aaron?"

"Yes." The man actually gave her a smile. "I'm Kevin, and I think you're his wife."

"Yes." She smiled back, and how she pulled that off, Eloise would never know. "I'm not sure where Aaron is right now." She hooked her thumb over her shoulder. "Weren't you upstairs with him?"

"I came down to check out the other breaker boxes."

"How many others are there?" Eloise asked.

"One in the basement, and one in the garage," Kevin said. "Oh, and the host is here, and she said she didn't even know about that room on the third floor." He smiled again. "I think Jerry and I can get this figured out tonight."

Hope bloomed in Eloise's chest. "You do?" She pulled her phone from her pocket. "Let me text Aaron." She did that while Kevin ducked back into the garage, and then she faced the house again.

The bustling activity in the kitchen, the dining area, the living room. Almost forty people all-told, and Eloise pressed her eyes closed and prayed as much as she ever had. The candles continued to flicker, and the power stayed steadfastly off, but Eloise could rejoin everyone now without feeling like the walls would crush her where she stood.

"How are things looking?" she asked Robin, who stood at the stove, whisking, whisking, whisking the turkey gravy.

"Good," she said. "When this timer goes off, it's going to be the rolls." She nodded to a pair of oven mitts. "Could you get them out. I'm afraid of leaving this for even a moment."

"I've got it," Eloise said.

"I have the butter and jam on the table," Alice said. "Along with the salt and pepper."

"Thank you," Robin said, flashing a smile as she kept whisking. "The potatoes need butter and cheese added to them, and I told Mandie to get out all the pies from the freezer, because we're going to lose them anyway."

Eloise's heart crashed somewhere down near her stomach. The frozen pies they'd bought were for the pool party tomorrow, not for dinner tonight. But Robin was right. If they didn't eat them, they'd lose them. Eloise had lived through a storm or two that had knocked out the power, and she couldn't describe how drippy and wet everything was as it thawed from a freezer that didn't work.

"I don't see any pies," Eloise said.

"She got a phone call," Robin said. "She ducked out onto the deck."

"Okay." Eloise moved over to the freezer and opened it to get out the pies. With several people helping, everything got done and laid out on the countertop and island, where they'd all file past the food and fill their plates. With the soft glow of candlelight, it was almost fun.

"Okay," Robin called loudly. "It's time to eat. Come on over, and we'll get started."

People started to get up from the couches and come out from where they'd settled in the formal dining room. Eloise automatically opened her arm for Billie and Grace to stand under, which they did.

"Where's Dad?" Billie asked.

"He's dealing with the electricians," Eloise said with a forced smile. She found Ben and Maddy in the room, with Julia, Liam, and Ian, then Scott, Clara, and Lena, and Alice stood with Mandie and Charlie at the end of the table. Jean, Kristen, AJ, Kelli, and Laurel hovered right behind the back of the couch, all of their kids in their arms.

She didn't see Duke or Paul or Aaron, and Robin apparently wasn't going to wait for them. "Okay," she said. "The food is done and hot, and we can eat by candlelight."

"Are we going to have to leave the house tonight?"

Robin hesitated, so Eloise took a step forward. "We don't know yet," she said. "Anyone who doesn't feel safe should, uh, make their own decisions about what they want to do. We have electricians here, and they're doing their job."

"Let's eat," Alice said. "Everyone has to eat." She nudged Charlie forward, nodding toward the kitchen where the platters, bowls, and dishes waited like soldiers, all lined up and waiting.

Charlie and Mandie led the way into the kitchen, which got the other teens to go, with the adults bringing up the rear. Eloise felt a little lost without Aaron, but she attached herself to Robin, who didn't have Duke either. She'd folded her arms, and she watched as Jamie picked up two rolls and balanced them on the edge of her plate.

"What are you going to do?" Eloise asked. She didn't have to spell out what she meant.

Robin sighed, rolled her head, and said, "I don't know. Mandie and Charlie just got here."

Eloise nodded, because she didn't want to pull Billie and Grace from their vacation either. Heck, *she* didn't want to leave the manor. But if it was unsafe...

"Let's get some food," Robin said as Alice glared them down while she and Arthur went by. Eloise filled her plate with sliced turkey, gravy, mashed potatoes, and creamed peas, then grabbed a roll and a can of ginger ale before following her friends into the formal dining room.

She sent a quick text to Aaron. *Food's ready. Can you come eat?*

Be down in a minute, he sent back, and Eloise relaxed enough to pick up her fork and take a bite of mashed potatoes and gravy.

Sure enough, Duke, Paul, and Aaron returned to the first level only a few minutes later, and their appearance stalled all the conversation happening across the two tables.

"All right," Aaron said. "I know everyone wants to know exactly what's happening, but that's kind of impossible."

"They're going to rewire the electrical box on the third floor," Duke said as he picked up a plate. "The other two have passed inspections—and fun fact: there are doubles of some places."

"Doubles?" Robin asked from where she'd gotten up and leaned in the doorway leading into the kitchen from the formal dining area.

"Yeah." Duke loaded mashed potatoes onto his plate. "What did he say, Paul?"

"The pool has two breakers," he said into the gap. "One being controlled from the garage, and one from that wonky electrical box upstairs." He glanced around the room, his eyes landing on Laurel, and then Eloise. "They think that's why the heater in the eaves has been going crazy. It's actually wired twice."

"Wired twice," Eloise repeated in a whisper. "This is insane."

"Maybe they can just deprogram that one upstairs," Laurel said.

Paul grinned at his wife. "I don't think you *deprogram* electricity, babe."

She smiled back at him too. "You know what I mean."

"They're pulling the wiring out now," Duke said. "Apparently jobs like this can take a couple of hours."

"And cost thousands," Aaron said. "They've been talking to the host."

Eloise nodded, and she waited for her husband to join her in the dining room. She gave him the best smile she could, and he beamed light back at her. He swept a kiss along her cheek and whispered, "I think they're going to be able to fix it."

"Do you?"

"I do," Duke boomed. "It's going to be fine."

"Duke," Robin chastised. "You're so loud."

"Well, it's going to be fine." He pulled out a chair next to Robin and sat down. "Neither of the electricians is moaning and groaning. Neither one of them said we should evacuate the house." He looked around at everyone, finally meeting Aaron's eye.

"They didn't," Aaron said. "He's right."

"Everyone should do what they want, though," Robin said. "The last ferry off Rocky Ridge is at nine o'clock."

The clock had just ticked to six, so there was still time.

Eloise met Aaron's eye. "We're not going to leave, are we?" she asked.

"I don't think we need to, El," he said. "I can ask the girls if they're scared."

She nodded, though she didn't want to leave. Since

she'd lived alone for such a large part of her life, she sometimes still had to get used to the idea that decisions got made
that she may not have made, based on how someone else felt.

Aaron set his phone next to his plate. "I just texted
them."

"They're in the next room."

"And they'll answer me honestly if I text them." He
gave her a smile and tucked into his turkey dinner. Eloise
looked down the table to Robin, who'd started talking
with Alice about the pool party tomorrow.

So apparently, they'd stay too, and somehow that
made Eloise feel even more safe.

Aaron's phone buzzed, and he craned his neck to
look at it. "Billie doesn't want to leave."

"Then we'll stay," Eloise said, and she met Kristen's
eye across the table.

"You're staying?" she asked.

"Yeah," Eloise said. "What about you?"

Kristen looked at Kelli and then Shad. "What are
you guys doing?"

"We haven't decided yet." Kelli twisted to look at
Parker, who sat beside Grace and Ian, and he fit so well
there. When Kelli faced her again, she wore pure indecision on her face. Eloise knew this look, and it would be
up to Parker whether they left the manor tonight—and
he wouldn't want to leave.

Eloise hid her smile behind a buttered bite of roll,
because maybe if they got the house fixed up electrically,

the next nine days would truly be made of Christmas magic.

Chapter Twenty

K risten leaned against the cool, antique dresser in her room, her gaze fixed on the open suitcase sprawled across the bed. A couple of sweaters lay inside, their bright colors muted in the dim, candlelit room. She rubbed her eyes, exhaustion seeping into her bones as the flickering light danced on the walls.

She'd spent the past hour in a state of indecision, torn between two choices: stay in the manor despite the questionable electrical situation, or brave the cold night and return to her condo on Diamond Island. Leave everyone she loved here. Leave the holiday house and all its festivities.

She let out a long breath, trying to weigh the risks, then a flash of annoyance sparked through her. She hated feeling this indecisive, but the idea of leaving the manor felt wrong, too. She didn't want to abandon everyone else or cut short the holiday Eloise had so lovingly planned.

Yet, the thought of an electrical fire lurking in these old walls sent a shiver down her spine. At least in her condo, she knew she wouldn't wake up to smoke or flames.

Her phone vibrated on the dresser, a faint glow piercing the darkness. Kristen picked it up, the screen lighting up with a message from Julia: *Are you staying?*

Kristen pondered her response for a moment. She hadn't heard from Maddy or Tessa, and the idea of being one of the few to leave felt isolating. She replied quickly with, *Haven't decided yet. You?*

The reply came almost instantly: *Liam and I are staying. Power can't stay off forever, right?*

Might get cold, though. Kristen allowed herself a small smile, fueled by Julia's optimism. Her heart felt a little lighter, knowing she wasn't alone in her thoughts. She didn't want to leave, and as her suitcase still sat mostly empty, she knew she wouldn't.

Kristen set her phone back down, determined to make a decision. With a deep breath, she removed the sweaters, closed the suitcase, and slid it under the bed. As she lay down, her mind wandered to the electricians still working somewhere in the manor.

"I hope they can get things sorted out," she murmured to the flickering candlelight in her room. She'd turned off her flashlight to preserve the battery, and darkness pressed down on her open eyes.

With a sigh, she finally closed her eyes, exhaustion pulling her under. She drifted in and out of sleep, her thoughts a jumble of wires, floating curtains, and flickering lights.

Sometime in the deep of night, she woke to the sudden hum of power returning. The soft glow of the bedside lamp flickered on, and a laugh bubbled up from her chest as relief washed over her.

She plugged in her phone, the tiny battery icon glowing reassuringly. She felt the chill in the air as she got up to switch on the fan beside her bed, simply to have the noise. Then she quickly snuggled back under the covers, whispering a silent prayer of thanks for electricity and the warmth it provided.

———

"THEN YOU JUST BRUSH THE BUTTER ON." Kristen's heart lifted as she instructed Billie for what to do next with the cinnamon rolls. She loved working with her hands, loved the scent of yeast and cinnamon and sugar, loved the feeling of sticky dough against her fingers and of flour dusting her apron.

Billie, Jamie, and Grace stood around the counter, eagerly waiting for her to tell them what to do. She had Jamie make a roll with butter, cinnamon, and sugar, and she now cut the rolls into one-inch rounds with a piece of unscented and unflavored dental floss.

Grace was still sprinkling on her cinnamon-sugar

mixture, and Billie had waited the longest to get her piece of dough for the cinnamon rolls.

Kristen was just so glad they'd all gotten up early with her to make breakfast for the whole manor, and she smiled as the three of them talked and giggled. Their presence filled the kitchen with a warmth Kristen hadn't realized she'd been missing.

"Look what is happening in here." Robin entered the kitchen wearing a pair of Spandex exercise pants and a sporty jacket. She smiled at her daughter and Eloise's. "This feels just like the Seafaring Girls."

Kristen gave her a fond look, then a side-squeeze. "Except we made cookies for Seafaring Girls."

"Right." Robin lifted a visor and put it on. "I'm going running."

"Okay," Kristen said.

"My pin is on," she said. "I'm not going to go far, so check with Duke if I'm not back in forty-five minutes."

"'Bye, Mom," Jaime chirped, and Robin slipped out the back door to the deck. Kristen watched as she breathed in deeply, lifting her shoulders into a tight box. Kristen's heart pumped out an extra beat full of worry for Robin, because she knew that stance.

She knew why Robin needed to go running this morning, and it was so she could pound out the frustrations and irritations from her life.

"Then I roll it up," Grace said slowly, and Kristen focused back on the baking happening in the kitchen.

"Okay, you want to get that first fold pretty tight," she said. "Use the parchment to help."

Grace went down the length of the roll, folding it over tightly, and then it started to roll up nicely, with cinnamon and sugar spilling out both ends.

Making cinnamon rolls here in The Starlight Manor did remind her of baking cookies with her Seafaring Girls. The memories warmed her, and the newfound lightness settling in the manor lifted her spirits.

"Maybe I'll tell Mom this should be our new family tradition," Jamie suggested, her eyes sparkling with excitement.

Kristen smiled, thinking of all the traditions that had come and gone in her life. "I think that's a wonderful idea, Jamie," she said, knowing full-well that Robin would not do that.

The girls continued to chat as they worked, and Kristen watched them fondly. In each of their faces, she saw hints of the young women they were becoming, and a swell of love moved through her. They were kind and capable, and she was grateful to be a part of their lives, even in this small way.

The kitchen became a flurry of activity as Alice arrived and made coffee. After that, a steady stream of adults moved through the room, filling their mugs and stirring in cream and sugar. The rolls raised, and Kristen got the oven preheating to the correct temperature.

The day promised to be bright and clear, the perfect backdrop for the holiday getaway Eloise had envisioned.

That Kristen really wanted for everyone—and herself. For the first time in days, she felt truly at peace.

"What time is the pool party today?" Grace asked, her voice breaking into Kristen's thoughts.

"I think it's at one," Kristen said, carefully bending to place a tray of cinnamon rolls into the oven. "Alice said she'd send a text."

"I'm typing it up now," Alice said.

"I can't wait to see the candy cane raft," Billie said. "Maybe it'll be big enough for me and Ian."

"You better watch it with Ian," Grace said. "And it's Mom you need to worry about. She's been watching you two."

"She's the one who sent us to the movies together with Dad," Billie said.

"She just wanted to be alone for the afternoon."

Kristen simply listened, because she knew Eloise worried about Billie and Ian. She didn't need to say anything, and the girls weren't asking for her advice.

No matter what, it felt good to be talking about boys and parents instead of something crazy that had happened with the lights.

As the scent of baked bread and cinnamon filled the house, Kristen got out the strawberries and cantaloupe and started cutting up the fruit. It didn't need to be refrigerated, and thankfully, the power hadn't been out for long enough to ruin too much.

Then she said, "Jamie, we need to make the frosting." She detailed how to do that with the cream cheese, icing sugar, butter, and a touch of milk, and Jamie put together the first batch.

The over timed beeped, and Kristen handed the oven mitts to Billie. "I've got a cooling rack right here."

Billie pulled the first tray of cinnamon rolls out of the oven and slid them onto the tray, and Kristen nodded to Jaime. "It's best to put the frosting on while they're hot," she said. "It'll melt down into all the little crevices of the roll." She smiled, because she loved nothing more than perfectly golden cinnamon rolls with such a perfect swirl.

"Breakfast is ready," she called to the house, but she didn't have a great big voice like Robin, so only the few people sitting at the table looked up.

Ben got to his feet and came to refill his coffee. "This looks amazing," he said as he took in the tray of cinnamon rolls. Jamie continued to spread the frosting across the tops of them, and it melted down in just the way Kristen wanted it to.

"Breakfast!" Billie yelled.

Grace quickly laid out plates, and within moments, the girls had assembled a beautiful spread on the kitchen island. "Oh, the juice," she said, and she quickly stepped over to the fridge and pulled out a bottle of orange juice and one of apple.

Eloise came into the kitchen, her eyes lighting up at the sight of breakfast. "Oh, this looks amazing," she said, taking a plate from Grace. "I knew I could count on you, Kristen."

Kristen waved her off, though the compliment filled her with warmth. "It was all the girls. They're the real experts here."

El gave her a quick hug. "How'd you sleep?"

"Good enough," Kristen said.

El watched her, but Kristen moved to help Billie check the rise on her rolls. "The ones in the oven still have twenty minutes, and they'll be ready then."

"Maybe we should've waited until all three trays were done."

"It's eight-fifteen," Kristen said. "I don't even see half the people down here yet." None of the boys had come down from the third-floor male bunk room yet, and she hadn't seen her son or daughter or their families yet either.

She set another pot of coffee to brew; Robin came back from her run; the third and final tray of cinnamon rolls went into the oven, baked, and came back out.

Billie frosted them, and she put the mixing bowl in the sink with a big sigh. "And now, we eat," she said with a smile.

She took two ooey gooey cinnamon rolls and put her fruit in a bowl, then took it all over to the table. She sent a text before she started to eat, and Kristen hid her smile when Ian showed up less than sixty seconds later. "Wow," he said as he crashed into the seat next to her. "You made these?"

"Go get one," she said with a flirtatious smile, and Kristen looked around for El. She didn't see her, but

Aaron sat in the living room, looking at something on his phone.

"Miss Kristen," Jamie said. "Can we make cinnamon rolls every year when we come to the holiday house?"

Kristen blinked at her, because she didn't know how to answer. Putting together a twenty-three-day retreat for people to come and go certainly wasn't easy, and Kristen wouldn't be volunteering for the job.

"If we do this again," she said. "We should definitely make sure we take a breakfast slot so we can make cinnamon rolls."

As a round of laughter lit up the kitchen, Kristen felt like they'd made it through the darkness—literally. Now, they could embrace the light and create memories that would last a lifetime.

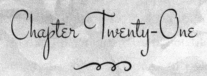

Chapter Twenty-One

Alice stood at the edge of the pool, her fingers tapping rhythmically against the side of her leg. She took a deep breath, inhaling the crisp winter air that mingled with the salty tang of the ocean coming up over the cliffs. Everything about the day should feel wrong—after all, it was December, and they were hosting a pool party—but somehow, it didn't.

The electric blue of the pool stood in stark contrast to the surrounding landscape, a vibrant oasis amidst the rustic charm of The Starlight Manor. The holiday-themed floaties—Santa, a candy cane raft, and a nearly life-sized reindeer—bobbed gently in the water, their bright colors adding a playful touch.

The heaters had been blowing for hours, because it was almost Christmastime, and that meant it certainly couldn't be categorized as warm.

"Mom," Charlie called from where he stood near the

outdoor kitchen. "How many mocktails do you think we'll need?"

Alice smiled, the ache of distance from her twins easing as she looked at her son. "Double what you think," she said, raising her voice to be heard. The teens had gone a little bananas for her mocktails, which only made Alice go to the store more often to pick up the sparkling water she needed to make them.

Mandie joined Charlie, and they started setting out the plastic cups. The two of them looked so at ease together, which was a complete one-eighty from when they'd arrived yesterday afternoon.

A lot had changed since then, actually, and Alice felt like the weight of the world had been lifted from her shoulders once the electrical boxes had been fixed. The mystery of The Starlight Manor explained.

"Is everything ready?" Kristen asked, coming to stand beside Alice. She planted her hands on her hips and surveyed the scene like a queen monitoring her kingdom. Her presence was always steady and reassuring, a grounding force for Alice.

"Almost," Alice said, glancing back toward the outdoor kitchen where Arthur had taken command of the grill. "Arthur's got the burgers and hot dogs going. Mandie and Charlie are making drinks, and I'm about to set out the snacks."

"You've outdone yourself," Kristen said, patting Alice's shoulder. "Really."

Alice breathed out a laugh, some of the tension

leaving her frame. "Well, we haven't started yet," she said. "Give it an hour, and someone will be crying."

"I hope it's not you," Kristen said, giving Alice a hug. She'd received many hugs from Kristen, but this one felt especially needed. She'd enjoyed her time in the manor with her friends, even though sometimes they just turned on a movie and didn't speak.

In fact, that was the best kind of friendship to Alice.

Kristen went to sit with Jamie and Grace, who'd taken up residence on a pair of lounge chairs near the pool, while Robin bustled around with bags of potato chips. Aaron and Paul distributed towels to each person, then started draping them over the empty chairs and loungers too.

Clara and Lena came outside, both of them wearing their swimming suits, and Clara nodded over to Billie, Ian, and Parker. "Look, Lena. Aunt Jean is right there next to Parker. Looks like she saved you a seat."

Jean had definitely saved that lounger for Lena, and the young woman lumbered that way. Clara met Alice's eyes and sighed. "She's got a new swimming suit, and I hope everyone will comment on how amazing it is."

Alice smiled and looked over to Lena. Her suit boasted the brightest pink the world had to offer— Lena's favorite color. "I'll make a big deal of it when I talk to her," Alice said.

"Thank you." Clara picked up a handful of sour cream and onion chips. "She likes Billie and Parker, but she says she's not sure about Ian."

"I think El and Aaron feel the same way." Alice grinned as Clara did, but she was able to tear her attention away from that small group to where AJ sat with Asher and Matt, Kelli and Shad. They seemed to have made up just fine, and Alice sure was glad of that.

"You waiting on anything else?" Eloise asked, and Alice turned toward her.

"My own bravery?"

El smiled and linked her arm through Alice's. "I watched you with your twins," she said. "And tried to take notes, because I knew I'd need to have someone to look to with Billie and Grace."

"You should've picked Robin," Alice said.

El just shook her head. "The teens love you."

"I'm sure," Alice said dryly. She took a deep breath and then blew it all out. "Okay," she called, because the pool party just needed to get started. Once it did, then it could end.

Her attitude surprised her, because Alice typically loved beach day in the summertime—and a pool party at a ritzy house was nearly the same thing.

"We're going to start with some floatie races," she called. "Everyone who wanted to participate signed up during breakfast this morning." She turned to pick up the sign-up sheet. When she faced the pool again, both Robin and El were shuttling people closer to her.

Gratitude streamed through her, and Alice started to relax. "Okay," she said again. "I've made a bracket for the races. You can choose your floatie from the several we have." She glanced around and the teens and adults gathered near her.

Of them all, she thought Liam wore the most determined look, which made a smile widen across her face. He was a cop, though, and they tended to be a little more competitive, a little more alpha. No wonder Julia liked him.

"We'll go in pairs, and the winner of each round advances to the next." She held up the paper, not really expecting people to be able to see her hand-drawn bracket. "So up first." She looked at the paper, a hint of happiness bursting through her. "Liam and Aaron."

"Oh, boy," Liam yelled, and he took a few steps away to start swinging his arms back and forth. He rolled his shoulders next as his boss simply stood on the patio and grinned at him. "It's on."

Aaron laughed then, as did several others, and Alice cleared her throat. "Whoever is the youngest gets to pick their floatie first."

Liam had been in their class in high school, so Alice didn't know who exactly was younger. Aaron raised his hand and said, "I'll be fifty in February."

Liam rolled his neck, still stretching out as if this pool floatie race might hurt him if he didn't. "I'm not fifty until June."

Aaron bounced on the balls of his feet, clearly going to get into this now too. "Pick your poison, deputy."

Liam grinned and moved over to the end of the pool where all of the floaties had been pushed. He looked at the ring, the raft, and the reindeer, then turned back to Alice. "Do you have to be on it? Or can you use it as a floatation device?"

All eyes came back to her. "You and the floatie have to get from one side of the pool to the other," she said coolly.

"I'll take this here Santa circle." Liam bent down and plucked it from the pool.

Aaron joined him. "I'll take the reindeer."

No one had successfully mounted the reindeer for longer than three seconds, and Alice honestly had no idea if Aaron was taking this seriously or not. It was a Christmas pool floatie race, so she sincerely hoped he wasn't.

"Everyone to the sides," Alice said. "Cheer for our racers, and—" She consulted her paper again. "Billie and Laurel are racing next."

Alice moved to the far end of the pool while Aaron and Liam completed their pre-race warm-ups. "Ready?" she called, and Aaron crouched like he'd explode off the side of the pool, hoping to win Olympic gold. "Three, two, one, go!" she yelled.

Aaron did, in fact, leap into the pool, him and the reindeer flying through the air. Liam tossed his floatie out onto the water, and then dove after it.

Cheers and hollers started from the group, with Grace yelling, "Come on, Dad! You got this!" and Billie whistling through her teeth.

Ian called, "Go, Dad! You can beat 'im!" which made Alice's heart so happy.

Aaron came up first, the bulky reindeer bobbing too much for him to make much headway. But he managed to muscle it behind his head, and he held onto it with both strong arms. Then he started kicking in a backstroke way, making good progress toward the side of the pool where Alice stood.

Liam came up about halfway across the pool, his head poking up from the center of the Santa ring. How he'd done that, Alice would never know. She wasn't exactly the most athletic person. But Liam and Aaron sure were, and as Liam started to kick in a front stroke way, she knew she'd started with the right people.

The encouragement and yelling continued, the noise level through the roof, as both men tried to get to the end of the pool first. Liam could lift up the front of his floatie, which reduced the drag, and he started to pull ahead of Aaron, who's bulky reindeer kept trying to push him back to the starting line.

The Santa circle got pushed up onto the deck near Alice's feet. Liam slapped the pool tiles there, then shot out of the pool with a triumphant yell. He raised both hands above his head as he dripped and splashed water everywhere, and the group went wild.

Alice started to laugh and laugh. She was so glad she'd started with this, because this—plus lunch and mocktails—could be the whole party, and people would love it.

As Liam hugged his son, Aaron reached the end of the pool with Rudolph. Alice wrote Liam's name on the bracket sheet; Billie chose the candy cane raft for her floatie of choice, and Laurel took the Santa ring. Alice wouldn't be shocked if Rudolph sat out for the rest of the races, because Aaron had just shown how difficult he was to manhandle through the water.

"Okay," Alice called. "Settle down. Settle down, now."

"Quiet!" Arthur yelled from a few paces away in the outdoor kitchen, and Alice tossed him a grateful smile. People actually did quiet then, and Alice looked across the length of the pool to where Billie clutched the over-sized candy cane raft to her chest while Laurel had the Santa ring hanging lazily over her forearm.

"Ready," she yelled down to them. "Three, two, one, go!"

Billie tossed her raft out into the pool the way Liam had, then she turned around and jogged back a few paces.

"Come on, Bills," Ian called. "Don't let her beat you!"

Laurel jumped into the pool with her floatie, clearly not intending to use it at all. She just needed to get it and herself across the pool.

As the candy cane raft bobbed with the movement of the water, Billie ran at it. Pretty fast too, and Alice's heart stopped for a moment. The mothers in the group had spent weeks telling their little children not to run on the pool deck. It was slippery when wet, and no one wanted to go to the emergency room for Christmas.

Billie launched herself into the pool while everyone cheered, and she landed near the edge of the raft. Her forward momentum moved her through the water—and right past Laurel. She then employed a similar tactic as Liam, leaning on the back of the raft and lifting most of it out of the water.

Grace moved along the edge of the pool with her. "Keep going, Bills!" she yelled. "Only a little further. Fifteen feet. Ten...five...you're there! Throw the raft up!" She jumped up and down and clapped as Billie pushed the candy cane raft up onto the pool deck and slapped the tiles the same way Liam had.

Billie gasped and labored for air, but Alice could not stop smiling. Ian came over and hauled her out of the pool, hugging and congratulating her while everyone else continued to cheer for Laurel.

She finally made it with her one-armed ring-floatie, and she too congratulated Billie on her win.

The races continued, until finally, it came down to Liam and Charlie. They'd both used the same floatie—the Santa circle, which Charlie chose again, as he was far younger than Liam.

"I guess I'll take the raft," Liam said, picking up the bigger item and squeezing it like he could test for air pressure that way. The trash talk from the crowd started, and Alice felt like she'd lost control of this beast already.

Arthur hadn't participated in the races, and he had

all the hamburgers and hot dogs ready. They'd eat right after this, and then Alice had found a volleyball net in the pool house, and she planned to simply let people do that—or not—make mocktails, and enjoy the winter sunshine and heating elements in the deck roofing.

"Ready," she yelled, and Charlie crouched. Liam poised the raft above his head, the front and back ends bowing outward. "Three, two, one, go!"

Charlie was young and agile, but Liam had muscles and sheer athleticism. They both threw their floaties into the pool and went after them, and they came up out of the water evenly.

Alice wasn't sure Charlie had the gas to beat Liam, not when it came to kicking or stroking. Robin stood on one corner of the pool, with Eloise on the other, and Alice hoped she wouldn't have to be the deciding vote when the two men made it here.

Then, somehow, Charlie's ring slipped under him and spurted out the back—the wrong way. A groan moved through the crowd, because he'd have to go back and get it.

He turned on a dime, but that left the win for Liam. He slid his raft onto the deck and propelled himself out of the pool too, clearly the winner. Instead of bellowing and prancing like he'd done last time, he started clapping and calling for Charlie to, "Don't give up! You've got it."

Charlie retrieved his ring and finished the race to plenty of accolades and support. That somehow made Alice love her son and her friends even more, and she hugged him, wet as he was, when he finally emerged from the pool.

Then she turned to Liam. "That makes you, Liam Coldwater, our official floatie race winner!"

Everyone whooped and hollered for him, and Alice turned to get out the prize she'd gotten for such a thing. She pulled out an oversized pair of Christmas tree sunglasses and showed them around to everyone on both sides of the pool.

"For the winner," she declared, handing them to Liam. He laughed as he slid them on and modeled them for everyone. He was such a good sport, and he sure seemed to get along with everyone.

"All right," Arthur called. "Time to eat."

The spotlight left Alice, and she faded into the background as the activity moved from poolside to the outdoor kitchen and then the loungers and tables where people ate.

She waited until almost everyone had food, and then she got herself a hamburger and some potato chips. She spotted a seat at a table with Robin and Duke, Kristen and Jean and Rueben, and she headed that way. "Can I sit here?"

"I saved it for you, dear," Kristen said with a smile.

Alice sank into the seat. "Thank you."

"That was amazing," Robin said, grinning. "Thank you so much, Alice."

"It's a pool party," she said.

"But it was amazing," Jean said.

Alice took a bite of her burger, and she decided to accept their praise. The floatie races had been amazing. She did make a delicious mocktail. She could throw a good party for all ages.

And she loved her friends, so she reached across the table and squeezed Robin's hand. Then gave Kristen a side-hug and nodded to Jean. "Thanks, you guys," she said. She glanced around the deck and patio, where all of them—except Ginny and Bob, who couldn't come this weekend—hung out.

"This has been amazing," she said. "Even with the electrical weirdness."

"Best Christmas ever," Robin said.

"Best Christmas ever," Alice, Jean, and Kristen echoed back to her. Then they all laughed together, and that made Alice ridiculously happy too.

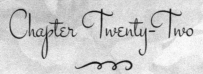

Chapter Twenty-Two

"Mom?" Kelli turned at the sound of her son's voice, which had been changing a lot in the past several months.

"Hey," she said as brightly as she could. She'd just gotten out of the shower and gotten dressed after the pool party, and Parker still wore his swim trunks. "What's up?"

He came into the suite where she and Daphne slept, and he glanced around. "Your room is huge," he said with a smile.

"I told you it was." She nodded toward the couch in the sitting area. "You could totally sleep there if the bunk room is bothering you."

"No, it's fine," he said as he came toward her.

Kelli had put Daphne down for her afternoon nap, and she expected her to sleep for quite a long time after all the fun they'd had in the pool. She sank onto the bed and propped up all of her pillows to sit up against them.

Parker surprised her by doing what he'd done as a little boy—climbing onto the bed and over to her. She brought him right into her side, tears almost coming to her eyes at this sweet moment that she had lost. She hadn't even realized it until now.

"You tired?" she asked.

"A little," he said. "The bathrooms are all being used."

"You can shower here," she said.

"Maybe I will." But he didn't get up to get his clothes or to get in the shower.

Kelli wasn't sure what she should say. Parker would be fifteen come spring, and Kelli honestly felt like she was simply muddling through every day the best way she knew how—which wasn't at all.

"Are you guys going to put a movie on this afternoon?" she asked, because the silence made her uncomfortable somehow.

"I think so," he said. "Not sure what."

"Well, no horror, okay?"

"Liam and Billie don't like horror," Parker said. "So we won't watch anything too scary."

"Good," Kelli said.

He lifted his phone in front of his face, started looking at something. Kelli told herself over and over that she didn't need to ask him another question, that they could just sit together. It quickly became one of the harder things that she'd ever had to do, and she really wished there were as many books on raising teens as there were on raising babies.

At the very least, infants couldn't roll their eyes and scoff and make her feel two inches tall and dumber than a post. Yes, teenagers had a real knack for such things.

"Ian says the bathroom upstairs is free," Parker said a few minutes later. "Think I'm gonna go shower up there."

"All right," she said as brightly as she could.

He scooted to the edge of the bed and turned back to her, catching her watching him. "There's only two days of school next week, and I don't think any of the others are going," he said. "Could I maybe stay here too?"

"Oh," she said. "I hadn't heard that."

Well, she knew there were only two days of school next week before the Christmas holidays, but she hadn't heard that Billie, Jamie, Grace, and Ian would not be attending. Parker didn't get the greatest grades in the world, but he wasn't a bad student either, and he never got in trouble at school.

Kelli and Daphne had been staying at the manor, while Shad had been getting Parker to school and then going to work on Diamond Island. Her husband still had to work this week, but that didn't mean Parker had to go to school.

"Do you have enough clothes?" she asked.

He blinked, as if clean clothes were the last thing on his mind.

Kelli smiled. "I suppose this place has a laundry room, and we can wash anything you need."

"Yeah," he said. "I'm sure I'll be fine."

"All right," she said. "Let me talk to Eloise and see what's going on. If no one else is going, you can stay here too."

His face lit up with a smile, making him the most handsome boy in the world. Kelli's motherly heartstrings chimed at her as he turned and said, "Thanks, Mom." He came around the bed and hugged her, and Kelli wanted to freeze time in that moment forever.

"If you don't like the movie—"

"I know," Parker said, a hint of that frustration coming into his voice. "I can leave, I can say you need me, I know what to do."

"Okay," she said. "Well, I think I'm going to stay here and take a nap with Daphne." She smiled at her son, glad that he seemed happy to be here. As far as she knew, he didn't spend a bunch of time at school with Grace or Jamie. Billie and Liam were older than him, and truth be told, Jamie was a grade ahead of him as well.

He left the suite, and as the click of the door signaled its closing, Kelli murmured, "He could be a lot more unpleasant than he is."

She tried to sleep for fifteen or twenty minutes, and when her nap didn't take, Kelli got up and checked on her baby girl in the portable crib. Daphne snoozed like the dead, and Kelli eased out of the suite. She went downstairs to the living room, where plenty of activity was still happening.

Julia slid a tray of crispy rice cereal treats onto the dining room table in the kitchen. It already held half-eaten bags of potato chips, leftover cinnamon rolls from that morning, and an assortment of bagged candy. Through the windows, Kelli could see several people still at the pool, mostly adults, as the kids had decided they wanted to come in, shower, and watch a movie in the theater room.

"I've got a batch of peanut butter chocolate chip coming up," Julia said.

Kelli smiled at her. "These look great," she said. "I'm kind of a crispy treat purist."

Julia laughed as she went back into the kitchen to make another pan of sticky treats.

Maddy sat at the bar with Tessa, and they talked about something going on at the library. Kelli's first inclination was to go out to the pool. Her childhood friends still lingered out there—Alice, Kristen, AJ, and Robin. She wasn't sure where Eloise had gone, but she knew AJ and Jean had taken their kids inside, cleaned them up, and put them down for naps too.

Kelli told herself that she enjoyed meeting new people and getting to know them, and just because she had a baby didn't mean she couldn't converse with people who didn't.

So she found herself migrating over to the island where Maddy and Tessa sat.

"Hey," she said. "Is this seat open?"

She slid onto it as Maddy grinned at her and said, "Absolutely."

Tessa now sat in the middle, and instead of turning toward Maddy and boxing Kelli out, she sat straight so that Kelli could participate in the conversation too.

"We were just talking about a new library program I'm hoping to start next summer," Tessa said.

Kelli smiled at her. "That's great," she said. "If you have flyers and things, let me know. I can put them at Whole Soul."

"Oh, I'd love that," Tessa said. "Thank you."

Her phone chimed, and all three of them looked at it.

"It's probably Dave," Julia said in almost a singsong voice.

Tessa slapped her palm over the phone, but Kelli had already seen that it totally was Dave.

"It is," Maddy said.

"Stop it," Tessa said, her voice somewhat cross.

"What's going on with you and Dave?" Kelli asked, and that brought every eye to her. "You don't have to tell me," she added quickly. "I mean, I get it. It's none of my business."

"Of course, it's your business," Maddy said. "Tessa's just dragging her feet a little bit."

Kelli looked at Tessa, into her deep, dark eyes, and

she found a soul sister. Tessa didn't jump into things with both feet the way some other people did. Kelli never had either.

"It's okay to drag your feet a little bit," she said.

"We've only been dating a few months," Tessa said. "As I've told Julia and Maddy *many times*."

"Is it serious?" Kelli asked.

"He wants it to be," Maddy said.

"And you're unsure," Kelli filled in for Tessa.

"I'm not *unsure*, exactly," Tessa said. "I just—he runs a very busy business on Diamond Island. It's not like we see each other every day. And I don't know..." She rolled one shoulder and then stretched her neck forward and then back. "I feel like we're still getting to know each other."

She didn't say what Dave had done to try to advance their relationship, and Kelli certainly wasn't going to ask. Robin might, and obviously Maddy and Julia had, but Kelli simply patted Tessa's hand that covered the phone.

"At least he's employed, right?"

A beat of silence followed, and then all of them started to laugh, including Kelli. After the fight with AJ, the tension in the house, and all of the flickering lights, then the problems in the tension-filled night, where none of them were sure if the power would come on, stay off, or cause the whole manor to burn to the ground, laughing was such a welcome release.

"He's employed," Tessa said through her giggles. "And he's not like my last boyfriend, who wouldn't leave his business behind. He does. He takes time off. He sees me when he can."

"And if you were living together," Maddy said. "You'd see him even more."

Tessa threw her a sharp look. "Not all of us live together before we get married, Maddy."

"She's just saying," Julia said as she came over to the counter and poured a massive amount of crispy rice cereal into a big bowl of melted marshmallows and peanut butter. "That Ryan likes him, and your son's opinion means a lot to you. You guys had a great Thanksgiving together, and I can see why Dave wants to take it to the next level."

"Yeah, and he's losing his apartment," Tessa said. "Let's not forget that."

Kelli simply let them bicker back and forth because she could see Tessa's side as well. Maybe Dave *did* want to move in with Tessa simply because it was convenient, and he was losing his lease at his condo.

"I just don't want to feel like I'm being used," Tessa said. "I'm not his landlord. I'm his girlfriend."

"And you have a really great beach bungalow," Julia said. "Even I'm jealous of it. I would love to move in with you if I could."

They laughed again, and Kelli turned her attention to Julia as she stirred and stirred to get everything coated. "What about you and Liam? Are there wedding bells in the future for you?"

Julia answered by pouring out the now-coated cereal

into a pan. "I can admit we've started talking about marriage." She reached for the bag of chocolate chips and sprinkled them on top.

Maddy gasped. "You have not told us that, Julia."

Julia grinned at them. "Maybe we just started talking about it this week." She gave Maddy a pointed look. "And I don't have to tell you everything the moment it happens."

"She's not wrong about that," Tessa muttered.

Maddy scoffed, her blue eyes wide as she looked over to Tessa and then back to Julia. "I don't make you guys tell me things the moment they happen," she said. She glanced over her shoulder toward the sliding glass door, then looked back at her friends. "I'm not like some of the other ladies here. Love them, but...I don't do that."

Kelli enjoyed sitting there with them. They reminded her a lot of the relationships she had with Alice, Robin, Eloise, and AJ.

"Ooh, marshmallow treats," AJ said as if summoned by Kelli's thoughts. She took the last barstool at the island and gave Kelli a side hug. "No nap for you either, huh?"

"Not today," Kelli said. "But Daphne was out like a light."

AJ grinned and took the super-soft peanut butter chocolate chip crispy treat Julia extended toward her. "Thanks."

She took a bite and then looked around. "I interrupted something, didn't I?"

"No," Kelli said in a bright voice. "I'll sum it up for you: Dave wants to be serious with Tessa by moving in together. She's not sure about it, doesn't want to feel used, like her beach bungalow is just a rental for her boyfriend because it's convenient for him. Julia and Tessa think Maddy sometimes wants them to tell her things too soon."

"Which is totally not true," Maddy grumbled.

"And Julia and Liam just barely started talking about getting married this past week."

AJ pulled in a breath. "Wow," she said, her wide-eyed gaze landing on Julia. "Just...wow."

"What does that mean?" Julia asked.. "Is there something about Liam I need to know?"

"No," AJ shook her head. "No, no, absolutely not." She looked over to Kelli. "I mean, unless maybe we should tell her about that time he snuck into the school and spraypainted the bulldog..."

Kelli burst out laughing—actually tipped her head back and laughed and laughed and laughed. AJ joined her, but none of the other women did, as they hadn't grown up in Five Island Cove the way AJ and Kelli had.

"Well, now I've got to hear it," Julia said.

AJ nodded. "You totally do. This is a classic Liam story."

"Who's telling Liam stories?" Aaron asked as he came in. He glanced around at all the women and picked up a bag of chips. "You know what? I'm just gonna let this one slide." He grinned at them all and went right back outside, though he probably had plenty of Liam-stories about the man, as Liam worked on the police force with Aaron.

That caused them all to laugh again, and then Kelli said, "Okay, but for real, Liam was a little bit of a prankster in high school..."

Chapter Twenty-Three

F rustration filled AJ as she tried to get Asher calm enough so that she could attend the Wednesday luncheon. She didn't get to go to every one of them, and it felt like their group had been more and more splintered into smaller groups in the past several months than ever before.

But they were all in the house this week: Robin, Alice, Eloise, Kelli, Maddy, Julia, Tessa, Jean, Clara, Kristen, Laurel, and Kristen.

Christmas Eve still sat a few days away, and AJ was anticipating the arrival of Matt's daughter, Lisa, for their last weekend of festivities before they would lose the holiday house and everyone would have to return to their own homes around Five Island Cove.

Maddy had catered today's luncheon, to be eaten in the formal dining room, from the Glass Dolphin, which was one of the best restaurants in the cove, and AJ didn't want to miss a moment of it.

Unfortunately, her three-year-old had been playing in the kitchen with Heidi, and he had gotten his fingers slammed in a cupboard door. She'd held ice to them for as long as he would let her, and then she'd been holding him in her arms while he hiccupped and continued to cry for the last twenty minutes.

She could bring him to the luncheon, but she felt like her attention would be too divided, and she wanted him to go down for a nap so that she could enjoy an adult event without him.

Sometimes she felt guilty about that. But she'd been seeing an online therapist for the last month or two, and she'd decided that it was okay for her, an adult, to want to have adult conversations and time where she didn't have to worry about anyone but herself.

It wasn't selfish. It was actually mentally healthy for AJ to take time for herself, outside of being the main caregiver for Asher and the one who held everything together at home for her and Matt.

She started to hum, and Asher quieted, his eyes blinking slower and slower until he finally closed them and went to sleep.

Relief rushed through her, quickly followed by panic that she would have to move him to his crib, where he might wake up and she'd have to start the process all over again.

She had no idea how close they were to having

lunch, as Maddy, Alice, and Julia had gone to Diamond Island to pick it up. They were supposed to be back on the twelve-twenty ferry, which would put them at the holiday house probably around a quarter to one.

AJ glanced at her phone on the loveseat next to her and gently reached over to tap it to bring up the time: 12:35.

She probably had a few more minutes, though she wished she could be more helpful in getting out everything they needed to serve lunch—plates, utensils, cups, mocktails. She thought of the many other women who were there who could do such a thing and told herself, *It doesn't matter, AJ. They all know that Asher hurt himself and that you're taking care of him.*

She let a few more minutes pass, and then she eased herself to the edge of the loveseat, then to a standing position with her three-year-old in her arms. She honestly should get a gold medal for such a feat. She took a breath, steadied herself, and then walked through the master bathroom to the closet, and laid him down in his crib-slash-playpen.

He groaned softly and then exhaled as she covered him with his favorite silky blanket. He seemed to smile in his sleep as he pulled it up to his chin, and he went right back to sleep. AJ also released her breath slowly, picked up the baby monitor, turned it on, and then slipped out of the room.

AJ found everyone in the kitchen, but she didn't

smell any evidence of food, which meant Maddy and the others had not returned from the Glass Dolphin yet.

"Go on," Robin said to Jamie, somewhat crossly. "The adults are having lunch today by ourselves. You guys got your food, and you can entertain yourselves either downstairs in your bunk rooms or at the pool."

"Fine," Jamie said, a little sass in her tone. She looked at Billie, and the two of them headed for the stairs that went downstairs.

Robin didn't apologize for her attitude, and AJ actually found it refreshing, because Robin was one of the best moms that she knew, and even she wanted some time just to herself with her friends.

As the teens went downstairs, AJ clapped her hands together. "What can I do?"

"I think we're about ready, dear," Kristen said. "We're just waiting for Maddy, Julia, and Alice to get back with the food."

"Oh, Alice just texted," Robin said, lifting her phone from the island. "We're having a hard time getting a RideShare," she read out loud. "We need an XL because we have so much food, it's like three passengers." She looked up. "She added a laughing emoji, but I don't think she's kidding."

AJ was quite sure she wasn't kidding because they were feeding a multitude of adults, and that required a lot of food.

Matt had gone to work at the golf course today, and Duke wasn't back from fishing yet. It was Arthur's first day off for Christmas break and Aaron had been here for weeks, but as far as AJ knew, no one had invited their men to the luncheon. They didn't during a regular week, and they all happened to be at the holiday house this week, so they wanted their time together.

"If they haven't even gotten a RideShare yet," Kelli said. "They'll be another twenty minutes probably."

"At least," Robin said.

AJ never ate much for breakfast, but she could wait another twenty minutes to sit down with her friends.

The time passed quickly, and soon enough, Robin said, "Alice just said they're here," and that caused a swarm to head for the front door to help them get the food out of the RideShare.

AJ went with them, and she ended up carrying in two plastic bags filled with salad dressing, sour cream, and other condiments.

Maddy took charge as she laid everything out on the eat-in dining room table in the kitchen. They'd serve themselves from there and then go into the formal dining room to eat.

AJ's mouth watered as she took in the trays of sesame chicken, braised beef, and vegetarian lasagna. Maddy had ordered steamed vegetables, green salad, tomato and mozzarella salad, corn on the cob, and conch fritters as sides. There were baked potato skins stuffed with bacon and cheese, an order of mussels, and more bread than AJ had seen in a long, long time.

Once everything sat where Maddy wanted it, she

looked up and around the group, her blue eyes shining like sapphire stars. "All right," she said, "I think we're ready."

Everyone looked around at one another, because they usually had someone who had initiated the meal, chosen the restaurant, or was hosting at their house, who would lead out for the luncheon. They all looked around at one another, and then Robin started to giggle.

"It's time for our one-day Wednesday luncheon," Eloise said over the laughter. "I'm so glad that we could do this once while we're here in the holiday house."

She paused for a moment, something burning bright in her dark, dark eyes. "I'm so grateful that all of you were able to come, and so many of us were able to stay here for such a long time together."

AJ reached over and took Kelli's hand, squeezing it tightly. The movement caused a ripple throughout the group as others did the same, and they created a connected oval around the table in the kitchen.

"I know sometimes we just sit by the pool and read," Eloise said, her voice somewhat tight and scratchy. "I know we just put the TV on and don't even talk, but it's been so nice for me personally to be here, away from all the busyness of my regular house, to just *be here* with you guys."

She nodded, and it took several long seconds before she could continue. "So thank you, and I hope that we'll be able to have many more lunches like this throughout the new year."

"And just know," Robin said. "That you're always invited to the Wednesday lunch. It's a standing invitation for anyone here. You don't need to get a special text or have a particular person invite you. All of us are always invited."

"That's right," Alice murmured.

AJ appreciated them saying so. They were the leaders of the group, whether she liked it or not. She had a somewhat dominant personality, but she usually didn't show it in her group of friends. She stuck with Kelli, who was far more mild and meek, and AJ had decided that she liked her place in the group where she was.

Sometimes she did feel left out, though, so the blanket invitation meant a lot to her.

"Okay," Julia said. "Let's eat before this gets colder than it already is. It's quite the ways from Diamond up to Rocky Ridge, isn't it?"

"That it is," Maddy said. "And now you know why Ben and I want to move to Diamond Island."

That sparked a whole new round of conversation, though AJ had heard Maddy say such a thing before. They hadn't made the move yet, but Maddy said, "I think we'll find a place this spring."

"This spring?" Tessa asked. "That's probably a good time to move."

Robin held up both hands, one of which held a chunk of dark brown bread. "We'll do news when we sit down," she said. "Everyone, just get your food first. We'll do news when we sit down."

"All right," AJ said with a smile. "Don't freak out, Robin."

Kristen put her hand on Robin's arm and leaned in to say something more quietly to her, and Robin lowered both of her arms. The intensity in her expression started to lessen.

"I just don't want to miss any news," she said much quieter, and AJ could definitely echo that.

Chapter Twenty-Four

The flickering flames in the fireplace cast a soft glow over the living room, illuminating the Christmas tree in muted shades of green and gold. Eloise smiled as she took in the sight. The red and green plaid stockings hanging over the mantel, the twinkling lights of the tree, the pile of presents beneath the boughs.

All of it represented countless hours of hard work, planning, and preparation, and she was so glad she'd been able to do it. She watched as Matt helped Asher put out the milk and cookies for Santa. Every man who'd been here had helped around the manor in some way, from grilling during the pool party, to working on the electrical issues, to keeping the firewood stocked.

Everyone had taken a turn with meals here and there, some more than others, but all had helped in some way. Eloise felt full to bursting, because Robin and Kristen had done an enormous ham feast for tonight's

Christmas Eve dinner, and Eloise couldn't get enough of Kristen's cheesy, delicious, "miracle potatoes."

Eloise watched as Asher carefully placed a carrot next to the plate of cookies and then watched it roll. His chubby fingers reached out and brought it back, and then he smiled proudly at it when it stayed where he wanted it.

"That's perfect, buddy," Matt said, ruffling his son's hair. "Santa's gonna love it."

The warmth of the scene enveloped Eloise, and she found herself blinking back tears. This was what she'd hoped for when she'd first conceived of the idea for this holiday getaway—moments of joy, of family, of togetherness.

"El." Aaron's voice came from behind her, soft and questioning. She turned to find him holding two mugs of steaming hot chocolate. "Hot chocolate is done."

"Mm, is this the mint?" She took in a long breath of it and smelled the peppermint on it.

Aaron's arm slipped around her waist as she took her first sip, and she leaned into him, savoring the moment. Billie, Mandie, Ginny, and Jamie worked in the kitchen, finishing up the dessert for tonight's single-gift opening. They had plans to put a movie on downstairs later, after everyone got one gift from beneath the tree a day early.

"Who's picking your gifts?" Duke asked, pausing in front of them.

"I am." Eloise handed her hot chocolate back to her husband and followed Duke into the living room.

They'd agreed that tomorrow, they'd go around and open their gifts, then show them to the group, but that tonight, they could each get their present and open it at the same time.

So Eloise bent to pick up the four gifts—one for each person in her family—from where she'd stashed them under the Christmas tree.

The couches and chairs and hearth got filled quickly when they all gathered here, and Aaron started bringing over some of the dining table chairs. El simply waited for him and Duke to get enough seating for everyone, and then she went to check on the girls in the kitchen.

She found Billie eating the bottom round of a snowman, and she froze as El joined the younger girls at the counter. "These look ready," she said as she drank in the brightly decorated sugar cookies. Reindeer, sleighs, Santas, snowmen, snowflakes, and stars.

She smiled at the girls, and Billie grinned back at her with cookie crumbs on her lips. "We ready?"

"Yes." Mandie picked up the platter of cookies and gave Eloise a side-eyed look.

"All right," Eloise said lightly. "Let's head into the living room."

She waited for Jamie and Ginny to follow the cookies, and Billie quickly crammed the last of the snowman in her mouth before she went with them too. Eloise brought up the rear, and when she reached the row of chairs behind the couch, she clapped her hands together.

"Everyone find a seat," she called, noting that Billie

camped right next to Ian on the floor, their backs resting against the couch behind them. Mandie and Charlie sat on the sofa behind them, their legs tucked up under them. Billie grinned at her lap and laced her fingers through Ian's, then peered up at him through her eyelashes, almost like she thought her father wouldn't see her.

"Let's pass out the gifts," Eloise said, and she turned to pick up the presents she'd already plucked from the pile. She leaned over the couch and gave Grace's to her, then tossed Aaron's gift to him, and then crossed the room and handed Billie hers with a stern-feeling look on her face. Billie had the sense to release Ian's hand to take the gift, and when Eloise had sat next to Aaron in one of the dining chairs and faced them again, Billie had put a few inches between them.

Smart girl.

A chorus of excited voices filled the air as packages continued to get distributed.

"Everyone have a gift?" she asked as Alice settled into a seat, and then Laurel, then Clara, Jean, and Kelli.

"We're ready," AJ said, and Eloise smiled.

"Okay," she said. "Let's open them." She didn't wait to se what others were doing; she tore into her gift. She already knew it would be the orange-ginger lotion she loved, as the body care store only sold it during the holidays, and she restocked every year.

Exclamations of delight and gratitude chimed in the air as gifts got opened, some faster than others. "Thank you, Dad," Billie called, holding up a delicate silver necklace with a star-shaped pendant. "Thank you, El."

Eloise grinned at her, then watched as Ian put the necklace on for her.

Laughter erupted as Charlie opened a gag gift from Mandie—a book titled "How to Survive Your First Year of College Without Your Girlfriend."

"Very funny," he said, rolling his eyes even as he grinned.

"Open the real one," Mandie urged, handing him another package.

As Charlie unwrapped a framed photo of the two of them on their first day of their sophomore year, Eloise felt a pang in her chest.

A shriek of delight from across the room pulled Eloise from her thoughts. Lena was bouncing up and down, clutching a stuffed, sparkly purple unicorn. "Mom! Dad! Thank you, thank you!"

Robin's girls got new pajamas, and Jean and Rueben had gotten Heidi a toy vacuum cleaner. She currently pushed it around the a small patch of carpet in the living room, pure joy on her face. If only she'd like vacuuming half as much later in her life.

New ties, new shoes, new jackets—they all got opened, and Eloise recognized the abundance in all of their lives. Just the fact that they could pool their resources and rent a house like this for over three weeks testified of how much they all had.

"Eloise, look what I got." Parker arrived in front of

her, wearing a bright green jersey. "It's my favorite player." He turned around so Eloise could read the name there. She had no idea who he was, but she knew Parker loved basketball.

"That's amazing," she said, and the teen smiled at her.

"Thanks for doing this," he said, and he semi-lunged at her and hugged her awkwardly.

Eloise could barely pat him on the back before he pulled away, and he moved back over to Ian and Billie. Eloise caught Kelli's eye, and her friend mouthed a silent "thank you."

Ginny stood up and held one of the platters of cookies. "Time for dessert," she said, and she moved around the room like a cocktail waitress, lowering the tray so others could take the cookie of their choice.

It didn't take long for the little kids to start yawning, and AJ scooped Asher into her arms, saying, "Come on, buddy. Santa won't come if you're still awake."

"That's right," Aaron said. "Everyone to bed."

"Bed?" Billie asked. "Dad, it's eight o'clock."

"Movie time, then," he said. "Santa will be flying by soon, and he won't want to be seen."

Eloise grinned at him, because she knew he'd told his girls the same thing when they were younger so he could finish getting their presents ready while they played or colored in their bedroom.

"He's not a young as he once was," Duke said,

joining in on the game. "We definitely all need to get to bed a little early tonight."

"Let's go put on a movie," Billie said.

"And when the boys go up to their bunk room, they should pretend like this floor doesn't exist," Liam said, really puffing out his chest. "Santa's presents disappear if they're seen before Christmas morning."

"Sure, Dad." Ian rolled his eyes at his father, and then he followed Charlie and Parker downstairs.

"Be careful with that frosting," Eloise said to Grace as she went by with a plate of cookies. "We don't own this house, remember."

"Okay, El." Grace smiled at her, and Eloise sure loved her.

Finally, only the adults remained in the living room, and Robin set down a bottle of wine and a couple of glasses. "Who wants a drink?"

"There's eggnog too," Alice said.

"And I have some of those whiskey chocolates," Kristen said as she moved into the kitchen to retrieve them.

"Let's get the presents out and done, so we can go to bed," Aaron said, and Eloise wasn't going to argue with him. She poured herself half a glass of wine and retrieved a laundry basket from the top of the dryer. She handed it to Aaron and said, "All of our gifts are in the master closet."

She didn't want to climb up and get them, but Aaron grinned and said, "I'll be right back."

"I can't believe how fast this month has gone," Alice mused, carefully swirling her wine. "It feels like we just got here yesterday."

Eloise nodded in agreement. "I know. Part of me doesn't want it to end."

"Well," Kristen said, a thoughtful look on her face. "Who says it has to? I mean, not this exactly, but...why can't we do something like this every year?"

The idea hung in the air, full of possibility. A spark of excitement ignited in Eloise's chest. "It's not a bad idea," she said. "But it's a lot of work."

"Many hands make light work," Laurel said as she joined them. She sipped from a can of ginger ale. "As my mother would say." She smiled at everyone, and Eloise reached to put her arm around her.

"It's something to think about," Eloise said, but she didn't want to do that right now. She only had two more days before they'd have to all pack their bags, pull the sheets and towels out of their bedrooms and bathrooms, and return to their own houses.

Eloise would have to go back to the Cliffside Inn. Regular life would resume, and the bubble the holiday house had provided for her would burst.

But they still had Operation Santa to finish, and Christmas Day, so the holidays weren't over yet.

Chapter Twenty-Five

R obin led the way downstairs, her husband right behind her. She'd sent out a text to everyone at the holiday house last night after their Christmas Eve festivities, saying they would be opening presents as a group at eight a.m. She still had fifteen minutes to spare, but she wanted to make sure that everyone had whatever they needed before the gift wrap came off.

"I wonder if people will really wear their pajamas," she said, feeling a flicker of self-consciousness at the blue and green plaid pants she wore with a dark green shirt—her pajamas. She hated feeling nervous and anxious about what she looked like or wore, as she felt too old to have to deal with those things.

"The girls will be," Duke said. "I am. You won't be alone."

Robin didn't do well alone. She wanted to belong and feel like she belonged wherever she went.

"Did your dad say if they were coming?" Robin asked as they reached the second-floor landing.

"Yeah, he texted about ten minutes ago," Duke said. "He said Mom isn't feeling well, so they won't be here."

Probably for the best, Robin thought, because her mother would be, and for whatever reason, Jennifer Golden had never taken to Duke's parents. El's mother had decided to come as well.

So Robin wasn't surprised to find Dawn in the kitchen with El and Aaron, all three of them sipping coffee.

"Merry Christmas," Robin chirped, relief flowing through her when she saw that Eloise still wore her pajamas and Aaron wore a simple T-shirt and a pair of basketball shorts.

"Merry Christmas," El said with a grin. She got up and hugged Robin and added, "Well, we made it."

"Almost," Robin said, glancing around for her mother, but she hadn't arrived yet.

Christmas had fallen on a Sunday this year, but they'd decided to have their own festivities at the holiday house. Anyone who wanted to go to church could, and Robin simply wanted to be with the people she loved most and create the memories that she could take with her into the future, and that was right here at the holiday house. No sermon needed.

She and Duke emptied the coffee into their mugs, and Robin set a new pot to brew as more and more people emerged from their suites and rooms.

She didn't see Jamie or Mandie. She wondered if she'd have to go wake her girls to come open presents. What a difference from when they had been little and come climbing into bed before six a.m., so excited that Santa had come. Robin loved every stage of her children's lives, including this new one where they were independent, did a lot on their own, and still got excited about Christmas—just at a later hour.

An excited squeal lifted into the air from the living room, and Robin looked over to where Asher stood next to the pile of presents. AJ and Matt watched him with such fondness, even as AJ gently corrected him that he couldn't pick up the presents and start opening them right then. He could say some things that Robin could understand, but right now, he babbled something unintelligible, probably due to his excitement.

Robin took her cup of coffee into the living room and pulled a kitchen chair over near the Christmas tree. Since they had so many families celebrating in the Starlight Manor, the gifts seemed to go on in waves out from underneath the pine boughs.

El had asked her to hand them out and try to make sense of the chaos that would be gift-opening on Christmas morning, and Robin had happily said yes.

Later, Jean, Clara, and Laurel and their families would make a waffle breakfast, and then they didn't have anything else planned for the rest of the day.

Robin loved an easygoing, casual Christmas Day

where people could enjoy their gifts, enjoy the weather, and enjoy each other.

"Mom," Charlie said as he came downstairs, and he seemed just like a little boy on Christmas morning. "Did you see it's snowing outside?" He glanced around. "Oh, my mom isn't out here."

"I'm right here," Alice called from the formal dining room, and Robin hadn't known she was there either.

"It's snowing," Charlie said, hurrying that way. "We opened the windows in the bunk room upstairs, and it's *snowing*."

He acted like he'd never seen snow before, but he definitely had, as it snowed in the cove every year, and it definitely snowed in New York City. They didn't get much in the cove, and it didn't stick around for very long due to the more temperate environment of the islands, but it definitely snowed.

Robin got up and moved over to the sliding glass doors and pulled open the curtains so that she could see the snow too. Something magical accompanied snow on Christmas morning, and she smiled as a sense of nostalgia and wonder filled her.

Someone came to stand next to her, and Robin glanced over to her daughter. "Merry Christmas, Mandie," she said softly.

Mandie put her arm around Robin's waist and leaned her head against her shoulder. "Merry Christmas, Mom."

Robin had not asked her a single question about Charlie, though they talked about school and their jobs and how things were going in the city. Both of them had given her some fairly enthusiastic answers in somewhat false voices, but Robin hadn't called them on it.

They'd each only completed half of their second year of college, and they'd been navigating all of the challenges of those classes, jobs, and their deepening relationship. No matter how she sliced it, they both had a lot on their plates, and she wanted them to deal with whatever things they needed to, knowing that Mandie would come to her if she wanted her advice. Since she hadn't, Robin had decided to keep her mouth shut.

It had been one of the hardest things she'd done, though she'd lain in Duke's arms at night and poured out her worries and fears to him. They'd talked through it all, but that didn't mean that Robin had to bring it up with her daughter.

Now, though, she wondered if she could ask a question and get a decently honest answer. So she pressed her ear to the top of Mandie's head, though her daughter stood taller than her, and asked, "Do I need to put a date for your wedding on my calendar? I usually get a lot of calls in January and start scheduling spring and summer weddings, and I'd hate to book someone else when it could be yours."

Mandie straightened, and a sigh slipped between her lips. "I mean, I don't know," she said. "We've talked about marriage, and of course, I want to get married on the beach, or maybe our backyard, or maybe the light-house—I don't know—but here in the cove."

Robin nodded and lifted her coffee mug to her mouth again so she wouldn't ask another question.

"But he hasn't asked me..." She trailed off, her voice becoming a little more uncertain. "And I don't know, maybe it will be another year."

"And that's okay with you?" Robin asked. She personally didn't understand it. Mandie and Charlie already lived together. Why not go ahead and get married? She didn't know what there was to wait for or how a person could possibly be ready for marriage until they did it.

No matter how prepared someone could be, it would never be enough. Marriage didn't work that way. Heck, *life* didn't work that way. And the best part about marriage was that she could figure it out as they went, day by day, situation by situation, in the good times and in the bad.

But Robin simply said, "Okay, well, let me know as soon as you know, would you?"

"Of course, Mom," Mandie said, and she gave her a small smile. "I love him, Mom, and he loves me. We're going to get married."

"Okay," Robin said, and she found the idea didn't bother her nearly as much as it had a few months ago. She certainly couldn't object to people getting married young, as she and Duke hadn't been much older than Mandie and Charlie. She'd fallen for him hard and fast, and her mother certainly hadn't approved of the wedding, though it was because it had happened too fast, not the other way around.

"All right," Duke called, and that made Robin turn away from the gently billowing snow outside. "It's time to open presents." He glanced over to Robin, and she realized that she'd lost track of the time as she'd stood at the window talking to Mandie.

"Yes," she said, raising her voice to be heard above the din, as Asher clapped his hands and bounced on his little boy feet. "It's time to open presents." She set her coffee cup on the dining room table and took up her perch on the chair. "And I know who the first one goes to." She picked up a long rectangular box and said, "Asher."

He looked up at his mom, pure delight on his face.

AJ said, "Go on, go get it," and the little three-year-old came toddling over to her.

Robin handed him the gift, and he took it back over to his parents to open it.

With most people focused on him, Robin quickly handed out several more gifts. As Asher finally unearthed a long white toy semi-truck, he held it up with both hands and yelled, "Truck!" as if he'd just gotten the greatest gift imaginable.

Scattered chuckles and giggles ran through the crowd, and Robin nodded over to Laurel. She started opening her gift, as did Mandie, Jean, Kristin, Julia, and Parker. Since they were older, the gifts got unwrapped much faster, and they each held up what they had gotten.

Mandie, an insulated mug that kept things hot that should be hot, and cold when they should be cold.

Jean, a luxurious skin care kit.

Parker, a wireless gaming headset.

Julia, a gift card to the spa where she liked to get pedicures and massages.

As Kristin held up the sweater that Alice had gotten for her, Robin handed out another round of gifts. Present by present and person by person, they went through everything on and under the tree, only pausing for the small children to open their gifts alone.

It didn't take long, and Robin knew that Matt and AJ had put a little tree in their suite for Asher as well, and that they would have their own private family Christmas together. Maybe they'd already done it; Robin didn't know.

She knew Alice had something planned for her family after breakfast, and she glanced over to her best friend. Alice had been nervous to tell her about it because she wanted Mandie to come...but not Robin.

Robin could still hear herself saying, "Of course, of course," in that super fake voice, because she did feel like she was missing out.

With the last of the presents opened and shown, Laurel, Jean, and Clara got up to move into the kitchen to start breakfast. Duke appeared at her shoulder and handed her another cup of coffee.

"Good job, babe," he said as he swept a kiss along her cheek. "You're staring at Alice pretty hard."

Robin tore her eyes away and got to her feet. She turned into him, and he put his arm around her, further concealing her from the rest of the group.

"We've had Mandie for twenty years," Duke said quietly as they moved into the formal dining room and over to the windows that overlooked the yard. "It's okay to share her."

Robin had not thought of it like that. And of course, Alice would want her son's very serious girlfriend and soon-to-be wife involved in their family traditions as well. She would want Mandie to feel comfortable and accepted. And Robin nodded, grateful for the steady wisdom of Duke.

"Let's go for a walk before breakfast," she said.

"All right," Duke said. "In our pajamas?"

She grinned at him, tipped her head back so that he would kiss her. He did, always able to read her cues so well. "No," she murmured against his mouth. "Let's go get dressed first."

"Maybe we could get undressed and then redressed," he murmured.

Warmth filled Robin as he pulled her against his side, and she laid her head against his chest. "That does sound nice," she murmured, but neither of them moved from their perch at the window quite yet.

Behind them, the bustling activity of Christmas continued with various toy noises, video game sounds, and people talking. But the warmth of the manor enveloped her, and the scent of yeast and bacon filled the air, and the sight of snow and the good feelings of Christmas reminded her of how very, very good her life was.

Chapter Twenty-Six

M andie squeezed Charlie's hand as he led her into Alice and Arthur's suite. A full-size Christmas tree had been set up in the corner, and the couch had been staged across from it to open up the sitting area.

Ginny and Bob had already arrived, and they canoodled on the couch, talking quietly to one another. Arthur had just entered the room ahead of Mandie and Charlie, and he said, "I've got the treats." He set a carton of milk and a plate of cookies on the credenza beneath the TV.

This room didn't have a fireplace like some others, but Alice had hung six stockings from the back of the couch, pinned in place with what looked like giant quilting needles.

As always, she looked like she'd been dressed by the most famous fashion designer in the city, as she wore a pair of navy blue slacks that flowed like warm water around her legs and a Christmas sweater tastefully done in white, with a beautiful Christmas scene on the front in matching blue.

Mandie always felt underdressed in front of Alice, and today especially so, as she and Charlie had not changed out of their pajamas after the group Christmas present exchange and breakfast. Ginny hadn't gotten dressed either, but Bob had, and he glanced up at Charlie and Mandie as they came around the couch.

"Hey, we'll make room," he said, and he scooted over so that Charlie and Mandie could fit onto the couch as well. Since Charlie was tall and lanky and barely had any body fat at all, he didn't take up much room, and Mandie sank into the space between him and Bob and gave Ginny's boyfriend a smile.

"Are you as nervous about this as I am?" Bob murmured.

Mandie leaned her head closer to his so she could hear him. "A little," she admitted.

"Has she ever done this before?" Bob asked.

Mandie shook her head. "No."

"It's going to be fine," Ginny said, a little bit of bite in her voice. She'd obviously told Bob this before. "It's a few gifts and some cookies."

"We already did a few gifts and a whole meal," Bob said, articulating how Mandie felt as well.

"She just wants something for us," Ginny said. "Mom's always done this."

"She's right," Charlie said, his voice quiet as Arthur and Alice spoke about something only a few feet away. "My dad would sometimes only be home on Christmas for a couple of hours, and Mom would then do something just with us after he left."

Mandie reached over and took his hand in hers. Charlie hadn't admitted it, but he carried a lot of anger and resentment toward his dad that he would need to eventually work through. They talked a little bit about it, and he'd said that his mom had put him in therapy after the divorce, and he had enjoyed speaking with a counselor.

Mandie had told him he should go again, but he'd shaken his head and said, "I can't afford it."

She'd mentioned that his mom would pay for it, and Charlie had simply said, "I don't want my mom to be paying for anything."

She hadn't brought it up again, and she hadn't realized that big family gatherings and special occasions probably triggered him a little bit, bringing forward memories that weren't so great on Christmas Eve and Christmas morning, New Year's Eve, and birthdays.

In this moment, she wished they had their own room so that she could lay in his arms and reassure him that he had plenty of people who loved him and would never leave him, even if one of them wasn't his father.

"All right," Alice said, finally turning toward them. "Did you guys get everything you wanted for Christmas?"

She smiled in that sophisticated, beautiful way she had, and Mandie smiled back at her.

"I didn't," Ginny said good-naturedly. "Unless you've got a suitcase of cash over there." She laughed, and Charlie joined her. Alice did too, and this must be some sort of inside joke that Mandie, Bob, and Arthur didn't know, because the three of them simply smiled and looked at the Keltons that they loved.

Ginny hadn't said that Bob had told her that he loved her. She hadn't said very much about the two of them getting married, but Mandie could see the adoration playing on Bob's face.

He'd fallen for Ginny quickly and hard, and he was probably simply waiting for her to dictate the next step of the relationship. Mandie realized then and there that she was doing the same thing with Charlie, and she decided that after this was done, she would ask him about getting married again.

"I just want my grades to come in," Charlie said. "Have you got that wrapped up under the tree?"

Alice giggled and shook her head. "No. What other impossible gifts do you guys want from me?"

Mandie realized that this was their game, and she looked over to Bob, who wore confusion plainly on his face. "I'll take my degree now," she said.

Alice nodded and said, "I bet you would."

"Oh, is that what we're doing?" Bob asked, finally cluing in. "Then I'd like my own law firm set up and full of paying clients."

"That's a good one," Arthur said. "I think I'm going to be the noble one and say..." He rooted around through some presents. "I think we've got world peace under here somewhere."

They all twittered again, and Mandie did enjoy being here in this smaller core family that was so much like hers and yet so different.

After this, they'd be leaving The Starlight Manor and going to Alice's dad's house for the afternoon, where they would be fed dinner before they returned here, and excitement stole through Mandie because it was fun to experience a different kind of Christmas with Charlie's family.

"Okay," Alice said, and she bent down and picked up a couple of gifts. "It's not much, and I don't want it to be a big deal, but Arthur and I got each of you something, and we wanted to give it to you here, privately."

All four gifts were identical—white boxes with red bows tied around them—and Alice could hold all four of them in both hands. Curiosity pricked at Mandie, because what could she possibly get for Bob that Mandie would also want?

Charlie leaned over the arm of the couch as Alice started handing out the gifts, and he lifted the plastic sack that he'd brought in.

"Here, Mom," he said, as Mandie took her gift. Charlie took his next and then passed over the plastic bag. They'd gotten gifts for his mom, Arthur, Ginny, and Bob as well, and Alice passed those out.

Ginny looked at Bob and asked, "What did we do with those candy bars?"

He bent over and picked them up from his feet. "They're right here," and they had giant king-sized candy bars for every person.

"Thank you," Mandie said as she took one with toffee in it. "I love these."

"Peanuts for me," Charlie said, as he did love a good chocolate-covered nut.

Mandie then looked down the row of people on the couch to decide if she should open her gift from Alice and Arthur or not.

"Go on," Alice said, and Mandie untied the bow and lifted the lid.

A certificate sat there that said *One Month of Free Rent*. Mandie blinked, sure this couldn't be true. An apartment in the city—even as small as hers, Charlie's, and Ginny's—was a lot of money. Alice was going to pay the rent for a full month?

"Thanks, Mom," Charlie said, and she glanced over to his box. He had the same certificate lying there.

Then Ginny got to her feet and flew into her mother's arms and said, "Thank you, Mom," in a genuine, sincere voice.

Mandie knew they'd just been given three months of free rent in the city, and that would take them almost through the end of their sophomore year.

"Wow. Thank you, Alice," Bob said, and Mandie glanced at his box to find that he had a Visa gift card sitting there. "This is amazing." He got to his feet and hugged both Alice and Arthur together, and Mandie got up to do the same thing.

When Bob stepped back, she took their place, and she said, "Thank you so much."

Alice held her tight with one arm, and Arthur said, "Of course, sweetie, and you let us know if there's anything else you need."

She nodded, suddenly emotional. Her parents would never be able to do anything like this. That didn't mean they loved her or Charlie any less; it simply meant they didn't have as much expendable income.

Charlie hugged his mom and stepdad as well. And then Alice and Arthur opened their two gifts from their kids, making a big fuss about them.

"I love this scent," Alice said about the candle set Mandie and Charlie had found in the clearance section of the home goods store. She leaned over and sniffed it and everything. "Thank you."

She peered into the bag and pulled out the eye mask. "Oh, this is one of those you can put herbs in."

"It comes with them," Mandie said, hoping Alice liked lavender-scented things. "It's got gingko-biloba and this Thai herb." She looked over to Charlie, aware her eyes had gotten too round. "What was the name of it?"

He grinned and her and lifted her hand to his lips. "I have no idea. You think I'm going to remember that?"

"You're going to pharmacy school," Ginny said.

"You should know what reduces puffiness around the eyes."

"I'm not in pharmacy school," Charlie shot back.

"My eyes are puffy?" Alice asked. She turned to Arthur and blinked at him. "Tell me the truth."

Arthur looked like he'd been hit with a brick, and this conversation had spiraled fast. "Your eyes are not puffy," he said dutifully, and that made Mandie smile too.

She snapped her fingers, and her memory fired at her. "Hibiscus," she said. "It's got that in it too."

Alice looked down at the care kit she'd been given, then lifted her eyes to Mandie's. "Thank you." She came over and pressed a kiss to Mandie's forehead. "It's very thoughtful."

"Your turn, Arthur," Bob said, and Arthur pulled the paper off the box Mandie had wrapped. "It's from all of us."

"We pooled our money," Ginny added.

Arthur lifted the lid on the box and laughed as he pulled out a handsome charcoal-gray sweater vest. "I love sweater vests," he practically yelled.

Alice grinned and grinned at him, and he swept a kiss across her cheek made mostly of a smile. "He sure does. Says they make him look like he knows what he's talking about when he has meetings with parents."

They all laughed, and Arthur moved down the row of them sitting on the couch, and Mandie leaned into his quick squeeze before he moved on to Bob.

With the presents now open, Mandie wasn't sure what would happen next. She glanced over to Charlie, but he gave no indication that he'd get up and leave. They didn't have anywhere to go anyway.

Alice looked at him too, and Mandie got the distinct feeling that they'd had a conversation without her. Of course they had. They talked often, the same way Mandie spoke to her parents, especially her mother.

Charlie cleared his throat, and he did scoot to the edge of the couch and get up. "There's one more thing." He went around to the back of the Christmas tree and pulled something from the branches.

He faced them all again, and Mandie knew someone had moved on her left side. She somehow knew without looking that Ginny was recording, and that meant—

"Mandie," Charlie said, and he cleared his throat again. His face started to turn a deeper shade of red, and he glanced over to his mom. She gave him an encouraging nod and subtly pointed at the ground. So subtle, Mandie almost didn't see it.

She couldn't see anything but that deep, dark blue velvet box in Charlie's hand.

He dropped to his knees, and Mandie tracked him. "I'm in love with you," he said quietly, earnestly, using the voice he did when he told the same thing as they made love.

"I sort of freaked out this month on you, and it's because I spent every last dime I have on this ring." He opened the box to reveal the diamond. "I don't really want to drop out of school. I just...panicked for a minute."

He swallowed, and Mandie did too. The diamond wasn't enormous or elaborate. It was a round cut on a white gold band, and it screamed her name.

"I don't want you to lose the best wedding planner in the cove." He grinned at her. "And I want to be your husband so dang bad, so I figured I better ask you: Will you marry me?"

Tears rushed into Mandie's eyes, and she wasn't sure why. Her heart pounded and thrashed against her breastbone, and finally, she figured out how to make her head nod.

A tear splashed down her cheek, and she quickly wiped it away. "Yes," she said, her voice throaty and cracked. She cleared it and said, "Yes, I'll marry you."

Alice started to clap, and Arthur whistled through his teeth. Bob said, "All right!" like he was ready to attend the world's biggest and best event.

Charlie slid the ring on Mandie's finger, cradling her hand in both of his while they both looked at the sparkling diamond. Then he raised his eyes to hers, and she moved her hands to hold his face as he leaned in and kissed her.

So many things made more sense now, and she sincerely hoped Ginny had stopped recording. She pulled away so they wouldn't have a scandalous kiss on the video she wanted to show her parents as soon as possible.

"I hope your mom won't be too upset," Charlie whispered, leaning his forehead against hers.

"You could've told me about the ring."

"Then it wouldn't have been a surprise." He pulled away, his eyes searching hers. "I'm going to freak out about many more things in our lives. If you don't want that, you should—" He swallowed again, a hard edge entering his gaze.

"I can handle it." She grinned at him. "I can handle you, because you handle me."

He grinned, kissed her again, and then got to his feet. "Come on," he said, lacing his fingers through hers. "Let's go tell your mom and dad."

Chapter Twenty-Seven

K risten pulled her sweater tighter around her as she paused on the front steps of The Starlight Manor. She gazed into the horizon, noting that almost all of the grass had been covered by snow. She'd meant to bring her camera outside with her that morning, but in the madness of getting all of her presents and things packed up and out of the house, she'd forgotten it.

Maybe Rueben would snap a few for her. She watched the sun rise over the top of the distant trees. He'd have Heidi with him, and Kristen could entertain her while he took the pictures. She had plenty of wall space that would benefit from a framed picture of the sun rising over Five Island Cove, the snow glistening in the light, the trees black against the orange and pink sky.

The snap of a suitcase handle made her turn, and AJ paused as well, a grin on her face. "Taking pictures again?"

"Just with my eyes," she said. "I forgot my camera."

"Well, get moving," AJ said. "You're going to miss it."

"Maybe," Kristen said, and she stayed right where she stood. She'd seen so many sunrises in her life, but each one brought a new measure of joy. She liked to stand back and watch the water too, and she couldn't imagine living anywhere but Five Island Cove.

Kristen hugged AJ tight and said, "Text me when you guys get home." She stepped back and smiled at the woman she'd been helping and guiding for so long.

"I will," AJ said with a smile. She sighed and looked up into the sky as Matt came outside with his arms full of their bags, the car seat, and their little boy. "I'm just glad the ferries are running." She bent down and picked up her suitcase. "Ready, guys?"

"So ready," Matt said, and he paused to kiss Kristen's cheek. "I'll come look at your dishwasher this week."

Kristen had forgotten she'd asked him to do that. "Okay," she said, a glimmer of hope in her life now. And how pathetic was that? But she'd be returning to an empty condo, and she'd so enjoyed the bustling atmosphere of The Starlight Manor, electrical mishaps and all.

AJ and Matt's RideShare left, and not ten seconds later, another car pulled up. The front door opened, and this time, Kelli herded her teenager outside. "Keep going, sweetie," she said. "The car should be here."

Chatter and noise came from inside the house, and

Kelli added, "I didn't see Kristen inside, and I want to tell her goodbye."

"I'm out here, dear." She took a few steps so Kelli would be able to see her, and she smiled as relief cascaded over Kelli's features. She carried Daphne in her arms and a bag swung over her forearm. She still moved swiftly into Kristen's arms and hugged her tightly.

"I'm going to miss you," she said.

"I'll come to Pearl this week," Kristen said, because she could, and because Kelli needed her to. She sniffled into Kristen's chest, then pulled away. She wiped her face with her free hand while Kristen kissed Daphne, and then took a few steps to hug Parker too.

"You be good for your mom," Kristen said. "And Shad too."

"I will," Parker said.

"AJ's talking about a New Year's Eve party at her house," Kelli said. "Watch for a text."

"I will," Kristen said, giving Kelli the best smile she could. Shad came outside, and they all started toward the waiting car.

El and Robin would likely be the last to leave, and Kristen should probably call a car too. They had families, and she couldn't just assume she could add herself to one of their parties. She cast the morning sun one more look before she went back inside.

Alice had just arrived downstairs with her suitcase, and Arthur reached for the handle. "I'll take these out front."

"I'll get coffee." Alice had just started to turn when she saw Kristen. She detoured over to her and embraced her. "When are you going?"

"I don't have a car yet," Kristen said.

"You could share with us." Alice stepped back and beamed at Kristen. "We're going to Diamond, same as you. We can share the whole way home."

"Our car will be here in fifteen minutes," Arthur said as he returned to the foyer.

"I'm already packed," Kristen said. "I'll go get my bag."

"I'll get it," Arthur said good-naturedly. "You go say goodbye to everyone."

Kirsten wasn't sure why it felt like her girls were leaving the cove for good, but it did.

She loved these women so much, and their children, and their husbands, and their extended families. She loved Alice's father and stepmother, and Robin's mother, and Eloise's girls. They all seemed like they belonged to her, and she pulled in a long breath to try to deal with all of the emotions running through her.

She went with Alice into the kitchen, where others had also gathered with their luggage to say goodbye. She joined the fray and hugged Laurel, Julia, and El.

"You are a queen for organizing all of this," she said to El. "Thank you so much for all you've done this Christmas."

El nodded and wiped her eyes. "Of course," she said, her voice mildly strained.

"It's going to be really quiet in my condo," Kristen said. "Maybe you could come over for dinner and bring everyone."

El laughed and swiped at her face again. "I'm sure Aaron would love that, and I know the girls would."

"Kristen," Aaron said, and she looked over to find the tall, athletic man she'd once known as a little boy. "Do you need a ride to the ferry?"

"I'm going with Alice," she said. "But thank you."

"You're going with Alice?" Robin stepped into her arms and held her tightly.

"I'm sure we'll all be on the same ferry," Kristen said. "If you're leaving in the next several minutes."

"I don't know when we're going." Robin stepped back and drew in a deep breath. The news of her Mandie and Charlie's engagement had swept through the manor like wildfire, and Robin had taken it really well in Kristen's opinion.

She'd laughed and cried and hugged Mandie, and then they'd sat down together to get a date on the calendar.

"Grams, we're going."

Kristen stepped back to hug her granddaughter, and she grinned as Lena clutched her back. "Text me when you get home, okay, dear?"

"Okay," Lena said, and she turned toward the front door. Clara paused in front of Kristen, and she reached out and took both of her hands.

"We'll see you soon," Clara promised. "We're

coming to Diamond on Thursday. We have that appointment with the doctor about Lena."

"Great," Kristen said. "I'll make that pumpkin curry soup for lunch."

"Thanks, Mom." Clara hugged her quickly and quietly followed her daughter out of the living room.

Jean and Reuben had left first, before the crowd, so they could get Heidi home and hopefully back to sleep. Maddy and Ben had also left, saying they had a lot of things to do today, because Ben had to report to the Coast Guard and Maddy had to get to the restaurant on Diamond.

"Our car is here, my love." Liam put his arm around Julia and pressed a kiss to her forehead. "You ready?"

"I suppose." Julia sighed like she didn't want to leave the holiday house, and Kristen understood the feeling.

"Are you ready?" Alice asked, glancing back toward the foyer.

"Yes," Kristen said, clearing her throat. "I'm ready."

"Bye, Kristen," Robin called, and that got several more people to echo the same thing. Warmth filled her, and she grinned and grinned as she waved and then turned to go into the foyer.

She put one foot in front of the other, and before she knew it, she'd slid into the backseat of the RideShare and was on her way back to Diamond Island.

KRISTEN MIXED THE INGREDIENTS FOR HER cornbread cookies, the New Year's morning silence nearly drowning her in her condo. She'd been home for almost a week, and while she'd gone out to Pearl to see Kelli and Daphne, as promised, and she'd gone walking with AJ and Jean once, she had to find new ways to stave off the loneliness.

And today, she would finish these cookies and take them around to everyone on Diamond, then get up to Sanctuary Island tomorrow, where she could see El and Tessa.

So she measured and stirred, her thoughts roaming to all of her girls and their families. She'd gone to AJ's New Year's Eve party for a couple of hours last night, but she couldn't stay up until midnight anymore. She hadn't for years, in fact.

She'd just scooped the first balls of cornbread cookies and slid them in the oven when her phone chimed. She closed the oven door and straightened, a moan coming from her mouth she didn't have to stifle. There wasn't anyone here to ask her if she was okay, or what hurt, and as Kristen had passed eighty, everything hurt.

She picked up her phone and saw Eloise had texted. *Happy New Year, everyone! I want to do a Texting Tell-All, and I'll go first.*

Kristen picked up the phone to open it even as it chimed again. Eloise had not given her Tell-All in the first text, but in the one that had just arrived.

I'm back at the inn, and it's just as crazy and busy

and stressful as before. *I was hoping a break would help me keep going, but I've decided what I need is a permanent break. I'm going to meet with a commercial real estate agent next week, and I'm going to list the Cliffside Inn for sale.*

The air whooshed out of Kristen's lungs. "She's going to sell the inn." She'd known El was tired, overworked, and worried about the girls. She was still surprised at this news.

She expected questions, but the Tell-All dictated no follow-up questions, and Alice's name popped up on the screen, in the Tell-All thread.

I'm terrified that both of my children are getting married this year. BTW, Ginny and Bob got engaged last night, and they've already set a date for October.

Shock waves moved through Kristen, mostly because she wished she could be with Alice face-to-face in this moment. She knew Alice was worried about Ginny's fast relationship with Bob.

Ben and I found a house on Diamond and our realtor is putting in an offer tomorrow! Maddy included a smiley face emoji with it, and Kristen found the same gesture forming on her face.

Parker told me he doesn't want to go to Jersey to see his dad this summer, Kelli said. *I honestly don't know what to think about it.*

Wow, Robin said. *That's a big one, El, selling the inn. And Kelli? I wish I could help.*

I'm sure you can, Kelli said. *I'd love some advice.*

Wednesday lunch next week, Alice said. *We can do a follow-up on this Texting Tell-All.*

I'll chime in and say I have nothing big, AJ said. *I finally feel settled into my new life as a wife and mother living in Five Island Cove.*

Tears pressed into Kristen's eyes, because AJ had been fighting that battle for years now. She'd given up a lot when she'd left behind the bylines and her journalistic life.

Mine is super easy too, Jean said. *We feel settled enough with Heidi that we're getting a kitten!* She sent a picture of the cutest gray and white cat, and Kristen had to lower her phone and look out the window as she tried to contain her tears.

Congrats to all who've found themselves this past year, Clara said. *We just got done doing a planning session with Lena, and you'll all die at what she said.*

Kristen's heartbeat pounded in the back of her throat, and she wondered what she'd put on this text string. She'd have to type up something, but for now, she waited anxiously for Clara's next text.

She wants to take some budgeting classes and some cooking classes so she can move into that assisted living facility on the south side of Diamond and...live by herself.

"Oh, my goodness." Tears spilled down Kristen's face, because she'd never thought Lena would be able to live on her own. And Scott and Clara had sacrificed so much for their only daughter. She couldn't even imagine what they'd do without her just down the hall from them.

That's amazing, Laurel said, as another text came in from Clara.

This one had come only to Kristen, and it said, *Mom, Lena would like to do the cooking classes with you. Is that a possibility?*

Of course, dear, she quickly sent back.

I don't have much either, Laurel said. *Paul and I have an appointment in a couple of weeks to learn the gender of our baby. I guess that's it.*

I'm worried I won't be able to pull off three amazing weddings this year, Robin said.

"Three?" Kristen asked herself and the silent solitude of her condo.

You will, Julia said. *Because I'm counting on my June wedding with Liam to be the event of the summer.* A picture started to generate after that, and soon enough, a crisp photograph of Julia's hand—her left hand—with a diamond ring on her fourth finger shone from Kristen's screen.

The texting slowed a little, and then Tessa said, *By my count, I'm not quite last. Thank goodness. You guys are such fast texters. But Dave found a place, so he's not going to be moving in with me. I'm...happier about it than I probably should be, but there you go.*

She didn't say more, and Kristen went back through the messages to see who else hadn't gone yet. When El finally texted, *Kristen?* she realized they were all waiting for her Tell-All. She still wasn't sure what she should say, and to her great relief, Robin sent another message.

Really quick, Charlie just texted to say he got an A in his molecular chemistry class that he was sure he'd fail!

Congratulations and celebratory texts poured in then, including one from Kristen.

So now everyone knew she had her phone and that it worked.

And that she'd seen this text string.

She typed quickly, her old fingers moving over her screen as she tapped out, *My life is full, and I love all of you so much. I love hearing your news, both good and bad, and celebrating with you and commiserating alongside you too.*

Kristen could say more, and because it was a Tell-All, and no one would judge her, she added, *If I'm being super honest, my biggest trial right now is loneliness. It's ever-present, and I fight it the best way I know how. So you've been warned: Everyone will have cornbread cookies either today or tomorrow.*

That made her smile—and the timer sounded on the very cookies she'd deliver to her loved ones, so she got up to go take them out before they got too crisp.

Chapter Twenty-Eight

Eloise stood in the foyer of the Cliffside Inn, her heart beating out a steady rhythm. Aaron threaded his fingers through hers and squeezed, and she looked up at him. He wore a kind smile, and a lot of the stress that had been in his face for the past few months had disappeared.

She knew he loved his job, but his job brought a lot of stress into their lives. He dealt with all of the islands in the cove, and they were each different and unique, with seemingly their own cultures and types of problems.

While she and Aaron had talked about her selling the inn, and what she'd do once it was gone, they hadn't had a discussion about him retiring from the force. She wondered if he'd like to, but she knew he'd never bring it up. After all, he had a very good job that he enjoyed, and he'd be fifty next month. He had plenty of years left in him to keep the peace in Five Island Cove.

She might drown under the politics, but Aaron didn't seem to mind them.

Either way, Eloise would wait until the inn sold, and then they'd have the conversation. After all, they'd have a huge influx of cash, and they didn't need two salaries to support their family.

"The photographer is here," Aaron said, and Eloise turned toward the door. A tall, thin man with a camera looped around his neck came into the inn right behind the realtor.

"Morning, Eloise," Prue said. "This is Sam. He'll be taking pictures for the listing and the brochure."

"Nice to meet you, Sam," Eloise said, her experience with people shining through. She could pretend when she needed to, that was for sure. "Hey, Prue." She hugged the realtor who'd been walking her through everything for the past couple of weeks since Eloise had decided to sell the inn.

She turned as her mother joined them. "This is my mother, Dawn." She smiled at her mom and then around at everyone. "We all want to walk through it with you," she said. "If that's okay."

"Totally fine," Prue said, taking the extra people in stride.

Eloise had gone to high school with Prue, and she'd started a new career as a realtor only a couple of years ago. She was one of the only commercial real estate agents in the cove, and Eloise liked how personable she was and how quickly she responded to messages and questions.

"All right." Prue gestured toward the lobby, which Eloise and Aaron had spent the past thirty minutes arranging with the water and lemonade they normally served during check-in. Eloise had baked the cookies last night, but they'd still look fresh in the pictures.

"This inn has been a desirable piece of property for years," Prue said. "I don't think it'll stay on the market for long."

Eloise swallowed, because she'd gotten offers from bigger hotel chains and conglomerates, and she told herself—not for the first time—that it wasn't up to her what happened to the inn.

She'd decided to sell it, plain and simple, and she didn't get to dictate what the new owner did with it.

She'd be free from it, which was what she wanted.

Prue continued to direct Sam what to shoot, and he snapped and clicked so often the sound grated on her nerves. "How many square feet?"

"Twenty-four thousand," Eloise answered. "Six guest rooms."

And the thought of being free from it made her heart beat out a new song. She reached for Aaron's hand and squeezed it as they led the way into the kitchen, then the laundry facilities, as they toured the pool, and as she unlocked the one-bedroom apartment attached to the back of the inn, where her day manager lived.

"And all the guest rooms are upstairs," Eloise said. "On the second and third floors."

"Elevator works," Prue said as it chimed its arrival. They all crowded on, and Eloise checked the time. She had to leave by eleven-twenty to get to the ferry on time, so she could make it to the Glass Dolphin for the one o'clock Wednesday luncheon.

Her heart pumped out a couple of extra beats as she thought about today's luncheon, because everyone knew about today's walk-through with the realtor and photographer. Eloise didn't usually sit in the spotlight, and surely everyone would exclaim over Alice's twins getting engaged within a week of one another.

They'd all go over how Robin could make three weddings completely different this year. And of course, Kelli had asked for advice too.

So Eloise might not have to say very much at all.

She almost scoffed out loud at the idea. Of course she'd have to tell them everything. She'd fought hard to take ownership of the Cliffside Inn several years ago, and it felt surreal and almost like someone outside of herself had made the decision to sell it.

"Eloise," Prue said, and she clued into the fact that they'd entered the largest guest room. "This looks amazing. The baseboards came out well."

Prue had come through the week after Christmas and made a list of things that needed to be repaired, replaced, or redone, and Eloise had been working harder than ever around the inn. Her mother had brought the girls, and they'd all pitched in before school had started up again in the New Year.

Eloise had painstakingly cleaned and straightened every inch of the common areas of inn over the past week, and the place looked spectacular. She was a bit of a neat-freak anyway, but she'd taken it up a notch for this. The housekeeping crew did a nice job in the guest rooms, and she'd asked them to get them done in time for today's photography.

"Do you have a price in mind?" Prue asked as she pulled back the heavier drapes in the suite.

"I have no idea what something like this would sell for." She glanced at her husband, and Aaron nodded. They'd had this discussion a few times, and El was determined not to be greedy. While she'd poured money into it to keep it updated and running, she wanted it to go to someone who would care for it and the guests that came to stay there.

"Whatever fair market value is." She didn't need a huge, insane payday, though the inn was probably worth a few million dollars. She glanced over to her mother, who gazed around the room with a fond look on her face.

"You okay, Mom?" Eloise asked.

Her mother looked at her. "Yes," she said. "Just...remembering things I'd forgotten." She flashed a quick smile, but it looked a bit painful to Eloise. So much had gone on inside the walls of this inn, and that had been the demise of Eloise's parents' marriage, though she hadn't known that at the time.

"I'll leave you guys to go through the rooms," she said. The inn suddenly felt too suffocating for her to be trapped inside.

"Babe?" Aaron's fingers around hers tightened.

"I—We don't need to be here."

"I'll go through with them," her mom said, and she gave Eloise a much brighter smile.

"Thanks, Mom." Eloise headed out of the room and down the hall. The carpet needed to replaced out here, but big projects like that would cost too much and would most likely not impact the sale of the inn that much.

At least according to Prue.

So Eloise hadn't replaced the carpet. Such a thing would take a few weeks anyway, as the furniture store didn't come to Sanctuary Island every single day, and Eloise would have to pick out the carpet, wait for it to come, and then schedule the installation of it.

She honestly hoped the inn would sell in less time.

Outside, the mid-morning sun shone brightly, the sky a beautiful blue overhead. That didn't mean it was warm, and Eloise shivered in the cool air. She'd grown up right here on Sanctuary Island, and she did love how close it was to Diamond while remaining slower and calmer.

It truly had a small town island feel, and going to the

center island had always brought excitement to Eloise as she'd grown up.

She took in a deep breath, enjoying the hint of salt in the air and the way the oxygen renewed her.

"Tell me what you're thinking," Aaron said.

"I just wanted to breathe for a minute," Eloise said. "I'm not thinking anything."

"Haven't changed your mind?" he asked.

"No." She turned toward him and put her arms around his neck. "I want to be home with the girls in the morning and afternoon. I want to get back to doing things for us instead of for strangers."

She wasn't absolutely certain about her decision, but Eloise had rarely been absolutely certain about anything in her life.

"All right," Prue called as she came down the front steps of the inn. "We got what we need, and I'm going to go back to the office and run some numbers." She arrived in front of Eloise and gave her a light hug. "I'll call you later this afternoon."

"Sounds great," Eloise said. "Thank you so much, Prue."

"We'll get this sold, El." She smiled in that shark-like way she had, and then she headed to her sporty little car.

"Well," Aaron said. "I think that went well."

"I do too." She turned to him, and she grinned at him and then her mom. She linked her arm through her mother's and asked, "You sure you don't want to come to lunch with me?"

er mom said, and Eloise
hadn't truly expected her to. She'd come to a few things
at the holiday house, and Eloise's mind spun forward
another ten months, when she could begin looking for
another huge vacation rental where they could all spend
Christmas together.

And this time, she'd actually have the time to plan it
without feeling like she might lose her sanity.

"Then get a ride with us," Eloise said. "We'll drop
you at home on our way to the ferry."

"Now that, I'll do," she said with a smile that didn't
stay as long as Eloise would've liked.

"Mom," she said. "Selling the inn is okay, right?"

"It's yours, El."

"I know, but." She took a breath, desperate for reassurance that her actions were okay. "It was yours for a
long time too." She cut a look over to Aaron, who kept
his head low, his expression unreadable.

"It hasn't been mine—nor have I wanted it to be
mine—for a long time now," her mom said. "Maybe it is
time we let it go."

"Yeah," Eloise said, as she'd already made the decision to do just that. A bit of panic descended on her, and
then Aaron called for a ride, and by the time she slid into
the backseat with her mother, she'd breathed in and out
a few times, and the confusion in her mind had cleared.

And as the car moved away from the Cliffside Inn,
the weight of it became less and less and less. They

dropped off her mother, and Eloise said, "I'll call you later," before the car continued to the ferry station.

Once there, Eloise once again felt like she'd made the right decision for herself, for Aaron, and for Billie and Grace.

She and Aaron boarded the ferry back to Diamond Island, where Aaron would head to the police station for the afternoon, and Eloise would head to the Glass Dolphin for her friend luncheon. She normally didn't stay outside in the winter wind, but she did today, and she let it whip through her hair as the ferry cut through the water.

Aaron stood at her side, and she leaned against his strong shoulder. "I have the best life," she said.

She did, and she couldn't wait to spend the rest of it with her husband, her girls, and her friends.

READ ON FOR THE FIRST 2 CHAPTERS OF **THE HAMPTON HOUSE**, a brand new women's fiction novel that follows Mandie Grover 5 years in the future as she works with a prestigious historical preservation and reconstruction firm that restores and conserves abandoned mansions up and down the Eastern Seaboard.

Learn more about it and preorder by scanning the QR code below:

A Note from Jessie

What an amazing time I've had with the women in Five Island Cove! I sincerely hope you've found a place to belong among Alice, Robin, Eloise, Kelli, and AJ. I definitely identified with each of them at different times over the past eleven books.

I love Laurel and Jean too, with their quieter personalities. Kristen and Clara rounded out our Five Island Cove residents, and then I brought over my Nantucket Point ladies too. After the mysteries and events they'd been through, they all needed a fresh start, and there's no better place to do that than Five Island Cove.

I always feel like I'm visiting old friends when I come here.

So, while I have more ideas for this series, I've also been gnawing on the idea for another book. As I wrote this one, and realized so much of the focus was on Mandie Grover, that book came alive in my head.

She'll be a central figure in *The Hampton House*, the next book I'm going to release. It'll be set five or six years in the future, and you'll get to see her, Charlie, Ginny, Bobby, with some amazing cameos from the ladies in Five Island Cove.

I'm also not saying there won't ever be another Five Island Cove novel. I do have three more covers in this series, and as I've said, I have more ideas for the women here! But I'm going to take a short detour to The Hamptons, and I'll hope you'll come with me!

This new series will focus on Mandie and her team of preservationists who go into abandoned mansions and restore them, clean them up, and get them ready to go back on the market. With Alice's ties to the Hamptons, and Mandie's love of history—and those YouTube videos I'm obsessed with!—I'm super excited to bring you the beginning of a planned trilogy!

You can read more about *The Hampton House* and **then read it by scanning the QR code below.**

Oh, and I've written the first two chapters for you and included them here! Keep reading to get a taste for this next sweet romantic women's fiction novel.

~Jessie

PS. Look at this BEAU-
TIFUL COVER! I'm in love
with it! Read it now by scanning this QR code with your
phone.

Sneak Peek of The Hampton House, Chapter One:

〜✺〜

Mandie Grover took a sip of her coffee, now lukewarm, and told herself to go dump it out and get some water. She'd been experiencing heartburn more often than not on days when she drank the entire cup of coffee she picked up on the way in to work.

She set the to-go cup further from her and reached for the next file in the pile. Part of her job involved looking through prospective properties, and she really enjoyed browsing through the "slush pile."

At tomorrow's meeting, she'd be expected to have her top three choices for the next clean-up project, appropriately labeled CUP in her department, and literal tally marks went up on the white board as the team reviewed their personal favorites.

Mandie had two files in her favorites folder already, but she told herself to have an open mind as she looked at the picture of the mansion on the first page in the new file. "Sixteen thousand square feet," she said. In all honesty, most mega-mansions approached ten thousand square feet, with multiple bedrooms, twice as many bathrooms, and ornate staircases.

Her heartbeat pumped out an extra beat, because she absolutely loved taking the abandoned and restoring it to full glory. That, and her phone had just sparkle-chimed with her husband's assigned ringtone.

Charlie had said, *I'm so going to pass this Pharmacology final*, with a smiley face emoji. *To celebrate, I'm stopping by Lin Chu's for dinner. You want those chickeny noodles?*

She grinned at his use of "chickeny noodles," abandoned the file, and reached for her phone to answer him. *You're finished with the final already?*

Piece of cake, he said, which was Charlie-code for *yes, I'm done and leaving campus*. He only had the one final today, and Charlie hated staying on campus when he could leave it. She'd find him in their one-bedroom apartment when she got home, and he'd most likely time dinner to arrive only a few moments before her.

She and Charlie had been married for almost five years now, and he took very, very good care of her. Mandie loved him with her whole heart, and they'd even started talking about starting a family.

Everything Mandie did required her to go through a minefield of thoughts, and she often felt like she'd made the wrong turn and gotten blown back to the beginning. She envied others who could made quick decisions with confidence, because that had never been Mandie's strong suit.

See you at home, she texted Charlie, and then she got back to the file in front of her. She had to have her choices done for tomorrow, and then she had some appointments to make with a restoration company for an apartment building here in the city that had sustained some flooding damage.

She loved her job at PastForward Restoration Company—PFRC—because they helped people who needed it while showing respect to the history of the dwellings and buildings on the East Coast. Some properties here were hundreds of years old, and Mandie felt a sense of reverence every time she got to go out on a field assignment.

The house in the file intrigued her, and Mandie leafed through the floor plan, read the story behind its abandonment, and embraced the growing excitement within her. She didn't often make her choices based on pictures, checklists, and facts. She relied on her feelings, and she reached for a green sticky note, which she attached to the front of this file.

It got placed in the yes-pile, and Mandie sat back. She loved learning about old things, and since she hadn't been on a field assignment yet this year, she muttered, "So you'll bring it up in your meeting tomorrow."

Part of her yearned to get out of this office building, though she'd once been tickled and thrilled to be riding the subway from Brooklyn, where she and Charlie lived, to the Flat Iron building every day.

She still was, but she definitely felt like some of the glitter that had first coated her job had started to flake off. She stood and stretched her back, glancing across the partition that separated her desk from the one in front of her.

The man who worked there had various camera equipment littering his space, and Flint Rogers looked up. "Hey." He leaned back in his chair. "My eyes are starting to cross."

"Editing your latest film?"

"Final edits," he said. "It's due to production by tomorrow night, and it should air next month."

"That's awesome," Mandie said. By "air," he meant the complete walk-through of one of the abandoned mansions. He led a film crew on field assignments, and they documented everything from the first step the team took onto the property to the final walk-through when a place went up for sale.

If he was lucky, he could work on one project per year, as his post-production was far more detailed than Mandie's. She was involved in field assignments from the first step to the sale, and that was it. She didn't then have hundreds of hours of film to go through and edit into a ninety-minute documentary.

"I can't believe the Maryland Mansion is almost done," she said.

"Hopefully, there will be something new at tomorrow's meeting," Flint said. He wore a neatly trimmed ginger beard, with a full head of hair to match. He was what Mandie would call a "clean hipster," as he showered regularly and didn't wear his hair long. His emerald eyes always seemed to see more than Mandie could, and he wore loafers everywhere he went, even into dangerous, abandoned mansions.

He rolled his khakis at the ankle, always wore skinny jeans and skin-tight tees—if he didn't have on a too-small polo like he did today.

"You think you'll get another assignment right away?" Mandie asked. She leaned against the chest-high divider and took in more of his mess. How he worked in those conditions, she didn't understand. He had yellow legal pads filled with notes and numbers in black pen she couldn't read. But Flint somehow knew what it all meant, and she supposed that was all that mattered.

"Jo Ann's quitting," Flint said. "Which means they'll have to promote up another film lead, and last time Candace needed to do that, it took four months for me to go through multiple interviews, present my portfolios, and get named to the position."

Mandie drew in a breath. "Jo Ann's quitting?"

Flint looked away. "I guess that isn't common knowledge." He looked at Mandie with puppy-dog eyes. "Don't say anything, okay?"

"Yeah, of course not," she said.

Flint stood and stretched his arms above his head, his

tiny shirt pulling up over the waistband of his khakis. "You haven't been out in the field in a while."

"Tell me about it." Mandie rolled her eyes. "I think Candace thought I'd get pregnant, and she didn't want to assign me to anything."

"So you're not pregnant?" Flint grinned at her, and Mandie smiled and shook her head.

"Even if I was," she said. "That shouldn't exclude me from field work. It's pregnancy discrimination."

"Sometimes those old houses are full of mold."

"We have protective gear for that." Mandie folded her arms, becoming more and more determined to get an assignment tomorrow. She'd had enough of desk work, phone calls, and file browsing. She swatted at Flint's chest. "Plus, you tromp through those sites in shoes with barely any soles and no socks. It's a miracle you haven't contracted gangrene or something."

Flint bellowed out a laugh, and Mandie allowed herself to smile. As he quieted, she said, "All right, Flint. Tell me how to get assigned to something tomorrow."

"Step into my office," he said, and Mandie scrambled to go around the dividers and into his disorganization. If it would help her get a field assignment, she could sit among cameras, flash lights, and micro SD cards.

———

"So the final went well?" Mandie asked as she entered her apartment. She tapped the door with her foot to close it, then noticed the candles on the table. She froze. "What anniversary did I forget?"

Charlie turned from the back counter, a plate of orange chicken in his hand. "Final went amazing. There's no anniversary."

"There's something," Mandie said as she got moving again. She'd brought home her top three files so she could obsess over them while she and Charlie watched TV tonight. He sometimes had her quiz him, especially with anything math-related, but he'd already taken that final, so she anticipated an evening filled with some sort of action-adventure movie, and she could easily keep up with the plot while she looked through her files again.

"There's me finishing another year of school," he said. "That's it."

"Only one more," Mandie said as she dropped her bag over the back of the couch and shrugged out of her jacket. Springtime in New York could still be chilly, and Mandie hated nothing more than being cold on the subway.

She wrapped her arms around Charlie once he'd set down the plate of chicken. "You're amazing, baby. One more year of pharmacy school." She kissed him, glad she got to spend her evenings with her best friend in the whole world.

"Tomorrow, they're making assignments for the next major field assignment, and I want it so badly." She whispered the last few words, almost afraid to speak her desires.

"You'll get it," Charlie said. "You haven't been out of the office in a while."

"For six months," she said. "And I know Candace just got a whole heap of new funding. She might even schedule two projects."

"Where are they?"

"My favorite one is in The Hamptons," Mandie said as he pulled out her chair and she sat down. "It would be a dream to work on it. It's close, so I wouldn't have to live on-site. My other two favorites are out of the city. One in South Carolina—a really old plantation that would be pretty cool—and one up in Cape Cod."

"Mm." Charlie sat down too. He dished up some of her chickeny noodles, and Mandie simply watched him.

"Did you hear about the internship?"

"Another interview next week," he said casually, but Mandie knew he hated the multiple interview process. *Honestly*, he'd said. *If they don't know by now, I don't know what else to do to win them over.*

She smiled at him. "So we'll both have amazing news by this time next week."

"You'll have yours tomorrow." He grinned at her and took orange chicken and ham fried rice for himself.

"What if I don't get it?" Mandie let her vulnerability show. Only for him, and Charlie heard her and looked right at her. "She's been passing me over for some reason, and I just—what if I've gotten my hopes up and I don't get it?"

"You're going to get it."

She sighed, because frustration frothed through her. "Thank you, baby." She did like his confidence in her, but they'd been together long enough to see that sometimes confidence didn't always equate to getting what they wanted.

He hadn't gotten into the Pharm.D. program at Rutgers, for example. He'd had to settle for his second choice of St. John's, and while he loved his program there now, Charlie had definitely been disappointed.

"And if you don't," he said. "I'll have mint chocolate chip ice cream here tomorrow night, and we'll go away for the weekend. Go see your mom and dad in the cove." He raised his eyebrows. "Okay? It won't be the end of the world."

"It'll just feel like it," she said miserably.

"Hey, let's be positive," he said. "You've got a strong case for getting assigned, and they've picked your top choice the last four times."

"Yeah." Mandie twirled up some noodles and stuck them in her mouth. Salty, savory deliciousness moved through her. "Mm."

Charlie grinned at her, and suddenly everything was okay.

"And hey," she said. "If I do get it, I know I won't have to work with The Bulldozer."

Charlie choked on his chicken as he started to laugh. Mandie smiled too, though she truly didn't like working with Suzette Paxman. She'd been nicknamed The Bulldozer by everyone in the office, because she rammed through old houses like one. She held a degree in Anthropology, and she acted like she was the only human being alive who did.

In some cases, working with her meant Mandie didn't have to get her hands and feet as dirty, as Suzie wasn't afraid of anything. She'd go into any room, any broken-down pool house, over any surface, to get the footage and information they needed.

Every team had a bulldozer, actually, but none of the other employees at PastForward carried the nickname the way Suzie did.

She giggled with Charlie, because suddenly everything felt lighter. "I'm going to get it," she said, mustering up all the optimism she could. "And I'm going to have the best team ever, and it'll be the house in The Hamptons, and when we go home to Five Island Cove this weekend, it'll be to celebrate my new field assignment."

"There you go." Her husband beamed at her, and Mandie reached over and covered his hand with hers.

"Should I really get us tickets for the Steamer?" she asked.

He nodded. "Yeah, my mom would like it too. She'll take us to lunch to celebrate another semester done."

"Free food," Mandie mused. "I see how you are."

"Hey, I never say no to free food." Charlie grinned, and Mandie did too. She suddenly had so much to look forward to in the next few days, and her stomach flipped over tomorrow morning's meeting.

She just had to get a field assignment. She simply had to.

Sneak Peek of The Hampton House, Chapter Two:

~∾~

Alicia Halverson stepped onto the elevator ahead of Mandie, and when she turned, she gave the other woman a look that spoke volumes. Thankfully, Mandie could understand looks where words weren't spoken, and she edged behind a tall African American man to position herself closer to Alicia.

"What have you got?" she whispered on the third floor, when half the people in the elevator exited. "Lish, don't hold out on me. I'm here an hour early to go over files I have memorized."

"Please." Alicia half-scoffed and half-laughed. "You're here early so you can pace in the bathroom and pitch yourself to your reflection."

Mandie's shoulder shivered back and forth, her way of conceding to Alicia without words. Alicia laughed, because she knew Mandie so well. She reminded her of her younger sister, and a powerful wave of missing rolled through Alicia completely unbidden.

"My thumbs are aching from how much I texted last night," Alicia said as the elevator struggled to get moving again.

"It better have been with Michael." Mandie sighed, and Alicia felt her frustration. She hadn't been assigned a field trip in months either, and once Mandie had texted last night, Alicia had taken it upon herself to figure out how to get the two of them assigned to whatever went up on the board today at PastForward.

"Michael, I wish." Alicia rolled her neck, and the day hadn't even started yet.

"He's going to ask you out. You just need to keep stopping by for those chocolate croissants."

"Yeah, and then I have to run fifty miles on the tread-mill." Alicia shook her head now, the ends of her long, dark hair brushing against her elbows. She'd braided into pigtails today in an attempt to make herself look younger. Candace seemed to discriminate on any grounds she could, and only she knew what those were.

Alicia and Mandie had brainstormed that they changed all the time too, and it could be because Alicia left her food in the microwave too long or that she'd just turned thirty-five. No one really knew, and she wished there was a system for how people got selected for field assignments.

"Rory says there's no way Suzie will get picked,"

Alicia said once they'd passed the seventh floor. "She's still finishing up with the New Hampshire mansion."

"So we'll need another bulldozer," Mandie said, her eyes glued to the numbers above the doors. They were nearing ten now, and had five more to go. "Who?"

"Rory says the two of us would make a killer research and checklist team, with Flint behind the camera."

Mandie only hummed, but that said so much. Alicia knew she wanted this field assignment more than anything, and she'd known before Mandie had texted last night. She knew, because Alicia needed this assignment like she needed oxygen.

"You love Flint."

"Flint's the best," Mandie agreed. "So John as the third?"

"Could be." Alicia nodded as the elevator made another stop and then continued up. "Maybe Chevy. He hasn't been out since that Baltimore fiasco."

She and Mandie got off on the fifteenth floor and went past the ritzy real estate firm to their private historical restoration and reconstruction firm.

They both worked in the Preservation and Conservation Department, but they both also handled local clients who needed help getting natural disasters cleaned up when they weren't working on historical cases.

"I'm so bored," Alicia whispered as she opened the glass door and held it for Mandie.

"I might scream if I don't get assigned today," she

whispered back. "Just right out loud, in the middle of the meeting."

Alicia laughed lightly. "I doubt it. Assignments always come at the *end* of the meeting."

Mandie scoffed and veered off into her desk area while Alicia continued down another two rows to hers. She quickly put her purse in her bottom desk drawer, grabbed her files, and went back to Mandie's desk.

"Top three. We have to be in perfect alignment."

Mandie already had her folders out too. She loved sticky notes and color-coding, which was why she'd be perfect for any field crew. The woman literally never missed a detail, and she had three folders, one each labeled with a green note, a yellow one, and a pink one.

"Is pink above green or below?"

"Pink is the prize, my friend." Mandie smiled as she slipped the marked folder to the top.

Please let it be the Hampton House, Alicia prayed as Mandie seemed to fall into slow motion. Alicia really couldn't leave her children for an off-site field assignment, and she wondered if Candace had somehow found out about her recent divorce.

She commuted from Queens, from the tiny two-bedroom house where her son slept in the second bedroom while her daughter shared her room with her. She and her ex had been living there for a few years now, so that hadn't changed. It would simply be difficult to be on-site for any amount of time, and she'd chosen the Hampton House as her top pick simply in the hopes that it would be chosen, and she could get the field assignment.

She earned more when on assignment, as they received a per diem for food for every day worked out at the site. Plus, the house held a magic to it that leapt off the printed page and permeated the air.

"I knew you'd like the Hampton place too." Alicia grinned widely when she saw the pillared mansion on the front page inside the pink-sticky-note-marked folder.

"It's the best property," Mandie said. "Though I did like that one in the Appalachians."

"The Mountain Mansion?" Alicia fake-swooned. "Isn't it amazing? Even full of someone else's stuff and those ghastly all-terrain vehicles. I can't even imagine the views." Alicia could admit she was somewhat of a romantic, but the images of her eight-year-old's and her five-year-old's faces grounded her. Brought her back to reality, and that meant she couldn't run off to Virginia even for an amazing mountain mansion.

"I didn't put it in my top three," Mandie said. "I don't really want to travel for the field assignment." She tucked her honey-blonde hair behind her ear as she bent over the Hampton House. "I'm worried that if it comes up a lot, Candace will choose it even if it doesn't have the most votes."

"She is so unpredictable," Alicia complained. "That's what I dislike the most. If I knew how things could go, if I could predict it, I wouldn't be so nervous."

She flapped her hands a couple of times, then told herself to stop it.

She got to her feet. "Look, you're the natural choice for the researcher. I'm the perfect fit for the financial advisor. All we need is a bulldozer and a film crew, and this is going to be the best summer and fall of our lives."

Mandie clapped her hands together. "Yes! This is the kind of pep talk we need."

No one else had come into the office this early, and Alicia had psyched herself up appropriately. "Okay," she said, pacing to get out some of her extra energy. "We are going to pitch ourselves today. I *want* this assignment."

"I *need* it," Mandie said. "I'm tired of assisting on research and then staying here while the team goes out."

"This is ours."

"What's yours?" someone asked, and Alicia's gaze flew past Mandie to another blonde, this one with plenty of strawberry in her hair and so not someone she wanted to talk to this early in the morning. Or ever, really.

"Hey, Suzie," she chirped in a falsely bright voice. "You're here early."

"I've got to get this last form filed for the West Hills Monster."

Mandie got to her feet, her irritation like a scent on the air. Suzie barely looked at her, as if Mandie didn't hold any importance at all. Alicia reached out and grabbed onto her forearm, and that stopped Mandie. Thankfully.

"Leave it," she hissed as Suzie went by them. "We'll play our cards in the meeting."

Several seconds passed while they both waited for the blonde bulldozer to get out of earshot, and then both she and Mandie sat down in Mandie's desk area. "She thinks she's going to get another assignment," Mandie said. "Unbelievable."

"She's not going to get it," Alicia said. "There are so many deserving people—like us."

"Like us," Mandie agreed with a nod. "Okay, more people are starting to come in. We can't be seen conspiring, or Candace will for-sure give the assignment to someone else."

"Right." Alicia squeezed her friend's hands, then stood, and made her way over to her desk. The office started to fill, and before she knew it, Candace had stepped out of the conference room, the silver bell in her hand.

"Let's go, people," she called as she started to ding the bell over and over and over. *Ding! Ding! Ding!*

Everyone got to their feet like dogs, like the bell had triggered something Pavlovian inside them. Alicia joined them, her three folders and her notebook in her hands. She deliberately didn't allow herself to migrate to Mandie's side. Candace didn't like it when friends tried to get on the same teams, and Alicia panicked that her friendship with Mandie—which was well-known around PastForward—would suddenly hinder her.

Fourteen people crowded into the room, and

Candace indicated the three trays in the middle of the oblong table. "First, second, third," she said, indicating a tray with each one. "Folders in."

Someone swore, and Jackson—another accountant with a degree in construction management—jumped to his feet. "I forgot my folders."

"Door's closing in ten seconds," Candace called after him, and though he was one of Alicia's main competitors for this field assignment, she hated seeing him humiliated. Candace had locked people out of meetings before, so her ten-second rule was not an empty threat.

Ten seconds later, Jackson sprinted into the room just as Candace said, "Doors, please."

He practically threw his folders into the trays. Candace glared at him as she pulled the first tray toward her. "Paula, please tally."

Another woman scrambled to her feet, and Alicia wondered why they all kept showing up here, day after day, to be ordered around and treated subserviently. Paula uncapped a blue white board marker, and Candace flipped open the first folder.

"Hamptons," she said, and Alicia shot a look over to Mandie. She sat very still, her gaze trained on Candace. "Cape Cod." Another folder. "Hamptons." She continued on until all the folders in the first pile had been read, and it was obvious that the majority of people in the office wanted to work on the Hampton House next.

Candace turned and looked at the tally marks.

"Nine, wow." She smiled as she turned back and picked up the second stack of folders. She read through those, and the Cape Cod Complex came in second.

Their boss didn't even turn to get the remaining pile of folders. She steepled her fingers and considered the board. "I'm a bit surprised more of you didn't pick the Appalachian Jewel." She simply let the words hang there, and Alicia had learned not to justify anything.

If Candace asked her a direct question, she'd answer. Otherwise, she wouldn't. If she didn't get an assignment today, Alicia wasn't sure what she'd do. Screaming, like Mandie had suggested, sounded about right.

She looked down the table to her friend again, and this time, Mandie's eyes darted to hers too. Then Candace spun, and Alicia jerked her attention back to her. The tension in the conference room pressed against the ceiling, against all the walls and windows, straining to get out. Alicia could barely get a decent breath, and she wondered if anyone else felt that.

"We might as well go over what's third." Candace started reading through those, and Paula dutifully tallied them all up. Candace, in all her bleach-blonde-bunned glory, turned to face the board again.

She never went out in the field, except to check-in once, maybe twice, during a project. She demanded detailed reports which she religiously read, and she'd email questions or call private meetings with teams. Alicia had never seen her wear anything but skirts that fell precisely to her knees, heels, and fluttery blouses.

Today's was pale blue, with a navy skirt and navy heels, and perfectly matching robin's egg blue earrings in the shape of dragonflies.

"Ah, there's my Appalachian Jewel." She grinned at the board, then swiveled back to the group at-large. "Thank you, Paula. Please take your seat."

Paula did just that, and Alicia looked down at her notebook, almost afraid to make eye contact with Candace. She forced herself to look up, because she couldn't show her boss any weakness.

"We have enough funding for two teams to get started," she said. "I'm going to send some of you to Virginia and this mountain mansion. I think it's the best in the bunch, and I'm honestly surprised it's not number one."

No one said anything, because it sounded like Candace had just started a lecture. Alicia gazed at her, and Candace looked her way.

"Let's start down there." Candace looked down at some notes in front of her. "Jackson." Alicia's heart started to pound through her whole body. If Jackson got the Jewel, she'd be the most logical choice for the Hampton House. "You'll manage the finances."

"Yes," he said, his smile spreading across his whole face. It only made Alicia want to squirm.

"Vanessa, I need you on point," Candace said.

"Yes, ma'am," Vanessa said.

"Chevy." Candace glanced over to him, and he was a bulldozer like Suzie.

"You got it, Candy," he said, and he was the only one

who'd ever called Candace such a thing. A thread of horror moved through Alicia, but Candace only laughed.

"And on film..." She paused and sighed. "I'm going to pause on that for a minute. I want you guys to clear your afternoon on Monday. We'll meet to go over everything then."

Murmurs of assent moved through the group, and the tension in the room skyrocketed. Alicia shifted in her seat, and Candace looked at her. Her eyebrows went up, and Alicia's did too. That was about as big of a challenge as she could lay down, and she hoped the message had gotten across.

"The Hampton House," Candace said, consulting her notebook again. A few seconds went by, then a few more.

"Ma'am?"

Every eye flew to Mandie. She'd half-raised her hand, and she'd gone pale, like she might throw up. Candace looked at her, blinking rapidly a few times.

"I'm in love with this house," Mandie said. "I'd love to take point on it. I've already sketched out a few things to get started."

"You have?" Candace folded her arms and considered Mandie, her gaze sharp and hooked. Alicia's mouth had gone dry, and she had no idea how Mandie had the nerve to speak up in a meeting where people didn't do such things.

"Yes, ma'am," Mandie said. "And I'm completely

available to meet with you and whoever else you appoint to the team anytime."

"Anytime." Candace nodded, though something cold definitely emanated from her. She leaned back in her chair and appraised Mandie for several long seconds. Then a couple more. Right when Alicia thought the air would snap, she said, "All right, Miss Kelton. Oops, I mean *Mrs.* Kelton. You can have point."

"Thank you, ma'am."

Alicia couldn't speak up now, but she wasn't a bulldozer, nor on film. If she didn't get named next, she wouldn't have an assignment. A voice started shrieking in her head, an internal monologue that left her feeling desperate, irritated, and hopeless all at the same time.

She had to get out of this room.

Now.

Get out. Get out. Get out!

She stayed right where she was, and Candace looked at her notes and then right at her. "Alicia, can you keep *Mrs.* Kelton within budget?"

"Yes, ma'am," she said, her voice grating like rusty nails against cement. "Absolutely, I can."

Candace nodded and looked around. Alicia's heartbeat now bobbed somewhere outside her body, but she still had enough wherewithal to pray, *Not Suzie. Please, not Suzie.*

"Brandt," she said. "You'll be on bulldozer, and Flint, I know you're just barely finishing up the Maryland Mansion, but I need you in The Hamptons."

"Sure thing," Flint said.

"Apparently, *Mrs.* Kelton has some notes already for us," Candace said dryly, and Alicia thought Mandie might blow her top. She'd turned bright red now, and since Alicia sat on the same side of the table as her, she could see her fisted hands.

"Mandie's the best," Flint said. "I'm sure she and Lish can get started without me and Brandt. We're more of the on-site crew." Flint threw Alicia a smile, and that settled some of the acid boiling in her stomach.

"I want the Hampton House team in my office first thing Monday morning." She got to her feet. "I'll have my own notes to go over." She gave Mandie a pointed look. "All right. Back to work."

She started stacking the folders, and Alicia filed out of the conference room along with everyone else...except Mandie. Alicia met her eyes and gestured for her to *come on! Don't stay in here with the Big Bad Wolf!*

Mandie shook her head slightly, her jaw set and her eyes filled with pure determination. Alicia moved out of the way, wondering if she needed to stay and back-up whatever Mandie said.

But Mandie asked, "Miss Ewing? Can I speak to you privately for just five minutes?" and Alicia ducked out of the room. She'd hear all about this five-minute meeting soon enough, and she didn't want to step on her friend's toes.

She closed the door behind her and practically rammed into Flint.

"What's she doing?" he murmured.

"It's suicide," Alicia said, turning to face the conference room. All of the blinds were open, but Mandie stood with her back to the office.

"So we'll be going to lunch today," Flint said easily. "If she's still alive, we'll hear all about it." He nudged Alicia with his elbow. "And hey, you guys got Brandt."

Relief filled her again and then again, and she finally felt like she could breathe properly. "Yeah," she said. "We got Brandt." Her gaze went back to the conference room. "And if Mandie doesn't get fired, we pretty much have the dream team for the Hampton House."

Then she turned and walked back to her desk, praying for her friend in a constant internal stream of words.

READ THE HAMPTON HOUSE ON YOUR favorite retailer by scanning the QR code below:

Books in the Five Island Cove series

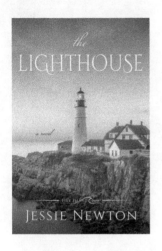

The Lighthouse, Book 1: As these 5 best friends work together to find the truth, they learn to let go of what doesn't matter and cling to what does: faith, family, and most of all, friendship.

Secrets, safety, and sisterhood...it all happens at the lighthouse on Five Island Cove.

The Summer Sand Pact, Book 2: These five best friends made a Summer Sand Pact as teens and have only kept it once or twice—until they reunite decades later and renew their agreement to meet in Five Island Cove every summer.

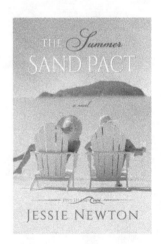

Books in the Five Island Cove series

The Cliffside Inn, Book 3:
Spend another month in Five Island Cove and experience an amazing adventure between five best friends, the challenges they face, the secrets threatening to come between them, and their undying support of each other.

Christmas at the Cove, Book 4: Secrets are never discovered during the holidays, right? That's what these five best friends are banking on as they gather once again to Five Island Cove for what they hope will be a Christmas to remember.

Books in the Five Island Cove series

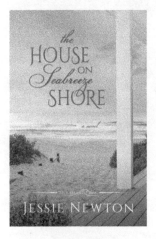

The House on Seabreeze Shore, Book 5: Your next trip to Five Island Cove...this time to face a fresh future and leave all the secrets and fears in the past. Join best friends, old and new, as they learn about themselves, strengthen their bonds of friendship, and learn what it truly means to thrive.

Four Weddings and a Baby, Book 6: When disaster strikes, whose wedding will be postponed? Whose dreams will be underwater?

And there's a baby coming too... Best friends, old and new, must learn to work together to clean up after a natural disaster that leaves bouquets and altars, bassinets and baby blankets, in a soggy heap.

Books in the Five Island Cove series

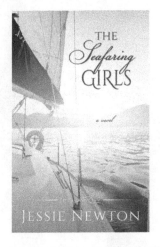

The Seafaring Girls, Book 7:
Journey to Five Island Cove for a roaring good time with friends old and new, their sons and daughters, and all their new husbands as they navigate the heartaches and celebrations of life and love.

But when someone returns to the Cove that no one ever expected to see again, old wounds open just as they'd started to heal. This group of women will be tested again, both on land and at sea, just as they once were as teens.

Rebuilding Friendship Inn, Book 8:
Clara Tanner has lost it all. Her husband is accused in one of the biggest heists on the East Coast, and she relocates her family to Five Island Cove–the hometown she hates.

Clara needs all of their help and support in order to rebuild Friendship Inn, and as all the women pitch in, there's so much more getting fixed up, put in place, and restored.

Then a single phone call changes everything.

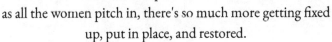

Will these women in Five Island Cove rally around one another as they've been doing? Or will this finally be the thing that breaks them?

The Glass Dolphin, Book 9: With new friends in Five Island Cove, has the group grown too big? Is there room for all the different personalities, their problems, and their expanding population?

The Bicycle Book Club, Book 10: Summer is upon Five Island Cove, and that means beach days with friends and family, an explosion of tourism, and summer reading programs! When Tessa decides to look into the past to help shape the future, what she finds in the Five Island Cove library archives could bring them closer together...or splinter them forever.

Books in the Nantucket Point series

The Cottage on Nantucket, Book 1:
When two sisters arrive at the cottage on
Nantucket after their mother's death,
they begin down a road filled with the
ghosts of their past. And when Tessa
finds a final letter addressed only to her
in a locked desk drawer, the two sisters
will uncover secret after secret that
exposes them to danger at their
Nantucket cottage.

The Lighthouse Inn, Book 2: The
Nantucket Historical Society pairs two
women together to begin running a
defunct inn, not knowing that they're
bitter enemies. When they come face-to-
face, Julia and Madelynne are horrified
and dumbstruck—and bound together
by their future commitment and their
obstacles in their pasts...

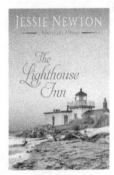

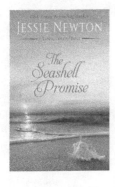

The Seashell Promise, Book 3: When two sisters arrive at the cottage on Nantucket after their mother's death, they begin down a road filled with the ghosts of their past. And when Tessa finds a final letter addressed only to her in a locked desk drawer, the two sisters will uncover secret after secret that exposes them to danger at their Nantucket cottage.

Books in The Hamptons series

The Hampton House, Book 1:
Mandie Kelton, Alicia Halverson, and Suzette Paxman are drawn together by the allure of forgotten elegance and the shadows of the past. They'll have to learn to get along if they have any hope of keeping their jobs, and as they restore an abandoned mansion in The Hamptons, they'll also discover the lost and hidden parts of themselves that make them into the women they're meant to be.

The Yacht Club, Book 2: Mandie Kelton, fresh from the triumphant restoration of the Hampton House, faces a new challenge when her boss, Candace Ewing, reveals their next project: restoring a famous historical yacht once owned by a legendary figure. Tasked with breathing new life into the venerable vessel, Mandie, along with her

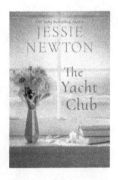

trusted friends and colleagues—Suzie, Alicia, and the enigmatic Candace—embarks on a journey that will test their skills and uncover long-buried secrets.

About Jessie

Jessie Newton is a saleswoman during the day and escapes into romance and women's fiction in the evening, usually with a cat and a cup of tea nearby. She is a Top 30 KU All-Star Author and a USA Today Bestselling Author. She also writes as Elana Johnson and Liz Isaacson as well, with almost 200 books to all of her names. Find out more at www.feelgoodfiction-books.com.

Printed in the USA
CPSIA information can be obtained
at www.ICGtesting.com
LVHW040724291124
797810LV00004B/87

* 9 7 8 1 6 3 8 7 6 4 2 0 5 *